YOU'VE GOT THIS

MAXINE MORREY

Boldwood

First published in Great Britain in 2023 by Boldwood Books Ltd.

Copyright © Maxine Morrey, 2023

Cover Design by Leah Jacobs-Gordon

Cover Photography: Shutterstock

A CIP catalogue record for this book is available from the British Library.

Paperback ISBN 978-1-80162-651-4

Large Print ISBN 978-1-80162-652-1

Hardback ISBN 978-1-80162-650-7

Ebook ISBN 978-1-80162-654-5

Kindle ISBN 978-1-80162-653-8

Audio CD ISBN 978-1-80162-645-3

MP3 CD ISBN 978-1-80162-646-0

Digital audio download ISBN 978-1-80162-649-1

Boldwood Books Ltd
23 Bowerdean Street

London SW6 3TN
www.boldwoodbooks.com

For D,
Thanks, buddy ;)

1

So this was how it would end. Plummeting to my death from a Welsh mountain. I knew this was a bad idea. Terrible. Quite possibly the worst ever, in fact. Jasper, of course, disagreed. Jasper thought it was one of his most brilliant ideas yet. An idea he'd had after a client he was currently schmoozing was marvelling over the amazing views on his recent trip to Snowdonia, thanks to being lucky with the weather.

'Have you ever been?' he'd asked.

'Oh God, yeah, but it was ages ago now.' Jasper had replied. 'Before it became so touristy. Be good to go back though.'

I'd kept my eyes fixed on the bone china plate in front of me, knowing he was lying – Jasper wasn't exactly what you'd call the outdoorsy type. But the more I'd come to know him, the more I'd realised this was his modus operandi. The thought that someone might have done something that he hadn't bothered him way more than it should, and he'd immediately begin rectifying the situation.

Sometimes I didn't mind. The trip to Capri was pretty nice and I certainly wasn't going to complain about the holiday to

Mustique. Although the ban on cocktails because they weren't included in the deal he'd swung was a bit of a downer. As a hedge-fund manager, Jasper had plenty of money, but he wasn't always keen on spending it on anyone other than himself. I'd tried to argue that I objected to him dictating what I could spend my own money on, but he'd gone into a huff and dropped a hint about as subtle as a tsunami that I was being ungrateful as he'd paid for the rest of the trip. I'd have happily paid my way, but as he didn't offer the best salaries in the sector that ruled out that option. As usual he'd missed the point entirely and I'd dropped my objection. I didn't expect anyone to pay for me and I'd done OK until I met him. It had been his idea for me to move into his place and to leave my long-standing coffee-shop job and take a position at his company. I'd known from day one that particular decision was a mistake but, by then, it was too late. But Jasper had really outdone himself this time. His never-ending obsession with one-upmanship had reached new heights – quite literally – with this latest endeavour.

I looked up at the looming mountain in front of me and felt my stomach swirl, the delicious home-cooked breakfast I'd wolfed down this morning threatening a swift reappearance. My eyes drifted up to the jagged ridge at the top. Oh God. This was *such* a bad idea. Thankfully I wasn't the only one who thought so. Jasper was currently in deep... let's call it 'discussion', with the climbing guide he'd hired for the hike.

'I'm sorry you feel that way,' Matt replied. 'But it's my job to keep people safe and, as much as I'd like to, I can't control the weather. Getting to the top today is out of the question. The cloud is too low and visibility will be poor to non-existent.'

'I hired you to take us to the top, not give up halfway! The word is you're one of the best guides around but I'm beginning to question the validity of your reputation.'

'Jasper!'

'What?' he snapped. 'I suppose this works out just perfectly for you. You were against this trip from the start.'

Oh good. And now we were going to have an argument in front of a stranger. Again.

'Never a great idea to piss off your significant other on the side of a mountain, mate.'

A giggle snuck out from under my defences and Matt shot me a momentary grin, which neutralised the dagger Jasper sent.

'Oh. Hilarious. I hope you're not charging extra for your "humorous" advice.'

Matt blew out a sigh through his teeth. 'Nope. Free of charge.'

'Good. And just to let you know, I'll be demanding a full refund for this so-called service anyway. Trade descriptions.'

Matt's reply was patient, his gravel-edged voice even as he spoke again. 'As I mentioned, unfortunately none of us have control over the weather. That point is stated in the booking details.'

'In the tiniest print possible, I suppose?' Jasper sneered.

'No. Same size. Actually, now you mention it, possibly a bit larger.'

I turned away, ostensibly to admire the view but in reality to hide a smirk.

'Oh, quite the joker, aren't you?'

'Nope. You asked a question. I assumed you wanted a reply.'

Jasper's face was thunderous, his high colouring beginning to turn an interesting shade of purple. He wasn't used to people questioning him. He was always the one in charge. The one throwing his weight around. Not that Matt was throwing weight around, which, by the size of him, was probably just as well. Had his trekking gear been white I reckon there'd be a spike in sightings of Yeti on the Welsh mountains.

'Look, I don't want to fall out with anyone. I love this area and I love getting to share it with other people too, but my first job is to keep clients, and myself, safe. I'm afraid it's just too dangerous to go to the top today for anyone, especially novices.'

'I'm not a novice! I've climbed plenty of mountains before.'

I glanced at Jasper's backside. Apparently the fire from his pants hadn't yet burst through his overpriced walking trousers. My gaze then slid to Matt. His bearing, unlike Jasper's, was relaxed and his expression was as steady and immobile as the mountain we stood on. Suddenly he flicked his gaze to me and I felt my breath catch. The striking ice blue of his eyes held mine for just a moment and, in that instant, it felt as if he saw right through me. It was also clear from that glance that he knew Jasper was telling the most enormous, and dangerous, porkie.

'That's as may be, sir,' Matt said diplomatically, 'but you hired me as a guide for Crib Goch and, as such, it's my job to keep both of you safe. Taking you further now would be irresponsible. You may be experienced but clearly you felt the need for some guidance on this particular mountain, which was a wise move. There are aspects which can easily lead to difficulties if you're unfamiliar with it. Perhaps we could try again tomorrow, if that's convenient. The weather is forecast to improve overnight.'

'No, it's not bloody convenient!' Jasper fired back at him. 'Today is the only full day we have here. Some of us have proper jobs to get back to.'

'Jasper!' I said, flushing pink on my boyfriend's behalf and sending Matt an apologetic look as Jasper clearly had no intention of doing so.

'What?' Jasper turned now, snapping at me again. 'This is all your bloody fault anyway! Hire a guide, you said, it's not safe without one, you said. And now look at us! I knew I shouldn't have listened to you. Bloody women. I'd be up there by now if it wasn't for you and your bright ideas!'

The blush I'd felt tingling at Jasper's earlier rudeness now came out in full force. At least now if anyone did get in trouble in the vicinity, they'd have a glowing beacon in the form of my face to guide rescuers to them.

'I did say I wasn't sure it was really my thing.'

'Oh, so now it's my fault? Of course it is.'

'The lady was right to suggest hiring a guide, and for someone who's never done anything like this before, she's doing well.'

Jasper issued a cold bark of a laugh. 'Flatter all the pretty women, do you? I see you're not wearing a wedding ring. You must keep yourself very busy up here.'

I lowered my gaze and looked for a massive hole in which to disappear. Even a small one would do – I wasn't fussy. Anything to extricate myself from this excruciating situation.

* * *

When I met him, I thought Jasper Hamilton-Grey was good-looking, charming and kind. I'd not long come out of a long-term relationship that hadn't ended well and my confidence, never high at the best of times, had taken a hit. So when Jasper showed an interest in me, I was entranced. That was really the only word for it. The rent on my flat was due a renewal in six weeks and somehow I let him talk me into moving in with him.

He made it sound like a financially wise, not to mention romantic, decision. And for a while it was good. But gradually I began to see beneath the shiny, sleek veneer and I wasn't a fan of what I saw. The sound judgement I'd been convinced of before didn't seem all that sound now. I was, in fact, in quite the pickle. I was not only dependent on him for a home, having given up my tiny rental, but also my employment. Jasper had assured me I wasn't fulfilling my potential making coffees for strangers and I should come and work for him as an assistant. Something I could build a career out from. I liked my job at the coffee shop but I knew it wasn't a career. It was supposed to have been temporary. The trouble was I was now in my thirties and still had no idea what I wanted to do when I grew up! But then there was Jasper with his promises of great pay and perks and I'd be working in a swanky office in the City.

The truth was, though, the pay wasn't all that brilliant. In fact, it wasn't much more than for my barista job and I didn't get tips here. I also missed the interaction with the customers, especially those regulars I'd got to know over the years. And the biggest poke in the eye was that my job, my promised swish admin job that would help me begin stretching my capabilities and 'showing the world what I could do' (Jasper's words) basically involved me making coffee for him, his clients and the rest of the staff. Most days I was bored out of my skull and secretly longed for my old job and – even more secretly – my old studio flat back. I'd bought new clothes, as Jasper had said my old ones didn't really suit the 'new me' – whoever the new me was. New, or old, me was sure of one thing though. Jasper was often capable of being a rude, embarrassing, entitled arse. And today he was outdoing himself.

'It's this way, I assume?' Before Matt could answer Jasper

strode off back down the mountain, still yapping away to himself.

Matt watched him go, the corners of his mouth tilted up ever so slightly. It was a really nice mouth. Not that I was leching, but it was hard not to notice he was pretty tasty in that I-spend-a-lot-of-time-outdoors-doing-outdoorsy-things way. Not like a weather-beaten Captain Birdseye, just sort of rugged. Yes, that was it. Matt was rugged. With ice blue eyes that looked straight into your soul. Those eyes now squinted at the bracing wind whipping up and ramming into the wall of rock behind us, but as he turned to me I noticed they too had a hint of the same smile. Jasper amused him. Whereas my boyfriend had clearly been going for intimidating, apparently all he'd done was entertain our guide.

'I suppose it's probably not the best idea to piss off your guide up a mountain either?' I said, shrugging my rucksack back on.

'You're a fast learner.'

'Sorry about Jasper. He was... he was just looking forward to it.'

Matt put out an arm as my boots hit a bit of shale and I slid forward with the momentum. I grabbed it automatically.

'Thanks.'

'You're welcome. Watch out for that, there's patches of it all over. Also, don't apologise for your boyfriend. He's the arse.' He gave me a look. 'Sorry to be blunt.'

'That's OK.'

'Fuck!' In front of us, Jasper was stomping along in a mood and did exactly what I'd just done but without the care Matt had warned him to take before we'd put one foot on the mountain this morning. Too busy throwing his metaphorical toys out of the pram, he'd now slid and fallen straight on his backside.

'You all right there, mate?' Matt held out a hand to help him up. Jasper pointedly ignored it, and its owner, and heaved himself up. Without looking back to see if I was OK, he stomped on.

* * *

'So, do you want me to take you back to the hotel or is there something else you fancy doing in the area today instead?'

'No, there isn't anything else I bloody fancy doing. What a sodding waste of time and money! As for you—' he pointed an expensively gloved finger at Matt, 'just wait until I get on Tripadvisor.'

Matt gave a kind of side nod that indicated that was Jasper's prerogative. I felt an inward groan. Jasper loved that site. The last time a hotel room hadn't been up to his exacting standards, he'd written a flippin' essay! I say he did. What actually happened was that he dictated it, striding about his penthouse, peering down on all the people below (something I realised now was actually the perfect metaphor for him), while I madly typed his venomous words into a review. What he didn't know was that the next day, I uploaded my own review, under an alias, giving the boutique hotel, which had really been quite lovely, a glowing five-star rating to try and balance out his unfair attack. It wasn't the first time I'd done it, and I could see I'd be preparing another very soon.

'Would you like me to drop you back at the hotel, then?' Matt asked again, his features still relaxed and impassive. Honestly, this guy was either a saint or on something. I somehow doubted it was the latter, seeing as he looked like an advert for an expensive health and lifestyle brand. Shame though. I could have done with something to help me chill out right now.

Jasper was almost puce with frustration. I wasn't relishing the trip back down south from Wales with a furious Ribena berry.

'Is there anywhere else we could climb?' The area was stunning and I'd have been happy to explore more now that the original, insanely scary plan had to change.

'I don't want to go anywhere else. I wanted to climb this one!' Jasper snapped, doing an excellent impression of a spoilt five-year-old.

'I know, but the weather is preventing us, so perhaps there's a compromise?'

'It's not the weather preventing us,' he growled at me, shooting Matt a dark look.

I let it go, as did Matt. He'd obviously sussed out pretty quickly that Jasper wasn't worth the breath he'd expend in arguing. Unfortunately, it had taken me rather longer.

'I can have a look and speak to another couple of guides on the satellite phone. The weather can vary a lot within a short distance up here so it's possible somewhere else might be more accessible, if that's something you're open to.'

'That would be great, if you don't mind.' I smiled at Matt, trying to make up for my boyfriend's unforgivable lack of manners.

'Do you want to ask if *I* mind,' Jasper interjected, throwing me a look as dark as the one Matt had received moments earlier, 'before you and he start making plans together? Perhaps I should just go? Leave you to it as you seem so keen to remain in his company.'

I stayed silent. I'd forgotten to mention the jealousy. Firstly it had been a little thrilling, in that strange way that the mind works. That someone wants you and the thought of others wanting you affects them deep down. But it soon morphed into more than that and then it wasn't so fun any more. Jasper liked his money and he bought possessions with it. Sometimes I wondered if he considered me as just another of those possessions.

'If there's an easier climb available, you may not need me anyway. Especially as you already have experience,' Matt said, looking at Jasper. Full kudos to him for keeping any hint of sarcasm out of the last sentence.

Jasper puffed up a little. 'That is true. OK, then. Make your calls.' He gave a flick of his fingers in a shooing motion. A tiny muscle flickered in Matt's jaw and I momentarily saw it tighten. Maybe a lot of people wouldn't, but I'd grown up watching for these tiny signs that indicated people's moods and the possible actions that might follow. A tiny knot curled itself in my stomach. Matt turned away to make the call, catching my eye as he did so, while Jasper stabbed madly at his own phone, trying desperately to get a signal on it. Matt's face softened and the knot miraculously unfurled.

'Two thousand pounds and it still can't get a bloody signal!' Jasper stomped off to another spot further away from me and I breathed out, turned to the stunning scenery we'd had our backs to and let my mind drift, concentrating on the view in front of me and nothing else.

2

'So, apparently the weather is better on the other side of the valley. I'm happy to take you walking over there, or I can take you and pick you up later if you'd prefer. There's also a bus to the village once every hour.'

'A bus?' Jasper looked at the man, astonishment sending his eyebrows so far up his face they nearly shot off the top of his head. 'A bus?' he repeated. 'Do I look like the sort of person who takes public transport of any sort?'

Matt wisely, and commendably, chose to remain silent about what sort of person Jasper looked like, instead waiting patiently for a reply to the question he'd asked.

'Well, I've already shelled out on your so-called services so I may as well get some use out of you.'

'That money can, of course, be very easily refunded if you'd prefer, sir.' Matt certainly looked as if he'd prefer it and I didn't blame him.

'No, come on. Where's this better weather, then?' Jasper stomped between us, heading to the four-by-four Matt had met us in.

'Sorry about this,' I said, keeping my voice low as Matt and I both turned to follow him.

His focus was on the way ahead. 'You're not responsible for other people's actions, so you don't need to apologise for them.'

'No, I know. But still...' I let the sentence drift off.

'But still what?'

'I... just...' I opened my mouth to continue, closed it when I realised I had no idea of what to say and then opened it again to try and fill the silence. Matt had glanced back to check the path ahead but now turned again. One dark brow rose a tiny bit, as if prompting me.

'I've no idea,' I said, exhaling. 'I just felt like I should apologise. He's not always like this.'

Matt paused before he gave a small nod of acceptance, which I got the impression was anything but. He was right, of course. It wasn't my fault that Jasper acted like a total knob at times but somehow I always felt the need to apologise to the perfectly nice people who got in the way of his imperious attitude.

Matt beeped the vehicle open and Jasper, with a long-suffering huff, yanked open the front passenger door and climbed in, slamming the door closed with more force than was strictly necessary.

'Guess you're in the back, then,' Matt said quietly.

'Guess so,' I replied, looking up at him as his hand wrapped around the door handle. And then he smiled. Just for a second. But it was enough.

* * *

'You two took your time,' Jasper harrumphed as Matt started the engine and pulled out on the road. 'Perhaps I should just leave you two to go off hiking.'

That might be nice...

'You strode off, Jasper. You could have waited for me.'

'I can't keep slowing down just for you to catch up. I told you if you wanted to come this weekend, you'd have to keep up.'

There were two things wrong with that statement. The first was that I hadn't actually been keen on coming this weekend anyway and had suggested he go on his own, especially as he had a guide for company. Jasper would, of course, disagree but I reckoned he'd been lucky to land Matt as a guide as he clearly had an enormous reserve of patience. But, of course, I had to come. Jasper had been appalled at the idea of me staying at home. What would people think if his girlfriend wasn't supportive? Well, I supposed they might think that I could do with a break from him. But we couldn't have people thinking his relationship, or anything else in his world, was anything less than perfect.

The second was that he was portraying himself to be some sort of expert at this mountain lark and he wasn't. Matt, on the other hand, clearly was a bona fide professional. A real-life action man. Now he had his jacket off, a semi-fitted T-shirt hinted at some serious muscles beneath it, rock-hard biceps poking out of the sleeves. He even had the buzz cut to go with the image. I tilted my head surreptitiously to look for the 'Eagle Eyes' switch at the back of his neck.

'Comfy back there?' he asked, turning his head as he waited for a car in front to turn off the road, timing his movement perfectly to catch me peering at the back of his head. Crap.

'Umm, yeah, fine, thanks,' I replied, stretching my neck to

the other side and doing that arm cross-over thing that stretched your shoulders or your back or something. I never was quite sure what it did. I just did it before I exercised because everyone else did.

'Good.'

'I'm comfortable too, you'll be glad to know,' Jasper added snarkily.

'Great. It won't be too long now.'

Jasper looked at his Rolex. 'Glad to hear it. We've wasted enough time already.'

Matt's eyes flicked up to the rear-view mirror, momentarily catching mine, before looking back at the road in front.

'This is stunning!' I said, looking out of the window at the swathes of green, punctuated by mountains reaching for the sky. A sky that was, as our guide had promised, completely different from the one we'd left behind. Soft edged white clouds chased through the blue sky above. There was still a breeze, but nothing like that on the other side of the mountain. I knew Matt wouldn't be taking us anywhere that would be risky. Jasper's manner often intimidated people and resulted in him getting his own way but it hadn't worked here and I'd inwardly, and possibly outwardly, drawn a sigh of relief at that. This terrain wasn't something to mess with. It didn't care how much money you or your parents had, what school you went to, or what car you drove. If you made a mistake, or didn't give it the respect it deserved, you'd still end up taking the quick way down.

'Beautiful, isn't it?'

'It really is,' I said, peering out of the window and smiling as a sheep looked up from her munching as Matt slowed to manoeuvre a particularly tight corner.

'Are we nearly there?' Jasper asked, looking up from his phone for two seconds.

'Not far now.'

Jasper returned to his phone. Probably composing his Tripadvisor piece while he was still all fired up.

'Isn't the scenery breathtaking, Jasper?' I prompted. Perhaps if he let himself appreciate the landscape, it might give his blood pressure time to lower and he could actually enjoy the time here. His head lifted, he gave a cursory look around and returned to his phone. 'Yes. Very... green.'

In the mirror, I saw the corners of Matt's lips twitch ever so slightly. Clearly we weren't going to get any conversation out of my boyfriend and I knew from past experience, and from his comment earlier, that if I struck up a conversation with Matt, Jasper would read more into it than there was.

* * *

There was a rush of adrenaline thrumming through me that I'd forgotten existed. Standing here, at the top of this ridge, looking out into the distance at the green, brown and slate colours mixing in the landscape. Tiny people walking below us looking like The Borrowers as they tramped along with rucksacks, various dogs scooting around, clambering up mountain sides far more easily than their owners. The sun had strengthened and I closed my eyes for a second, feeling its warmth on my face, my skin, blotting out everything but that sensation.

Jasper's puffing and huffing brought me back to reality and I reluctantly opened my eyes. Having refused my suggestion of sun cream and hat, he was now the colour of a perfectly ripe strawberry. He was one of those people who didn't tan but refused to believe it and continually kept trying, determined to bend genetics to his own will. I'd shrugged and left him to it, knowing from many previous occasions that to continue prompting was a waste of breath. He'd be sore tonight. Great. Something else for him to moan about. And it would, of course, be either my or Matt's fault. My money was on both.

'Damn boots. I knew that chap didn't have a clue what he was talking about when I told him what I wanted. I'd have been here quicker but they're not...' Jasper didn't elaborate, but instead began poking at them and adjusting the laces. The boots were fine, and the chap might have known what he'd been talking about, had he had a chance to get a word in. As usual, Jasper had marched in, demanded the most expensive boots they had and marched out.

Matt nodded sympathetically at him but, as he turned back, I saw the amusement in his eyes. OK, not that sympathetic, then.

* * *

'Did you enjoy that?' Matt asked as we all headed back to the car.

'It was great! Thanks so much. I've never done anything like this.'

'You did great. Obviously a natural.'

'I still think we still could have done Crib Goch,' Jasper sniped.

Matt checked his phone before answering. 'Looks like the weather that side of the valley only got worse today. A couple of the other guides had to turn back.'

'Perhaps they're not as good as they claim to be. I'm sure we would have been fine. I told you. I'm no novice.'

'I'm sorry you weren't able to get up there today, sir. Even for the most experienced it wouldn't have been a pleasant trek.' Matt had clearly got the measure of his client. The only terrain Jasper had knowledge of was walking his parents' dog on their estate when he wanted a cigarette.

In theory he'd packed up years ago, at his mother's request. She was the only one he didn't answer back to, so desperate was he for her approval. So if he ever got a craving, he pretended he had to take a very urgent phone call and walked out, taking the dog, and lit up once he was out of sight.

I had an idea that his mum knew exactly what he was up to. I'd met her once and she was sharp as a tack. Needless to say, I hadn't met with their expectations for their son. Jasper had dismissed my concerns out of hand so I didn't tell him I'd over-heard their conversation when I'd gone to find the bathroom (seriously, a map would have been useful!). The sound of his father's Old Etonian tones reassuring his wife that all men had to have their little dalliances with 'such women' before they settled down with the right sort. I didn't know if Jasper's dismissal of my concerns meant he agreed and had, at some point, plans to kick me out, or if he had decided to take a stand against tradition and closed views and make a life with someone not from the 'right' echelons. I'd have bet his Rolex on the first.

'Perhaps it's you that needs more experience,' Jasper grumbled as he glared out of the window. Matt drew in a deep breath, let it out slowly and we rode the rest of the way in silence.

* * *

'Can you believe that guy?' Jasper dropped his rucksack on the floor as we entered the room. I picked it up and put it to the side, sliding mine off my back as I did so and placing it alongside.

'We ended up having a good day, Jasper. Can't you just let it go? It's really not his fault that the weather wasn't good enough to do what we'd—' (*you'd*) 'planned. It did look quite challenging and neither of us have much know-how when it comes to hiking up mountains. So, it's probably for the best really. You can always do it another time.'

'I don't want to do it another time. I wanted to do it now.'

And we both knew that what Jasper wanted, Jasper got. I wasn't prepared to get drawn into the argument any further. I'd had a really good day. Matt was a great guide; patient, knowledgeable and not full of himself as some instructors could be. The only thing that had spoiled it was Jasper's intermittent digs about how he could have been at the top of Crib Goch by now. Matt hadn't taken the bait. I didn't know where he got his patience from. After the fourth time, I'd been close to pushing Jasper off the bloody mountain myself. As I'd swung a dark glance round from Jasper's back, it had connected with Matt's. He'd sent me a quick smile and given the smallest shake of his head – he'd known exactly what I'd been thinking. I'd blushed but Matt had just smiled more before turning his focus back to the path ahead of him. He might have been patient, but it was clear I hadn't been the only one having momentary lapses of tolerance with Jasper's sniping.

'Do you want a shower first or shall I go in?'

'You go.' He waved a hand without looking at me. 'I have some emails to answer.'

Standing under the rain-head shower, I let the warm water and soft bubbles wash away the stressful parts of the day, leaving me to enjoy the rest of it. The scenery had been breathtaking and I could have stood for hours just watching the colours change on the landscape as the sun warmed the crags and rolling green hills. Shadows had danced as soft-edged clouds scudded across the sun before it broke through again, illuminating the lush greens and glinting off the protruding rocks and shale falls.

I couldn't remember any of the names of the surrounding peaks or areas Matt had pointed out as we'd stopped to take breathers. He'd told us their names in English and then in Welsh, which a lot were reverting back to. It was clear he knew his stuff and the area well. Whichever direction I'd pointed in and asked about, he'd been there with an answer, and had seemed pleased that I was interested. Jasper hadn't asked any questions. He still hadn't forgiven Matt for not falling into line with his orders and, although he'd climbed the range Matt had taken us to instead, he'd kept his head down and trudged on ahead of us like a sulky child. I'd tried to get him to take notice of the incredible scenery, but he'd made up his mind and that was that.

It was hardly the romantic weekend he'd sold it to me as when he'd returned from the building's gym one morning bearing a bunch of red roses. He could just as easily have come alone. But as it was, despite Jasper acting like an idiot, I'd loved the hike, even though I'd struggled at times. Matt had been patient and understanding, suggesting breaks and sharing the odd tip for getting a better hold on the scrambly bits. Jasper had just rolled his eyes and mumbled about me holding them up, but I'd seen him guzzling the water on the breaks and turning a bit purple at times in the steeper areas. If he'd been the type to regret things, which he wasn't as he refused to believe he ever did anything wrong, top of the list today was probably those sneaky fags.

3

'What?' Jasper snapped once I'd finally got a chance to speak that night at dinner.

'I said just let it go. It was hours ago and it couldn't be helped.'

'It could be helped. That guide bloke wasn't the best and I'd specifically requested the best. He was obviously too much of a wuss to go up when there was a bit of a breeze.'

'It wasn't a bit of a breeze, Jasper. It was fifty-mile-an-hour winds and dense cloud.'

'Well, of course, you'd side with him.'

I sighed. 'I'm not siding with anyone, Jasper. I'm just stating facts.'

'Facts *he* gave us.'

'Anyway, I really enjoyed it. Perhaps if you hadn't been so hung up on not getting your own way for once, you might have been able to enjoy it too.'

Jasper snapped his head up and looked at me.

'What?'

'I said—'

'I heard what you said. I'm just rather surprised you have the cheek to be so rude after I shelled out on a romantic weekend away. This hotel is also supposed to be the best in the area.' He tilted his patrician nose skyward and peered around. 'God knows what the other places are like.'

'Jasper, shoosh!' I said, mortifyingly aware that the lady behind the bar, who I suspected was the owner, had already overheard the comment. Jasper never made much adjustment to volume even in public.

He waved my words away. 'I didn't have to pay for you, you know.'

'Jasper, I told you I didn't particularly want to come and I did offer to pay my half but you just went ahead and booked it. I'd actually have preferred to pay my way because your constant little digs about money are unfair.'

I had his attention now. 'I beg your pardon?'

I felt myself flushing. 'Can we put today behind us and move on?'

'What can I get for you?' a pretty woman aged around thirty asked, her hand poised over her pad.

'Some sense for my girlfriend here would be perfect,' Jasper snapped.

The woman's smile faltered awkwardly and I gave her a more genuine one, trying to smooth over the situation.

'Have you decided what you want, Jasper?'

'Yes, I have actually.' When he raised his gaze, it was so cold I had to suppress a shiver.

'Sorry, would you mind coming back in a few minutes?' I said, fixing on a smile for the woman, who nodded and headed over to another table.

'I want someone who appreciates me.'

'Jasper—'

'I'm done with this. With you!' There was a pause before he flung the white linen napkin on the table and shoved his chair back.

'You are, of course, fired,' he added as he stood up. More heads turned and my own snapped up.

'Jasper, you can't do that.'

He gave a cold laugh. 'Oh, for God's sake, the only reason you have that job is because I wanted to get you into bed. There was no vacancy. But...' he shrugged '... being the boss has its perks.'

'I have a notice period.'

'Not if you've indulged in behaviour deemed inappropriate by the company.'

'I haven't!'

He shrugged again. 'Your word against mine, I'm afraid, and, oh, that's right, it's my company, so sorry.' He gave a little finger wave along with a snake-like smile. How had I not seen this streak of outright cruelty before? Because he'd been careful not to show it, or because I'd been careful not to see it? 'I'll have your things removed to a storage facility for two weeks, which I will generously pay for. If you haven't collected them by that time—'

'Jasper—'

'I'll send you the address and any pay you are owed will be in your bank within the next fourteen days.' He turned away.

'Where are you going?'

'To pack and get back to civilisation. This trip has been one disappointment after another.'

I made to stand up.

'What are you doing?'

'Going to pack my stuff if we're leaving now.'

Jasper looked at me with cold eyes. '*I'm* leaving now. You

can do what the hell you want but if you think I'm driving you back, you're sadly mistaken.'

'Jasper! You can't just leave me here!'

'Actually, I can do whatever I want. Goodbye, Fleur.' With that he stalked out of the restaurant, all eyes on him until inevitably they all swung back, some less surreptitiously than others, in my direction. I sank back in my chair. Great. I was now without a job, a home and stranded in the middle of North Wales. Well done, Fleur. This was probably your most disastrous relationship yet.

'You OK, love?' The older lady from behind the bar jogged me from my reverie.

'Oh! Oh, yes,' I said, dredging up a smile. 'I'm so sorry about all that.'

'Don't be daft,' she said. 'Not your fault.'

'I think that would depend on who you asked.' I made an effort, but my smile was watery. Oddly I wasn't that upset about the break-up. I'd known some time ago Jasper wasn't the man I'd thought he was, but I hadn't yet worked out how to get out of the situation. I was, however, upset at being homeless and unemployed. 'I'm so sorry to disrupt your restaurant.'

'Better off without him, from what I saw.'

I agreed wholeheartedly with the sentiment of these words, but sentiment would only get me so far. The truth was I was well and truly stuffed.

'Do you want something to eat?'

'Oh... no, thank you. That's very kind. I'm sorry. I'm taking up a table.' She laid a hand gently on my shoulder as I made to rise. 'You sit there, love. Give him time to stamp around and collect his things.'

She had a point.

'Come on, let me get you something to eat. You were out walking today, weren't you?'

'Umm, yes. Yes, I was,' I replied.

'That's what I thought. Now, what can we tempt you with? On the house, of course.'

'Oh, no! I couldn't possibly accept that.'

'Of course you could. You deserve a medal for putting up with that man. I'd have clonked him with a frying pan before now if it were me.'

A giggle bubbled inside me.

'That's it. You've got a beautiful smile,' she said, having bent a little closer now. 'Don't let anyone smother that, my love. You're so much more than he could ever see.'

I wasn't sure what to say.

'Now. About this food...'

In the end, I agreed to some soup served with warm, home-baked crusty bread. My appetite had dissolved into nothing the moment Jasper had told me I was fired but Bronwyn, the hotel owner, was right. I'd burned a tonne of calories today and my body needed fuel.

As I ate, I typed out a message to my old boss.

I wiped the tears threatening to spill from my eyes as my phone vibrated and I turned it over to read the reply.

Sorry, doll. I'd take you back in an instant, you know that, but we're fully staffed at the moment. What happened with the other job? Xx

It had been a long shot but I'd desperately hoped it would be one that hit the mark.

Not worked out, unfortunately. Long story.

Sounds intriguing. Must meet up soon! Sorry can't help. Will let you know if I hear of any other positions. Xx

Thanks. That'd be great. Speak soon xx

'How was that?' Bronwyn asked as she came to clear the table.

'Lovely, thank you. I'd really like to pay though.'

'Not a chance. Now, what tempts you from the pudding menu?'

She was relentless but in a good way, fussing around me like a mother hen. I revelled in the unfamiliar feeling, storing the memory away for another time.

'Oh, no, not for me, thanks.'

'Now, that's disappointing.'

'I mean, they all look yummy but I'm really not hungry now. Thank you.'

Bronwyn gave me a long look before relenting. 'OK, I won't push you any more. At least you've eaten something. I'll clear these away.' Expertly, she stacked the dishes and with a soft parting smile she took them away.

So, next task. Find transport home. Actually, scratch that. Next task, find a home, then find transportation to said home. And find a job. Preferably all in the next few hours. God, Jasper was a shit. How had I ever fallen for his fake charm? I pulled up a letting-agency website on my phone and began scanning.

'Hi.'

I jumped as the deep voice with its edge of gravel broke my concentration.

'Sorry, didn't mean to make you jump.' Matt's striking eyes were shadowed with concern.

'Oh! No. It's fine. Hi. How are you?'

'Better than you, I think.'

'Wow. Blunt.'

'True.' There was a glimmer in those eyes now.

I gave a conciliatory smile. 'Fair enough. Did you stay for the whole show?'

'Afraid so. There's not much that makes me miss one of my mum's steaks.'

'Your mum?'

He pointed at Bronwyn. 'This is my parents' place.'

'Oh, I see. You mum's very kind.'

'Yeah, she's all right.' He grinned now as Bronwyn came closer and slid an arm around her son's waist. He towered over her, the love and pride evident in her eyes as she looked up at him.

'High praise, indeed!' She laughed, giving him a quick squeeze. 'You two have met, then?'

'Yep, I took Fleur and her boyfriend walking today.'

'Ex.'

'Huh?'

'Ex boyfriend. Very much so.'

'Ah. Yes. I was trying to be tactful.'

'There's a first time for everything.' His mother laughed as she turned to deal with another table close by.

'So, what—?'

'Oh, I should have known the minute I was out of the way, you'd be in there!' Jasper's pompous tones rang out from the doorway as he glared at Matt.

Matt turned to face him, his expression flat and unreadable. He held Jasper's gaze for a long moment before glancing back at me, sending the faintest smile before walking away.

'Looking for someone else's bed to keep warm, I suppose, Fleur?'

Matt stopped in his tracks and colour flamed to my cheeks. Hadn't Jasper embarrassed me enough for one day?

'I think it's best if you go now, sir.' Bronwyn had appeared from nowhere and had now placed herself square in front of my ex.

'I'll go when I'm bloody well ready.'

'No. You'll go now,' she replied, calm, even and unmoving.

'And what makes you think I'm going to take orders from someone like you?'

Across the room, another man stood and made his way to the doorway where Matt was now standing behind his mother.

'Oh, going to be the hero now, are you?'

'My mother said it was time for you to go.'

'Your mother. That explains things!' Jasper gave a laugh that was more of a snarl.

'What the hell is that supposed to mean?' The other man took a sudden step towards Jasper, who flinched, the supercilious look fracturing for just a second. Matt laid a hand on the man's arm. No words were exchanged but he stepped back. Why couldn't Jasper just leave? Why did he always have to make a scene? It was one thing treating me like crap, but these people had been nothing but kind and helpful. I pushed my chair back and walked up to the group, tapping Matt on the arm. He looked down, then stepped aside, his hand still on his mum's shoulder. I moved into the gap he'd made. Jasper's eyes fell on me.

'Please, Jasper. This is between you and me. There's no need to drag anyone else into it, or be rude to them. They don't deserve it.'

'Ha! He was making eyes at you the whole day, trying to make me feel inadequate.'

'Oh, for God's sake, Jasper. You're imagining things and also, as shocking as this might be, not everything is about you. If you felt that way, then that's entirely of your own making. Now, please. Just go home.'

He narrowed his eyes. 'My father was right about you. You're definitely not our kind of people.' He gave a cold laugh. 'I'm not surprised even your own parents didn't want you!'

'Please leave!' Bronwyn's voice became stronger.

'With pleasure!' And with that, he spun on his handmade shoe's heel and stalked off.

I could feel the eyes of all the other diners boring into the back of my head and all I wanted right now was to disappear.

'I'm so sorry,' I said for what felt like the millionth time. 'This is really a lovely place. He's just—'

'I think we all know what he is,' Matt interrupted, 'and you don't need to apologise for him. Come on, let's get you a drink.'

'Oh, no, really. I'm fine. I need to go up and pack.'

'And where are you going to go at this time of night without a car?' He looked down at me, his expression gentle.

'I thought I'd look up trains and buses while I was packing.'

'Nonsense,' Bronwyn said, shooing the other man away with a smile. 'My sons are very protective of me.'

'So I see. You're very lucky.'

'I am. Big lumps, they are, but lovely lumps.'

'I'm right here,' Matt said.

'We can hardly miss you, my love. You're the biggest of the lot!' She laughed melodically and gave his waist a squeeze. 'And my boy's right. Let's get you a drink and a good night's sleep and look at things again in the morning.'

Somehow I didn't think things would have miraculously improved by then but I went along with her instructions, mostly because I was suddenly exhausted. I hadn't realised how tiring being with Jasper was these days. I was always on edge –

being on alert had become such an automatic thing I'd stopped noticing. But now everything was becoming clearer, including the fact that I should never have told him about my history. At the time, he had still been in his sweet and caring mode. He'd seemed interested but I couldn't help but wonder now if he had just been trying to discover whether I was suitable to be introduced to the Hamilton-Grey stable. I'd clearly failed that test but had proved entertaining enough to be a stopgap, as his father had intimated, until a woman of the right calibre came along. I'd been a complete idiot.

'You look like you're beating yourself up over there.' Matt looked at me over the top of a cut-glass whisky tumbler.

'Not at all.'

He fixed that gaze on me and I crumbled. 'OK, fine. Yes, I was just vigorously questioning my taste in men.'

'He was an interesting choice, I grant you.' Matt definitely had a habit of saying it as it was. I felt a smile spread on my face and realised sadly that I couldn't remember the last time it had felt this natural to smile.

'Mind if I sit?'

I shook my head.

'He wasn't that unbearable when I first met him.'

'I'm sure.'

'I don't know what happened.'

'Sometimes people only show us what they want us to see.'

'Yes, I suppose you're right. I'm sure he will be demanding tonight's room fee back, by the way.'

Matt gave a shrug. 'We can only issue refunds up to 1 p.m. on the day of the booking. If he decides to leave early, that's his choice.'

'He has lawyer friends.'

Matt smiled. 'Stop worrying.'

I took a sip of the Baileys over ice Matt had prepared and savoured the creaminess. It was ages since I'd had one. It was yet another thing that Jasper hadn't approved of – for whatever reason. I'd given up asking in the end. It was easier just to let it go.

'So where is the nearest train station?'

'Don't you need somewhere to live before you think of going home?'

'I'm working on that at the same time.'

'Is there someone you can stay with?'

'Not really. I mean, I have a couple of friends who I'm sure would let me sleep on their sofas, but I need to sort out something more permanent. I don't like to put people out.'

'I'd noticed. It was hard enough work just getting you to take my hand earlier today over a couple of tricky bits.'

'It wasn't that. I was just...'

'Trying to avoid trouble with the boyfriend.'

'Ex,' I reminded him. 'And yes.'

'Worried he might beat me up?'

I snorted my Baileys and shoved my hand up to my face before it poured down my nose. Matt laughed, deep and rich and relaxed.

'Don't make me laugh when I'm drinking.'

'Sorry,' he said, looking far from it.

'And yes. I was. And with you out of action, there would have been no one to stop me pushing his complaining arse off the side of the mountain.'

'Good job I was there, then. I think.'

'Quite.'

'So what's the plan?'

I shrugged. 'Scan job and letting sites and try and get myself back on my feet again. Don't look at me like that.'

'Like what?' He appeared genuinely mystified.

'All intense and questioning.'

Matt sat back in the chair. 'Sorry. Totally unintentional.'

'No, sorry. It's me. I'm just... actually, I don't know what I am at the moment.'

'Tired for one thing, I think.'

Matt stood from the chair and held out one meaty hand. I took it and he hauled me up from the soft, comfy armchair I'd been ensconced in.

'Come on. Go up and have a good night's sleep. Things often look better in the morning.'

4

Not this time, they didn't. Unfortunately things looked exactly the same. Although I had at least had a good night's sleep. I'd fallen into bed and barely moved all night, missing my alarm and only waking when a nearby church bell began to chime. I lay there for a while, listening to the peals ringing out before pushing myself up and into the shower. The water cascaded over me and washed away a little of the stress of yesterday but it was soon replaced with a new level of anxiety as I thought about my predicament.

'Aah, there she is.' Bronwyn came bustling over when I walked into the restaurant. 'How did you sleep?'

'Not too bad, thanks. Considering.'

'Quite. Now, what can I get you for breakfast?'

'Oh, thanks, but I'm not hungry.'

'Still. Got to eat. It will make you feel better. You've got decisions to make and you can't go doing that on an empty stomach, can you?'

I got the feeling that fighting her on this would take more energy than I had.

'I'll get you a full Welsh breakfast. Sit yourself down there and I'll make you some tea.'

Bronwyn was right. Of course, she was. Having seen the size of her sons, and their automatic response to come to her aid last night – not that I thought she needed it – it was clear they were close and she'd aced mothering. Once again, I felt that familiar pain deep inside. Slamming the door in my brain loudly, I returned to scrolling through letting-agencies pages. I'd been at my last flat for ages. I'd liked it and the landlady and I had become friends over the years. I knew she could have asked for a higher rent than she was charging me, but she never did, and I was sorry to say goodbye to both her and my little studio flat. But Jasper had said all the right things, persuading me that moving in was for the best. God, how I wished I could turn back time.

Everything I looked at in my old area was horrendously pricey and the only options looked like either going somewhere other than London or sharing. I had no special ties to London. A few friends but only one close one, and she was moving soon anyway. I'd never been very good at making friends, as I'd learned from an early age that people you get close to inevitably either leave or let you down. I suppose that was why I'd hoped it would work out with Jasper. Or Peter before that. When it came to romantic relationships, I had a habit of pinning everything on my partner, every hope, every wish, and yet here I was again. Alone. But this time with the added bonus of being homeless and unemployed. And the truth was, I was done with it. This was absolutely the last time I was going to even attempt a relationship. I didn't mind my own company. Maybe I could take up a hobby. Well, once I found a place to live and a job in order to pay for said hobby. There was far less chance of a hobby leaving me either broken-hearted, or feeling stupid.

'Any luck?' The deep voice jolted me from my search. I looked up to see Matt, prepared for another day's hiking, resting on the back of the chair opposite, in front of a large window. There was a great view from the bedroom but here I could just turn my head and look out onto the wild beauty of Snowdonia. The sun was more in evidence today and chasing away the few clouds that danced lazily across the sky. The breeze of yesterday had dropped. It seemed Matt's prediction that today would be a better day for the climb was correct.

'Not really,' I replied. 'Prices these days are crazy.'

'True enough. Are you just looking at London?'

I shrugged. 'It's all I know, but I think I'm going to have to widen the search.'

'There are other places outside London,' he said, with a teasing smile that I couldn't help but return. It was a good smile. It was, in fact, a good smile on a great face, above a smoking-hot body. But all that was totally irrelevant. I was done with men. From now on, it was all about me.

'I know. I'm not one of those people who thinks London is the be-all and end-all.'

'I'm just winding you up. Although I get the impression the ex-boyfriend might have been.'

'Yes, he was rather. Although he did allow Mustique and Monaco into his hallowed arena of acceptable places.'

'Not been to Mustique, but I thought Monaco was a bit overrated when I took a trip.'

'Me too!' I said, pushing myself up straighter on the chair. The less and less luck I'd had in my search, the lower I'd sunk in the chair. 'Not that I have much to compare it with. But I just—'

'Couldn't see what all the fuss was about?'

'Exactly!'

'Maybe you need to be wealthy to fully appreciate its charms.'

'Oh dear. I don't think I'm in any danger of appreciating them any time soon, then!' I said, laughing. I had to laugh. The other option was sliding under the table and bawling my eyes out, and I'd already had enough mortification for one weekend.

'Makes two of us. But there's more to life than money.'

'Having some always helps though.'

'True. Talking of that, has Mum spoken to you?'

'Me? No. I mean, we chatted at breakfast but not since. Why? Oh God! Did Jasper get the bank to reverse the charge on his card or something?' I dug into my bag and pulled out my purse. 'I have some but—' Matt's large, tanned hand closed over mine.

'No, he didn't. Not that I'm aware of anyway. And even if he had, we wouldn't expect you to pay.'

'Well, you should. I was staying in the room. You're a terrible businessman.'

'Noted. Which is why I leave the running of the hotel to my parents and the running of the adventure business to my brother while I concentrate on the fun bit.'

'Sounds like a good plan. Although I don't suppose yesterday was one of your most fun days.'

'Nah.' He gave a small shrug. 'It was fine. I've definitely had worse days.'

'That's good, then.'

He began to smile.

'Oh!' My mind played the words back to me. 'I don't mean it's good that you've had worse days. I just mean that we weren't your worst day. I think that's what I mean.'

'I know.'

'What are you up to today?'

Matt glanced at a ruggedised watch. 'Meeting a client in twenty minutes to take them up Crib Goch as my weekend suddenly freed up, and the weather is better for it today.'

'Oh God, yes. We'd booked you for this morning too, hadn't we? Sorry.'

'Not a worry. This other couple were thrilled when I called them to say I had enough time to take them after all, so think of it as doing someone else a favour.'

'That's a nice way to look at it.'

'Always good to try and find a silver lining,' he said.

'I like the sentiment but I'm not sure I can find a good way of looking at my current predicament.'

'How are you, my love?' Bronwyn said, laying her hand on my shoulder as she came over to us.

'OK, thanks.' I smiled back. I wasn't. Obviously. But that was my problem not theirs, and maybe, as Matt said, I just needed a different viewpoint. Ideally that viewpoint would be one where I was standing grinning like a loon as I held the winning Euromillions ticket for an obscene amount of money. Slim chance of that happening! Especially as I didn't even do the lottery.

'Has Matt told you about our predicament?'

I glanced at Matt, then Bronwyn. 'Predicament? No.'

'I was just getting to that,' he said.

'What predicament?'

'Molly, one of our best waitresses, is going travelling for a year and we've not had any luck getting a replacement. Matt mentioned that you have some waiting experience?'

'Oh! Well, yes. I used to work in a lovely coffee shop before I met Jasper and took a job with him.' I took a deep breath. 'And please don't think I'm not grateful for you trying to help. Obviously it was difficult for anyone not to hear that I was fired last night, as well as evicted, but it's really not your problem. I'll sort something out.'

Bronwyn nodded and I noticed Matt flash her a look that suggested a sentiment of 'I told you so'.

'I do appreciate you trying to help.'

'May we?' Bronwyn indicated the spare chairs at the table.

'Of course, but I know Matt has clients and I wouldn't want him to be late.'

He checked his watch. 'I've got time.'

'Oh... OK.'

They both took a seat at the table. We were tucked in the corner by a window and the breakfast crowd had thinned now. It was a shame that Jasper couldn't have picked a quieter time for his performance yesterday, but then Jasper always had been rather impervious to minor details like that. In fact, he'd probably enjoyed the fact he'd had an audience.

'All right,' Bronwyn said, placing her hands flat on the table. Her nails were neat and short but manicured with the palest pink polish giving a sheen to them. She was an attractive woman and I guessed she'd been an absolute knockout in her day. 'I shouldn't have tried to wrap it up as something else. I apologise,' she said, laying her hand over the one of mine that wasn't having its nails nibbled. 'Yes, we'd like to help you. But the truth of the matter is, Molly is going travelling and the only applicants we've had aren't the right fit. I've been running this place for long enough to get a feeling for these things and I just know the ones I've narrowed it down to are still people that will stay for a bit then flit off. Ideally we'd like someone who's going to be a little more permanent than that.'

'I can see why. It's a lot of effort to integrate someone into the team for them then to leave after a short time. I know we had that a few times at the place I used to work.'

'Exactly.' Bronwyn turned to her son, who had remained silent throughout. 'I told you she was the one.'

'Umm... pardon?'

A broad grin immediately broke across Matt's handsome features. 'Mum's been trying to set me up for years but, don't worry, that's not what she means in this instance.' He turned to Bronwyn. 'For once!'

She rolled her eyes at me, but they crinkled at the edges at her son's teasing. 'I've long since given up on that front and accepted now that he's a lost cause.'

'Hallelujah!' Matt raised his hands to the sky.

She gave him a steady look then turned back to me. 'Honestly, I don't know how I've put up with them for so long.'

'Surely there should be some sort of medal for long service by now?' I giggled, in spite of myself.

'You'd have thought, wouldn't you?'

I glanced at Matt. He was resting back with his arms folded loosely across a solid broad chest, a smile on his face, accepting the teasing and clearly comfortable in his own skin. My thoughts drifted for a moment, wondering what that must be like...

'So, what do you think?'

'Sorry?' I said, jolting back to the present.

'About taking over from Molly? We'd be ever so grateful, and I know you'd fit right in.' She unfolded something out of her pocket and slid it across the table to me. 'I don't know what you were earning in London. Quite possibly more than that, but it's a decent rate for the area, and of course I wouldn't expect you to take my word for that. You're more than welcome to do some research before you give an answer.'

I looked down, studying the formal offer of employment in front of me. The salary was actually a bit more than I'd been on back in London plus here I'd get to keep all my tips and the shifts were good. Obviously things were a bit cheaper here than in town, plus the offer included live-in accommodation.

'If there's anything you have concerns about, I'd be happy to chat it over with you and, of course, we can show you the room you'd have before you make any decisions.'

'I don't really know what to say,' I replied eventually, looking from one to the other of them.

'You don't have to say anything yet. Matt, do you have time to take Fleur up to see the room?'

He nodded.

'Molly was local so it's not been used for a while, but it's recently had a fresh coat of paint and I've just put up some new curtains in there. You're welcome to put up your own pictures and things. Make yourself at home.'

'I... this is really too kind.'

'Nonsense. As I said, you'd be doing us a huge favour too. Now, pop up with Matt and see what you think. You don't have to give me an answer today. That room you're in isn't booked tonight so take the day to explore the area and see what you think about maybe staying longer here.'

'Oh, no, if I'm staying tonight, I really must pay.'

'We'll talk about that later,' Bronwyn said, rising from her chair as Matt and I both followed. 'Now, have a lovely, relaxing day – goodness knows you can probably do with one – and we'll catch up later.'

'Thank you, Bronwyn,' I said, my voice cracking on her name.

'Oh, my dear,' she said, pulling me into a hug before standing me back and taking my face between her hands. 'Now, go with Matt. I'm sure he can give you some ideas of places to see. Just get out into the fresh air and let nature do its thing. I'll see you this evening.'

I nodded, wary of betraying my emotions any more by speaking, before heading the way Matt indicated, with him following behind.

'Just up here,' he said, his deep, tones close as we walked up the stairs, past the paintings by local artists of the area that hung on the wall. I'd finally got a chance to study them once Jasper had left. Jasper had been into art but only if it lent him bragging rights. He'd once bought a piece of modern art by an artist everyone was talking about as being the next big thing. Of course, Jasper had made it clear he already had one of his pictures. When I'd admitted one night that I didn't really like it – it was huge and had taken up a good portion of a wall in the penthouse apartment, so it had been hard to miss – Jasper had admitted that he didn't really like it either but, apparently, 'that wasn't the point'. I got that he bought things as investments, which was sensible, but surely you had to like it too if it was going to be staring you in the face every day?

As it turned out, the artist had decided the bohemian life wasn't for him and had gone off to train as a lorry driver. Jasper had a thing against all lorry drivers from that point as the painting he'd bought, not only didn't appreciate as he'd expected it to, but actually fell in value. My attempt at a helpful comment that I supposed it was like his job in that investments he made for others could go down as well as up hadn't been received well, so I'd said no more about it and hadn't been particularly upset to come home one day to find something else hanging in its place.

These, though, were beautiful. The delicate watercolours

picked out aspects of the scenery and captured celestial sunbeams with such realism as almost to be photographic.

'You like them?' Matt asked as he stopped at a room at the end of the hallway on the top floor of the building.

'They're beautiful. I mean, I don't know anything about art but...' I shrugged my shoulders.

'I think the most important thing is to know what you like. And you clearly do.'

'I wouldn't know what was worth anything though.'

Matt opened the door to the room and stepped back, allowing me to go in first.

'Is that important?'

'For some people.'

He turned and closed the door before fixing his gaze on me. 'And what about you? Do you think it's important?'

'I... well, no. I don't really know. I don't think so.'

Matt studied me for a moment, then stepped further into the room and adjusted the curtains so that the view was revealed in all its glory. As he did so, I pondered his question. What did I think? I knew what Jasper thought and I could probably tell you what previous boyfriends had thought. But what Fleur thought – that seemed a little bit less defined.

5

_____

'So, the room's all pretty self-explanatory,' Matt said, pushing open an adjoining door. 'Through here is the en suite.'

I stepped closer to him and peeked my head into the room before taking a further step, feeling the smile break on my face. 'Matt, this is beautiful!' I touched the cold edge of the stand-alone roll-top bath placed near to a window that looked out onto countryside.

'There's a blind you can pull, but that area of ground is protected for the wildlife and rare flora so no one can enter it. It's entirely private.'

I smiled back at him as I walked around the room. It was small but not cramped, and filled with lush plants and modern fixtures, all crowned with that stunning view.

'Do you like it?'

'I love it!' I replied, automatically and genuinely.

'Good.' He waited as I studied the rest of the room. In the corner, near to one window, was the cosiest armchair I'd ever seen. Squishy and inviting, dressed with a soft wool blanket over one arm and a beautiful cushion depicting a peacock, the colours of its feathers shimmering in the light as the metallic threads used in the embroidery caught the light streaming in.

'That's one of Mum's makes,' Matt said, pointing to the cushion. 'And the blanket is from a couple up the road who breed their own alpacas, then spin, weave and create their own items to sell.'

'Really?' I replied, eyes wide with interest.

'Yep. They do tours some days. I can sort you out one if it's something you think you'd like to do – assuming you decide to stay, of course.'

'It's a big step.' I moved closer to the window and took in the lush greens, sweeping mountains dotted with sheep.

'Are those goats?' I asked, peering at some animals closer to us.

'Yep. Friendly enough. They'll just ignore you.'

'They have horns.'

Matt's lips curved. 'They do. But don't worry. They don't use them on people.'

I looked up at him. This took some doing as, at well over six feet, he had a distinct height advantage on me.

'You don't seem convinced.'

I shrugged and felt warmth creep into my cheeks as I looked back at my feet. 'Sorry. I don't really know much about the countryside. I've always been around the London area.' I risked another look at him. 'Don't come across too many goats there.'

'No, I imagine not. But that's nothing to be embarrassed about. Set me loose here, I'm fine, but I'll admit I've got lost on the Tube on more than one occasion and ended up going the wrong way.'

I grinned. 'Really?'

'Yep.'

'The Tube I can do with my eyes closed.'

'Bearing in mind there's a live rail there, I'd prefer it if you didn't. But it proves my point. We can't expect to know everything about everywhere straight away. Doesn't mean we can't learn though. If we want to.'

'I suppose you're right,' I said, sitting down on the bed. 'Ooh, this is comfy.'

'Good to hear it. So you like the room?'

'I love the room.'

'As Mum said, you can decorate it however you choose, if you want to stay.'

He rested against the end of the white painted bedstead. Tiny fairy lights had been wound through the metalwork.

'There isn't a thing I'd change. It's absolutely perfect.'

'Mum will be thrilled to hear that. But don't let this sway you. I mean, don't get me wrong, I'm glad you like the room, but you have to be happy with the whole thing. As you said, it's a big step.'

'You think she's placing too much faith in someone she just met.' It wasn't a question.

Matt shook his head, apparently not offended. 'No, not at all. I'm pretty good at sussing character. I had to be in my previous career, and it can certainly be a useful skill in this one. I'd spent the day with you yesterday so when Mum had the idea of trying to kill two birds with one stone and solve a problem for each of us, she asked my opinion of you, and whether I thought you'd be a good fit here.'

'Oh... I see.'

He dropped his head a little, trying to catch my gaze, as I was now studying a pale pink rug, the tiny gold threads in it catching the sunlight. 'Obviously I said yes, I did.'

'Thank you for that.'

'No need to thank me. She asked me a question and I answered honestly. Now, if she'd asked me about the bloke...' He pulled a face.

'Don't remind me.' I glanced out of the window at the serene view. 'He wasn't always like that. I mean, perhaps he was but I didn't see it for a while. And then it was all a bit late.'

'It's never too late to make a new start, Fleur.'

'Do you believe that, I mean, really?' I asked, looking up at him now.

'Yes, 100 per cent. I've seen it happen. You just have to know what you want.'

I sucked in a deep breath. Honestly, I had no idea.

'That sounds to me like you don't know.'

I chewed the inside of my cheek and gave a small shrug.

'OK,' he said, taking a seat next to me on the bed. 'Then a good place to start is to decide what you don't want. Is that any easier?'

Was that any easier? God, what sort of person was I that I couldn't even answer a simple question like that. I felt hot tears begin to thicken and burn my throat. Suddenly I realised that I didn't really know the answer to either of those questions. I'd spent so long doing my best not to cause ripples, trying to make myself as agreeable as possible, trying to fit in, that I'd never paid much attention to whether what I was doing was what I actually really wanted or what I thought other people wanted me to be doing. So who was I? And what did I truly want from my life? I couldn't think of a time I'd purposely sat down and considered it. Neither could I think of a time that anyone had ever asked me, not properly.

'Seems like such an easy question, doesn't it?'

I looked up from where I'd laced my fingers together so tightly they were beginning to turn white. Matt's expression was calm. In fact, serenity emanated from his whole being. I definitely needed to ask him his secret.

'It seems to be easy for a lot of people.'

'Less than you'd think,' Matt replied as he reached over to the bedside and plucked a tissue from an engraved silver tissue holder.

'Thank you,' I said, taking it from him and blowing my nose in a way that certainly wasn't going to win me any etiquette prizes. Right now, I didn't care. I liked Matt but, as for trying to impress him, that was the last thing on my mind. So after a good honk, I pushed myself up from the bed and dropped the tissue in the bin next to the desk.

'Do you really believe that?' I asked as I turned back to face him.

'What's that?'

'That lots of people don't know what they want from life. Everyone I meet seems to know exactly who they are, what they're doing and where they're going.'

'Or at least that's what they want you to think. Remember, Fleur. Not everything you see is the real picture.'

'No, that's true. You're right. I know people tend to show you what they want you to see. I suppose it's human nature. No one wants to show off their failures or flaws.'

'Sometimes it's the imperfections and vulnerabilities that make someone attractive, especially if they're willing to own their flaws. No one is perfect and the attraction of those who think they are can wear thin pretty quickly.'

'You sound as if you're talking from experience.'

A curve played at the side of his mouth. It wasn't quite a smile, but it wasn't serious either. It was something in between. Something enigmatic.

'Sorry, I didn't mean to be nosey. I shouldn't have—'

Matt held up a hand. 'It's fine. If you do decide to work and live here, I doubt I'll be left with any secrets anyway once Mum gets chatting.' This time the smile was clear and I felt it reflect on my own face as I looked around the room once more and out over the ancient landscape, before my gaze rested back on the handsome man sitting on the bed in front of me.

'I still can't believe that your mum's made this offer. I mean, none of you know the slightest thing about me and you offered me a job, and a roof over my head, just like that. It seems a bit of a fortuitous coincidence that you're looking for someone with waiting experience just as I visit here and lose my job all in the same day.'

'Something tells me you haven't come across a lot of fortu-itous coincidences, as you call them.'

I gave a shrug.

'I see,' Matt said, placing his shovel hands on rock-solid thighs and pushing up from the patchwork eiderdown that was folded across the end of the bed, contrasting with the crisp white duvet cover. 'Well, sometimes luck does land in the right place. But like we said earlier, don't feel pressured to take the job. Upping sticks is a big thing to—'

'I want it.'

Matt blinked. 'Umm... what?'

'The job... this,' I said, indicating the beautiful, homely room. 'I want it. And I promise you won't regret it. I'm a hard worker and I'm happy to do overtime or cover anyone and—'

'Stop!' Matt interrupted, laughing. 'I get it. Mum will be thrilled. And I know we won't regret it. But you don't need to take on all the tasks to try and please people. Yes, we've built this place on hard work, but we know how to play too, when to relax. And that includes our staff.'

'Yes, but I want to prove to you that you did the right thing.'

He'd moved to the door.

'Fleur, you don't need to prove anything to anybody. All you need to do is to be yourself. That's enough. OK?'

I nodded. 'OK.'

'I'll see you downstairs when you're ready. I'll leave you to tell Mum the good news.'

'Thanks. I'll be right there.'

'No rush.' He gave a smile, and headed down the corridor and stairs.

'Be myself,' I repeated quietly in the privacy of what was about to be my own room. Now the only thing I needed to do was work out who that was.

6

'I'm more than happy to start today,' I said to Bronwyn.

'I can see we're not going to have any trouble with this one skipping shifts.' She laughed as Matt sat on the back step lacing up his boots.

'I think the problem might be getting her to stop working.' Her son chuckled.

I felt a blush on my cheeks, which Bronwyn immediately picked up on. 'Oh, don't mind him. He's just teasing you. Goodness knows it's better to have a hard worker than someone who's there under duress with a face like a slapped bum, who you have to chivvy along all the time.'

I smiled at her expression.

'It's harder than you'd think to find people with a work ethic like you these days.'

'I know. We had a few people come and go at the coffee shop I worked at who just weren't prepared to pull their weight. As you say, sometimes it felt like they were doing you a favour even bothering to turn up each day. I promise I'm not like that, and that I won't let you down.'

'I know.'

I flicked a glance to Matt, who had by now finished preparing to go out and was standing, peering at his phone. With some kind of sixth sense, he switched his gaze from the screen to meet my own.

'Don't worry about it. She's been running this hotel a long time and has got used to reading people pretty well over the years.'

'Hadn't you better be going?' his mum asked, glancing up at the statement clock on the wall.

'Client's cancelled. Decided to go white-water rafting instead.'

'You going to charge them?' Bronwyn asked before turning to me. 'There's a twenty-four-hour notice period normally. It's lost earnings for him otherwise.'

Matt shook his head. 'Nah, they didn't have a lot of notice that I was going to be free anyway.'

'I hope you charged Jasper for it as he's messed up your plans?'

'I have done but I also fully expect him to query it either directly with me, but more likely the bank.'

'If he does, then let me know. I'll make sure you're paid.'

'No need for that, but thanks. The terms were there for him to read and they're pretty airtight. He won't get far trying to claim it back.'

'You don't know Jasper.'

'Jasper doesn't know me,' Matt returned.

'True. But he's used to getting his way.'

'He didn't get his way when he wanted to tackle a mountain that was far beyond both of your capabilities and with unsuitable weather.'

I thought for a moment. 'That's true. In fact, I think that's one of the few times someone has said no to him and stuck to their guns.'

'So, what are you going to do today, then, now you have an unexpected day of leisure?' Bronwyn asked as she took off her apron and folded it over her arm.

'I'm not sure.'

'Well, I'll get out of both your ways,' I said, going to turn away. 'Thank you again for your offer. The room is really beautiful.'

'Are you absolutely sure?' Bronwyn asked. 'I don't want to hurry you. It's a big decision moving to a place where you don't know anyone. Although, of course, you already know us.'

'It's fine. I've had plenty of experience going places I don't know anyone so that's really the least of my worries.'

'What are your worries?' Matt's face and tone were calm.

'Well, the first one isn't a worry. More a job to do.'

'Which is?'

'Find out where the nearest railway station is and get booked on a train back to London to collect my stuff.'

'OK. Next?' Matt asked as Bronwyn leant against the side-board, listening.

'Work out if I can get my stuff back on the train easily or, if not, whether I can hire a car for a one-way trip. Lots of places only want to do rentals that start and finish at the same place these days.'

'When were you looking to go?'

'Today if there are any trains, bearing in mind your mum won't let me start yet.' I gave her a quick grin, which she returned.

'Are you hoping to do it there and back in one day, or do you have somewhere to stay down there?'

'I could probably find somewhere, although I'd rather try and do it in one day.'

'It's kind of late to start today, then, and it's a bit of a faff to get to a main line station from here.'

'Then I'll go tomorrow.'

'Or we can drive down today. How much stuff have you got? Is there furniture, for example?'

'I... umm... no. Not really.'

Matt quirked a brow.

'No. Not furniture. The place I had before was furnished. I'd bought a new mattress because... well. You would if you could, wouldn't you?'

'I've probably slept in worse places but, yes, I know exactly what you mean.'

'But I left it behind when I moved in with Jasper. I don't really have a lot of stuff, to be honest.'

'We've got this.' He pointed out of the kitchen window that looked out onto a gravelled area. Parked there was a metallic grey pick-up with a cover over the back bed. The name of the hotel was written on the door. 'Do you think all your stuff would fit in there?'

I huffed out a laugh. 'A few times over, I should think.'

Matt didn't reply, or even look at me. He just nodded before turning away from the window.

'You don't need to take me. It will all fit in a couple of suit-cases. I can get those on the train.'

'The chance of getting a seat yourself these days is hit and miss, let alone when you have luggage.'

'It's fine. I don't mind, really. I'd rather do that.'

This time he turned, piercing eyes hooking my gaze.

'Not that I don't appreciate the offer.'

'Do you need to get the Tube to and from this bloke's place?'

'Yes. But it's not a problem. I grew up doing it.'

'Although presumably without a couple of suitcases.'

'Well, no. Not that often.' I dropped my gaze and my thoughts drifted back to the various pillars and posts I'd bounced around from during my childhood. Most of the times the shifts were by car, but there had been a couple of times when I'd needed to get myself out of a situation and I'd taken the Tube late. At the time there had only been the one bag. It was a bit sad to think that in all that time I'd really only gained another few suitcases' worth of belongings.

He had a point. I lifted my eyes to meet his. 'Is it the thought of spending several hours stuck in a vehicle with me?'

My eyes widened. 'No! No! Not at all. I'm more than happy to do that.' The slightest curve of a smile teased his lips. 'Not that I mean... I was just trying to say that that's not the problem.'

'So, what is the problem?'

'Nothing really... I shouldn't have said anything.'

'But now you have.'

'Are you always this insistent?'

'Depends on the situation.' He shrugged. 'If I think the situation warrants it, then yes. I want to help you and you won't let me and I'm curious why. I had a shower this morning, I promise.'

That much I didn't need to be told. When he'd pointed to the truck parked outside, the scent of a citrusy shower gel had drifted around me. Jasper had always used a designer brand that didn't smell all that nice, if you'd asked me. He'd flipped one time I'd left my lemon and lime Superdrug bargain brand in the shower. When I'd asked him why he was so upset, he'd stared at me and then asked me what people would think if they saw it.

'Well, I'd have asked them why they were in the en suite shower in the first place,' I'd returned. Jasper had stared, shaken his head and stalked off. Personally I'd thought it was a pretty valid question but then it seemed that, on the odd occasion I actually spoke my true mind, he and I disagreed. I just wished I'd realised that before moving in with him and chucking in my coffee-shop job. It would have saved a lot of hassle. Not to mention money on yet another wardrobe. When I'd worn a designer dress a friend had found for me in the donations at the charity shop she worked at, I'd been thrilled. Jasper had complimented me on it and we'd gone to dinner with some of his friends, all smiles and laughter. The smile had slipped when one of the women had glanced over at me during a lull in conversation at dinner and noted the designer.

'Chanel, isn't it?'

'Yes,' I'd said, doing my best to sound as though I wore high-end designer clothes all the time. The truth was I didn't know a Gucci from a lychee, but I'd been trying.

'I thought so. That's from their collection three years ago, isn't it? Or is it four?' Had her eyebrows not already been permanently raised from a rather intense facelift, I'd have imagined them rising in mock query. Everyone present had known she'd been sure of her facts and had enjoyed sharing that knowledge. So what? Did these people just wear things for one season after paying astronomical amounts for them? As I'd glanced around the table, I'd realised that was exactly what they did. And, judging by Jasper's frown, wearing something that wasn't of the current season was apparently a massive no-no.

'I've never been so embarrassed,' he'd grumbled on the way home. 'Where did you get it? Can't you take it back? If they're trying to sell the previous season to people who don't know any better, they should be taken to court for misrepresentation.'

I'd stared out of the windscreen watching the rhythmic swishing of the wipers, stinging from his words. Words he hadn't even realised had hurt me. No, I didn't know better. But then I hadn't had the privilege of his upbringing, his education, his... everything. I'd literally had nothing. Until that moment, I'd had the excitement of wearing a designer dress, but his so-called friends had dashed the joy from that too.

'I'll take it back tomorrow.'

'Good.'

Thankfully my friend had been understanding about the whole thing and had refunded me the full amount. Neither of which she'd had to do – and probably hadn't been supposed to. But she had met Jasper once and, according to her, once was enough.

'I'm sure I sound ungrateful,' I said, looking back up at Matt. He and his family had been so kind and supportive from the moment I'd met them. He deserved an explanation. 'I already owe you all so much. I don't really like being beholden to anyone so I'd rather do this on my own.'

'I see.'

'Please don't be cross.'

Matt's eyebrows shot up and, to my surprise, he began to laugh. 'Sweetheart, I'm not cross. Far from it. Why would you think that?'

He wasn't to know that was always my automatic assumption. It had been for a long time, and, no matter what I did, I couldn't seem to change it.

I gave a small shrug.

'Well, I'm not. OK? Not in the slightest. As for the rest, you don't owe us anything.' He bent his knees a little so that he was level with my face despite the fact I was refusing to look up.

'Of course I do. You've given me a job and somewhere to live.'

'Mum and Dad have been looking for someone to fill this position for ages. The hotel's got a good reputation and they need staff that have the ability to support that reputation. So far, none of the applicants have. Then you came along.'

'Someone you know nothing about.'

'Someone I'd spent several hours with,' he corrected me. 'Someone who mentioned during the day that she'd worked at a coffee shop for years until she'd met the bloke she was with, and loved it. Believe me, we had all the information we needed to offer you the job. The live-in accommodation was just a part of the deal, whoever took the position.'

'I'll do my best not to let you down.'

Matt grinned – but the smile faded when he realised my expression didn't match his own. 'Oh my God, you're serious.'

'Of course I am!'

Matt took a deep breath, which stretched the fabric on the T-shirt he wore, highlighting muscles that yesterday had been mostly hidden beneath a jacket.

'You are not going to let us down. OK? Just relax and be yourself.'

There it was again. Be yourself. He made it sound so easy.

'I hope not,' I said trying to put a hint of amusement in my tone, diverting him from the fact that I desperately wanted to know exactly how to do just that.

The stillness on his features showed me he wasn't buying it for a moment. 'I've met a lot of people in my time and some-times assessing what sort of person they were in a short time could be the difference between life and death, and not just my own. So, I had to get pretty good at it, pretty quickly.'

'Life and death?' I asked.

'Yep,' he answered, grabbing a couple of small bottles of orange juice out of the fridge. 'We can take these for the journey, but we'll stop for a coffee and to stretch our legs anyway.'

'I didn't know I'd agreed yet.'

Matt stretched his neck, tipping it from side to side slowly. 'Do you really want to lug cases on the Tube and the train?' That bright, intelligent gaze focused on me again, and I couldn't look away. Or lie.

'No.'

'Come on, then.'

7

'The views are amazing,' I said, peering out of the window as Matt drove away from the hotel. 'Have you always lived here?'

'Mostly. When I wasn't deployed elsewhere.'

'You were in the services?'

'Yep.'

'Hence the need to suss people out quickly.'

Matt glanced over. 'Yep.'

'I suppose that comes in handy in your current job too. For example, if someone tried to bluff you that they were more experienced than they actually were.'

His eyes were still focused on the road but I saw the grin and couldn't help joining him.

'I am sorry about that.'

'Stop apologising. One look at your face was enough to tell me that none of it had been your idea.'

'It's not that I don't like walking or fresh air or anything. Not that you get a lot of fresh air in London.'

'No, not exactly known for that, is it? But you'll be making up for it soon. And you can still enjoy walking without feeling the need to clamber up a mountain.'

'Exactly!'

'Shame though. You get some incredible views as you saw the other day. The higher ones are stunning, but it does take some effort to get up there.'

'You obviously love what you do,' I said, enjoying the enthusiasm in his voice as he spoke.

'I do,' he said, slowing the pick-up to a stop as we waited in a short line of traffic at a red light.

'Have you always enjoyed scrambling up mountains?'

'To an extent. But I really got into it more when I came back on leave. Getting out into nature, with nothing but the sound of the wind, and the odd goat or sheep. I found it a great way to decompress.'

'I can imagine.' I paused. 'Actually I can't. I'm not going to pretend I know what it's like to serve. I saw some of the photos on the walls back in the hotel. Was that Afghanistan?'

'Yep.'

'But I get how just going out among the wilds and silence could be therapeutic. I found it far more enjoyable than I thought I would, if I'm honest. And that's just coming from London.'

'You didn't exactly come across as relaxed.'

'No, I wasn't really.'

'Any particular reason? Apart from living with that bloke?' He shot me a smile. 'Seems like that would be enough to stress anyone out.'

'He's not that bad. I mean..."

Matt remained silent and, for some reason, I felt compelled to fill the break in conversation.

'He isn't, honestly. Not always, anyway.'

'Well, I only have the experience of spending the day with him acting like a spoilt child for most of that and then embarrassing you in front of a room full of diners, leaving you without a job or a place to live. And while I'm likely putting my size twelve right in it, I'm not sure he can just fire you like that when you haven't broken any rules.'

Matt's words resonated within my brain, bouncing around before coming back again and again to the same place. The place that said, 'This guy's right and you know it.'

'Sorry.' Matt blew out a deep breath between his teeth. 'I shouldn't have said anything. It wasn't my place and was pretty insensitive considering you've just broken up.' I saw his face tense and momentarily his grip on the wheel tightened, the long tanned fingers curling around the wheel. A silver scar traced along the back of his left hand, starting in two different points to the side of his palm before joining at a point just below his fore finger. It stood out against the tan and I wondered what had happened to cause it. Scars were funny things. Some people wore them like a badge of honour, some people hid them, and some didn't seem to think of them at all. Then there were those of us that had ours on the inside. Sometimes the ones no one could see were the deepest.

'It's fine, really.' I trotted out my usual response.

'No,' Matt said, certainty in his tone. 'It's not. I'm pretty good at keeping my opinions to myself normally. I'm the one who usually gets lumbered with the more... demanding clients because I've got the longest fuse.'

'Ah, I can see why Jasper and I were assigned to you.' Even in an email, Jasper had the ability to get people's backs up. Unless it was a client, obviously, when he could be as charming as I'd first thought him.

Matt slapped a hand to his forehead before dragging it

down over one side of his face. 'That's not what I meant at all. Although now that I've played it back in my head... Tell you what, I'll stop talking and you can enjoy the view in peace. Feel free to put the radio on if you'd like.' His tone was light but I could see the tension in his jaw, itself shadowed by a day or two's growth of dark stubble.

'Don't worry. That wasn't the first time someone's offered up such an opinion of my boyfriend.' I paused. 'Ex-boyfriend.'

'Not the point,' he replied. 'I still shouldn't have said anything.'

'I'm glad you did.'

Matt shifted his eyes to me for a moment before returning them to the road ahead. 'You are? Why?'

I let out a sigh as I watched a couple of sheep trotting across a field. 'Because I know where I stand with you.' I turned away from the dry-stone-walled field to face him. 'It's good.'

His smile was tentative but it was there and the sight of it made me smile too. Matt was unmistakably gorgeous, tall and muscular. Imagine a magazine editor requesting a good-looking, outdoorsy type, who could be both a clothes horse and look as if he knew what he was doing, and Matt would be the perfect choice. But I needed this job too much to start having a crush on the boss's son and I was pretty sure that Matt didn't look at me that way either. Mind you, he had one of those faces that could switch to unreadable when he wanted it to and I wondered idly if that was something he'd learned in his time in the armed forces where, I was sure, it would have been a useful trait. Even so, sometimes you could tell from the way someone looked at you, even briefly, if they felt an attraction, and with Matt there had been nothing.

Daft then that Jasper had felt threatened by him. Not that he would have admitted it – he'd have rather worn a polyester suit from a cheap fast-fashion outlet and spark his way through the office before admitting that someone else might be more handsome, cleverer or better at something than him. There was no denying that Jasper was bright, and good at his job. He was also nice looking. It was just a shame that, in the end, he'd turned out to be a complete dick.

The fact was I seemed to have a habit of attracting them. Rumi, the one friend who knew, and, most importantly, understood my history, tended to roll her eyes at me every time I finally introduced her to a boyfriend. Rumi wasn't one to pull punches – she'd thrown a few in her time when the occasion required it, one or two of them on my behalf. I wasn't sure I would have got through it all without her. She'd taken me under her wing from the start and, despite despairing of my choice in men, had stuck by me. I slid a glance to Matt. Had things been different, I got the feeling that Rumi would have approved of Matt. Typical! I made a note to give Rumi a call when I could. I'd given her a brief summary on WhatsApp but I knew she'd want a full play-by-play account. She loved a drama, did Rumi.

'You OK?' Matt asked. 'You're very quiet.'

'Yep.' I gave a brief smile. 'I'm fine.' If he thought I was quiet now, he should have met me as a teenager.

'I really am sorry,' he said again.

'Oh my God,' I said, bursting out laughing. 'Seriously. Don't worry about it. Jasper is everything you said and I should have left him ages ago. Yes, you were a bit blunt but that's OK. You and Rumi would get on like a house on fire.'

'Who's Rumi?'

'My best friend. She is of the same opinion as you about Jasper, and in fact most of the boyfriends I've had, and she's never been afraid to say so.'

Matt grinned as he waited at a zebra crossing, his eyes lighting up with mischief. 'I think I like her already. Is she in London too?'

'Yes, not too far from where I used to work although they're in the process of trying to move out of the city. She and her husband have a couple of kids now and want somewhere a bit more family friendly to bring them up.'

'Sounds like a good plan. Are they planning to move far?'

'Norfolk.'

'Blimey! One extreme to the other.'

'I know,' I replied, laughing. 'Rumi was a bit unsure at first too, but her husband has family there and he runs his own business from home so isn't tied to one place. They hired a cottage and spent the summer holidays there, as a trial of sorts. By the end of the first week, Rumi was totally sold and looking for properties. She can't wait.'

'And how do you feel about that?'

'Me?' I asked, turning in my seat a little.

'Yes. You're obviously very close and there's a good distance between London and Norfolk'

'True. But I just want what will make her happy. I think they'll have a better quality of life there. The place they're buying has a big garden for the kids to run around in and we can keep in touch by video chat and stuff. I know it's not the same but it's fine and, anyway, I'm moving now too. Not many people stay in the same place all their lives these days, do they?'

'No, that's true. And I'm sure we'd be able to work out a special rate for your friend and her family if they wanted to visit.'

'That's really kind, thank you.'

More scenery passed as the conversation ebbed and I watched the clouds chase each other across the sky on the light breeze that ruffled the early leaves. Once we joined the motor-way, Matt spoke again.

'Have you asked where your things are? Would they still be at his place?'

'I doubt it. Knowing Jasper, he probably hired someone to erase all trace of me. Once he gets an idea in his head, he tends to go at it full steam. I suppose that's part of the reason he is where he is. Sometimes it's for the good, and sometimes...' I let the sentence drift off. We both knew how it ended. 'I suppose I'd better call him and find out.' Speaking to Jasper was the last thing I wanted to do but, as Matt had been kind enough to drive me down to collect my things, I didn't want to take him on a wild goose chase. I pulled out my phone, scrolled to Jasper's number and rang.

'Fleur.' His voice was soft. Charming. Just as it had been that first evening I'd met him. So unlike the sharp tones that had gradually become more familiar. 'I was hoping you'd call.'

'Oh!' I said, momentarily thrown by the lack of hostility in his voice.

'Where are you?'

'Coming down to get my things. I need to know which storage unit you've had them put in.'

'I haven't.'

'Oh. Well, I've been able to collect them quicker than I thought but I also know how... efficient you are.' In my peripheral vision, I saw the corner of Matt's mouth tilt up.

'Yes. Ordinarily I am.'

'So? Where do I need to go to collect my stuff?'

'It's still here. At the apartment.'

'I see.' My stomach knotted. I had no wish to encounter Jasper today. I'd hoped I'd just be able to grab my belongings from a faceless unit, throw them in the back of the pick-up and head back to Wales. That, of course, would have been far too easy.

'I thought we could talk.'

'I'm not sure there's anything to talk about, Jasper.'

'Fleur, darling. Of course, there is.'

'You made it quite clear that there wasn't when you dumped me, fired me and left me homeless all in one fell swoop, with an audience at the restaurant.'

Jasper cleared his throat. 'Yes. Well. I may have been a little hasty. That's what I wanted to talk about.'

This was how it went. Every time. And not just with Jasper. Everything was fine until it wasn't and just as I found the strength to leave, I'd chicken out and get pulled back in, thinking things would improve. That the cracks in the relationship were fixed. But they weren't. They were, once again, just papered over. Jasper took my silence as assent.

'I knew you'd understand, my beautiful flower.'

But that was the thing. I didn't. Not this time. Something had shifted. Just the tiniest amount. But it was enough. I couldn't say if it was the support that Matt's family had surrounded me with or if it had been Jasper's parting shot, or a combination of both. But either way, there was now a tiny sliver of light. A minute shaking of the belief that I had to accept such behaviour.

'Fleur? Are you still there?'

'Yes.'

'OK. I'll order some food in and we can talk.'

I remained silent. Even when he wasn't on speaker, Jasper had one of those voices that carried and I knew Matt had heard every word.

'Jasper, I need to call you back in a moment.' Before he

could protest, I hung up. That alone probably had him fuming but he'd just have to deal with it.

'Please don't ask me what I think you should do,' Matt said.

'I wasn't going to.'

Matt momentarily turned his head to meet my gaze before returning his concentration to the road. How did he know that that was exactly what I had been planning to do?

'It's your decision.'

'But you've taken your day off to bring me down to get my stuff.'

'And had you decided to go back to him, I'd have still driven you down. Trying to get public transport on a Sunday from anywhere is a royal pain in the backside. Don't worry about it.'

'You'd have really done that?'

'Of course.'

'But you don't know me.'

A smile curled Matt's lips. 'You don't have to know someone to offer kindness, Fleur.'

'No, I know. Sorry.'

'What are you apologising for?'

'Because it sounded like I was saying that... well, that you wouldn't be kind, I mean, that you—'

Deep, rich laughter rolled around the inside of the cosy cab and Matt reached across, momentarily laying his hand over my clenched ones. 'Whatever it is that you're trying to say, or trying to apologise for, it's completely unnecessary. I didn't think anything, or take offence.'

'Right. OK. Thanks.'

His hand gave a momentary squeeze of mine then returned to the steering wheel. Jasper's name flashed up as my phone began to ring.

'Not the patient type, is he?'

'Not exactly.' I took a deep breath and answered.

'I was getting worried,' Jasper said before I'd had a chance to speak.

Unlikely. The thought popped into my head before I could stop it. He just wasn't really the type. In two years, the only thing I'd seen him stress about was work. Jasper was definitely one of those people that lived to work, rather than the other way around. He loved his job and he was good at it, both of which were qualities I admired.

'I needed time to think.'

'Think? About what?' I opened my mouth to answer but Jasper hadn't finished. 'It would seem that continuing our relationship is a harder decision for you than me.' He'd taken on the role of injured party expertly.

'Jasper. Yesterday there was no continuing. You made that very clear and therefore I'm sure you can understand my confusion now.'

'I was just cross and tired and having had that tour guide leering over you all day hadn't done much for my patience.'

I shot Matt a glance and he rolled his eyes.

'He wasn't leering, Jasper, and you know it. I was tired too. That still doesn't give you the right to treat me like you did. It was humiliating.'

'I apologised already, Fleur. Can we just move on now?'

'Actually, Jasper, you didn't.'

Jasper let out a sigh. 'Come on, Fleur. You're just quibbling over semantics now.'

Just agree. It's the easiest way. Less stress, less conflict. People don't like people who don't agree with them...

I looked over at Matt, whose face, once again, wore that inscrutable expression but, even through the shadow cast by his stubble, I could see his jaw was a little more tense than it had been earlier. Perhaps he was thinking about his parents and the position they thought they'd finally filled turning out to be a non-starter.

I thought back to the hotel, how kind they'd all been. The beautiful room and the warm feeling that had washed over me as I'd walked in and realised that this was the place I'd get to retreat to every day, surrounded by nature and fresh air and... everything I was completely new to. It was daunting but I also couldn't remember the last time I'd felt excited about something like this – or if I ever had.

Yes, going back to Jasper would be the easy thing to do but I wasn't happy. He didn't make me happy and I knew there was no future there for me. His parents had made that quite clear and, even if they hadn't, Jasper's parting shot last night had been so cruel it had shocked me. Even I hadn't thought he could stoop to that level of callousness.

'Are you still there? Fleur? Just let me know a time.' It was obvious he was doing his best to keep his temper but the initial cooing tone he'd begun with was thinning now.

'I'm coming to collect my things, Jasper.'

Matt turned his head briefly and I met his eyes. Something in them strengthened my resolve.

'What?' Jasper was clearly trying his best not to be snappy, but mostly failing.

'I said I'm coming to collect my things. You ended the relationship quite definitely and, now I've had time to sleep on it, I think you were right.'

'Of course I wasn't.' Frankly it was a good job I was sitting down as hearing Jasper actually admit he was wrong was quite the blue moon event. 'It was all just heat-of-the-moment stuff. You know how it is.'

I did know how it was. And usually I forgave people

because it was the easiest option. But this time was different. This time I didn't want the easiest option. I'd had a glimpse of a different life and, scary as that might be, I wanted to find out more about it.

'Now stop being ridiculous and let me know which train you're getting. I'll come and meet you and we can forget all this.'

'No, Jasper. We can't forget it. I can't forget it. You said some hurtful things and we both know this relationship can't go anywhere. And, with your help, I've realised that's probably a good thing anyway.'

'Bloody hell, Fleur. What have I told you before about being over-sensitive? You're really making far too big a deal out of this.'

'Well, you won't have to worry about that any more.'

'So you're just taking your things and going?'

'Yes.'

'Where?'

'I'm not sure that's relevant for you now, is it?'

'I see. It's like that, is it? Fair enough. Do you know what time you'll be here? I have things to do and can't wait about all day for you.'

Matt pointed at the satnav destination arrival time. We'd entered Jasper's address as a starting point until I found out where he'd had my stuff taken.

'I should be there in about an hour and a half. You can just leave my stuff in a couple of boxes with the concierge if you need to go out.'

'Yes. I might,' Jasper replied. 'It depends on my other plans.'

The plans he didn't have two minutes ago, I thought. How did I miss the foot-wide streak of childishness this man had? The truth was, I hadn't. I'd just accepted it. But not this time.

'OK,' I said with as much nonchalance as I could muster, which seemed to irk Jasper even more.

'I want my key back.'

'I didn't take my set with me. They're in the console table in the hall. I hadn't anticipated needing them this weekend.'

I caught Matt's smirk at my uncharacteristic dig about Jasper's flouncing off. At the other end of the line I could hear Jasper rummaging in the drawer.

'Right. They're here. Good.'

'I told you they were.' I did my best to remain calm but being accused of lying had always been a trigger for me. Something I'd stupidly told Jasper when I'd thought he was different from the others, but perhaps he didn't remember.

'I just wanted to check.'

He remembered. Jesus, what an arse. Why on earth had I wasted two years of my life with him? I'd thought the good breeding and expensive education meant something. All they meant was that he was just another loser, but with a posh accent.

'Goodbye, Jasper.' I ended the call before I said something I wouldn't regret and then flung my head back against the headrest.

8

———————

'You all right?' Matt asked.

'Fine.'

'That's the type of fine people say when they're exactly the opposite of fine.'

'It doesn't matter. Really.'

'Yes,' Matt replied, in a definitive tone. 'It does. There are some services coming up. Do you want to stop and get a drink and stretch your legs?'

I glanced at the timer on the satnav.

'He can wait a bit. And as you said, he can leave your things downstairs if his busy social life calls.'

Matt was right. I'd been running my life around Jasper's wants for the last two years. It was about time I stopped.

'Actually, that sounds great. And I'm buying the coffee.'

* * *

'Nice place.' Matt stood outside the heavy glass doors and tipped his head back to look up at the apartment block.

'It's probably better if you stay down here,' I whispered to Matt as we stepped through into the echoing, marble clad lobby.

'Do you need help carrying anything?'

'No, it's fine. There's a lift.' Now I was back, I could feel the edginess in my voice, the knot in my stomach. Part of me – quite a large part of me – would have been happy for Matt to come with me but I knew it would only wind Jasper up. And I could do this alone anyway. It wasn't as if that were an alien concept to me – which was probably exactly why I didn't want to. Why being on my own was something I'd pushed back against for so long now. Unfortunately, as I stepped through the doors and saw Matt disappear behind them as they closed silently in the expensive hush of the building, it was becoming obvious that being with someone never seemed to work out either. I leant back against the mirrored wall. I wished someone would give me a bloody clue what I was supposed to do with my life. My own choices, as Rumi had reminded me more than once in the kindest way she could, had been a bit rubbish. Now, as I left the lift and walked to Jasper's front door, I was about to come face to face with yet another poor choice.

'Oh... hi.'

The woman looked me up and down with a mixture of confusion and judgement. I got the feeling I didn't pass. 'Can I help you?' she asked, the cut-glass tones cool, as was her smile.

Jasper could have at least bloody opened the door. He knew when I was coming. The penny dropped with a loud, metallic clang. He knew when I was coming...

I mentally hiked up my big-girl pants until they were practically under my boobs and spoke again, trying to squeeze some strength into my voice.

'I've just come to collect a few things. Jasper's expecting me.'

'Really?' One expensively prepped HD brow did its best to fight against a dose or ten of Botox.

'Yes. Is he in?'

Of course he's bloody in.

'Jasper?' she called, only half glancing away as if she suspected I was about to make off with the door knob. A few moments later, she smiled at the approaching footsteps and stayed close as Jasper took her place at the door.

'Oh. Fleur.'

'Hello, Jasper. I've come to collect my things as we arranged.'

'Well. We didn't really arrange it, did we? You hardly gave me much time?'

I glanced at the mystery woman.

Doesn't look like you needed much time...

'I thought you'd prefer it if I got out of your way as quickly as possible.' Jasper made an almost imperceptible movement of his head that was neither a yes nor no.

'I suppose.'

'Can I come in, then?' I asked, as Jasper had yet to invite me into the apartment and Matt's pick-up was parked on the street, which was costing a fortune.

'Oh. Right. Yes. I suppose you'd better.'

I gritted back the automatic thank you as he made things as uncomfortable and awkward as possible.

'Will you be long?' the woman asked, the plummy voice now laced with irritation.

'I hope not.'

'Do you have any boxes?' Jasper asked, looking around as though I were about to produce a handful of boxes from the end of my sleeve like a magician's scarves. Their attitude was beginning to grate now. He was the one who had ended it and yet he was the one acting the most put out.

'No, Jasper. Clearly not. I'm pretty sure everything I have will fit in a couple of suitcases.'

'What suitcases?' He looked around again. I'd only taken an overnight bag to Wales and had left it in my room at the hotel. My room. I smiled to myself at how that sounded. A room of my own... Jasper cleared his throat, bringing me back to the moment.

'The ones I used for travel.'

'Oh.' He frowned as if thinking and I knew exactly where this was going. *Don't give up the day job, Jasper – there's definitely no Oscar waiting with your name on it.* 'I don't mean to be rude...'

I'm pretty sure that's exactly what you mean.

'But...' he turned his palms up '...those are actually my cases. I mean, not being funny or anything.' Although his features were arranged in an – almost – apologetic way, the eyes were cold.

Arsehole.

'Fine,' I said, with an equally fake smile on my face, and turned towards the kitchen.

'Jasper? Where's she going?' the woman asked without any attempt at lowering her voice.

'Getting these,' I said, returning with a roll of bin liners as I passed them both before heading into the bedroom.

I heard Jasper's footsteps behind me and turned, tilting my head in question.

'Thought you might want some help.'

Jasper had never knowingly helped anyone in his life. The only reason he knew the word was because it could be attached to the word 'hired'.

'No, you didn't. You're checking I don't take anything that you consider yours.'

'Now, there's no need for that.' He put on a wounded tone but I knew I'd hit a nerve.

'Isn't there? Why don't you invite your friend in here too to double-check? Or is she in the kitchen checking that I didn't stuff a Le Creuset dish up my jumper when I went to get the bags?'

'Her name is Lucinda, and there's no call to be nasty about my friends.'

'Perhaps now you know how I feel, Jasper. You were always mean about Rumi but I'm beginning to think she was right about you from the start.'

'I didn't like you associating with people like that. I was trying to elevate you, for God's sake! Obviously it was all a complete waste of my time.'

'Elevate me?'

'Yes. Just because people are born in the gutter doesn't mean they have to stay there.'

I spun around, unable to hide the tears in my eyes, my whole body vibrating with hurt and fury.

'There's someone else here now too.' Lucinda's voice sliced across the crackling atmosphere now engulfing the bedroom.

'What?' Jasper snapped as he turned. Lucinda flinched. The person she was referring to remained perfectly still beside her. Matt. And from the look on his face, he'd heard every word of the previous exchange.

'What the hell are you doing here?'

'I gave Fleur a lift,' he answered steadily before shifting his gaze to me. 'You OK?'

'Yep.' I nodded. 'Sorry, I won't be long.' I shook out a bin bag. Matt's eyes took it in.

'Hang on,' he said, leaving the periphery of the room he'd been standing on. Lucinda watched him go, an appreciative look on her face, which immediately disappeared when she caught Jasper's glare.

'What the hell is he doing?'

'Bringing these for Fleur.' Matt answered the question himself as he swung two suitcases onto the bed and unzipped them. 'I put these in the truck, just on the off chance we needed them. There's no need for you to put your things in bin bags.' He straightened and met Jasper's eyes. It had taken Matt less than a day to work out what had taken me nearly two years. And even then, I still hadn't thought he'd stoop to forcing me to leave the place with my possessions in rubbish bags.

'Thank you.'

'No problem. Need some help packing?' he asked, as if Jasper and his gawping friend weren't there.

'No, I won't be long now,' I said, pulling open a few drawers and lifting out the items that I'd bought for myself. I put a bunch of posh underwear on the side and left it there purposely. Jasper had bought it all for me and I didn't want it. I didn't want anything from him. If it was pettiness he wanted, that was exactly what he would get.

The cases weren't even full and represented two years' worth of wages mostly spent on clothes I wasn't sure I even liked all that much. I zipped up the cases and then stopped. Kneeling down, I peered under the bed and pulled a small bag out.

'What's that?' Jasper asked.

'Nothing of yours. Just the few items I brought with me from the gutter.'

Jasper's Adam's apple bobbed and a thick silence descended around us. 'I put it under there because you'd never look there.

Maria, the cleaner, knew and knew never to touch it. Funny, isn't it, that I could share something personal with her and not you?'

'You could have if you wanted to.'

'No. I couldn't. You wouldn't understand. You've never understood and your comments at the hotel and today proved that.'

'How do you know she's not stealing something valuable?' Lucinda chose this moment to enter the conversation.

Matt's head spun towards her, astonishment widening his eyes, anger tightening his jaw. 'What the hell is wrong with you people?'

'It's fine, Matt.'

'It's not bloody fine!'

'You're right. It's not fine at all. But to satisfy your curiosity, even though I have no idea who you are or what it's got to do with you, and because I suspect Jasper has had the same thought, I'll prove to you I'm not stealing anything. These things are precious, yes, but only to me.' With that I opened the fabric drawstring of the bag and placed a neatly folded flowery blanket on top of the suitcase. Next followed a soft teddy, slightly balding in patches from years of love and providing comfort and, lastly, a tiny silver bangle.

'What's that?' Lucinda homed in on the jewellery.

'For God's sake, Lucinda. It's clearly a baby's. She's not taken anything,' Jasper snapped, then turned to me, his expression softer now. 'Why did you never show me these?'

'Because you always made it clear my background was an embarrassment to you and now, I realise, you didn't deserve to share them. The only reason I'm showing you now is to prove to your "friend"—' I put an emphasis on the word that could have been taken in several ways, 'that I'm not a thief.' With that, I placed the three items back carefully in the bag, and held it close. My hand reached for the handle of the suitcase but Matt was there before me.

'Thanks.' I looked up, meeting his eyes, and saw the smile in them. There was something else there. Something I hadn't seen in a long time. Pride. He stepped back, allowing me to go first, and we walked out of the apartment.

'Oh my God,' I said, flapping my arms in the lift. 'I'm sweating buckets!' I paused in my flapping and looked up. 'Sorry.'

'Not a problem. Totally understandable. They certainly didn't make it easy for you.'

'No. Thanks very much for bringing the cases. I had no idea Jasper would be that petty about bloody luggage.' I let out a sigh as the lift doors breathed open and we exited. Matt gave a shrug and pushed open the door to the street with his shoulder.

'No problem. Says a lot more about him than you, acting like that.'

'Or it says that I was a pretty poor judge of character. Again.'

'We all make mistakes. Some people are very good at letting you see only what they want you to, especially at the beginning.'

'True. But I'm not sure what my excuse is two years in.'

'Sometimes it's even harder once you've invested in something. Leaving means giving up on that, which is hard. Even when you know it's the right thing to do.' He gave a shrug. 'Don't beat yourself up about it. Most of us have been in that situation in our lives at one time or another whether it's a relationship or a job. Sometimes the easier option is to stay.'

'I guess.'

'I know,' Matt said as he swung the luggage into the back of the pick-up. I stood there, staring at it. 'You OK?'

'Yeah... I mean, yes.' I forced a smile.

Matt shut the cover. 'Not buying it, but OK.' He walked around to the passenger door and opened it for me. I stepped up and belted myself in as Matt walked around to the driver's side and settled himself behind the wheel.

'I suppose I was thinking that a couple of half empty suitcases doesn't seem very much to show for my life so far.'

'Life's not all about possessions... despite what some people think.' Matt gave Jasper's building a slight glance as he said the words before pulling out into the traffic.

'No. I know.'

'You have the things that are most precious to you. That's what counts.'

'Yes. True.'

'So where now?'

I looked over at Matt. 'Back to Wales, I guess. Although I'm concerned at all the driving you're doing today. If it's insured I can drive.'

'I'm fine, but thanks for the thought. I wondered whether you wanted to see your friend if you might not get to see her for a while.'

I felt my face light up. 'Oh, Matt, that's so kind. But it'll make us pretty late getting back.'

'I don't have anything on tomorrow so it's fine with me. It's good to see the people who are important to you when you can.'

'Are you sure?'

'Yep. Give her a call.'

Rumi, true to form, insisted I come over that moment and tell her every single detail of the weekend's drama.

'Did you get the train? Do you need meeting somewhere?'

I now regretted making the call on speaker but couldn't take it off without it looking weird. I was hesitant to tell her about Matt. There wasn't anything between us, but I knew that wouldn't stop my friend's imagination from going into overdrive.

'No, I'm fine, thanks. You know I told you about Bronwyn, who owns the hotel?'

'Yeah?'

'One of her sons has driven me down to collect my stuff.' There, that sounded pretty neutral.

'Oooh! Is he single? Is he yummy? Is he the one that told Jasper he couldn't just do what he liked and endanger others on a mountain? I'd have paid to have seen that.'

'Rumi. You're on speaker,' I said, feeling heat radiating from my face. Rumi's only response was to laugh wickedly and say that she looked forward to meeting him.

9

'Sorry about that,' I said once I'd hung up.

Matt was grinning. 'She sounds great.'

My smile matched his. 'She is. Even when she embarrasses the hell out of me, I wouldn't change her for the world.'

'I take it you two go back a long way.'

'Forever, really.'

'It's good that you've managed to keep the friendship strong. It's not always easy when people move around.'

'True, but there are bonds that can't be broken no matter how far apart you are.'

'Yep. I totally get that. I've got a few friends like that. You go through stuff together and you're the only ones that get it. I mean, really get it.'

'Exactly.'

'You're not ex-services too, are you?'

'No. Ex children's home.'

'Right.'

'Rumi was already there when I got there and she took me

under her wing, even though she was only a few years older than me.'

'How old were you?'

'They think I was nearly one.'

'Wow.'

'Yeah...'

'You know that stuff that your ex said at the restaurant the other night was crap, don't you? About people not wanting you.'

I swallowed. Even I'd been surprised Jasper had plumbed those particular depths.

'No, I know.'

'He's lucky he didn't get decked there and then.'

'You'd have had to join the queue. I was just trying not to give your mum more mess to clear up.'

Matt threw his head back and laughed. 'I'd have cleaned up the mess myself to have seen you do that. God knows he deserved it.'

'Yeah, he did. I should never have put up with him when I knew it couldn't go anywhere. His parents made that very clear. Can you imagine? Bringing home someone of unknown parentage?'

'Well. You're done with it now. New starts and all that. Onward and upward.'

I giggled. 'Any more platitudes you'd like to throw in there?'

'Give me a minute, I'm thinking.' Matt grinned and I smiled back. They might indeed be platitudes but he was right. Perhaps this was a chance for a new start. A chance to actually find out who I was – figuratively if not literally.

* * *

'Oh my God!' Rumi squealed as she flung her arms around me at the door. 'I can't believe you're moving to Wales!'

'I know,' I replied, laughing into her shoulder. 'I'm not quite sure I can believe it myself.'

'It's going to be great,' Rumi said, standing me back and fixing me with the look she always gave people when she meant business. 'I can feel it in my bones.'

'Oh God, she's not on about her bones again, is she?' Rumi's husband, Ayaz, came to join us, laughing as he did so.

'And when have they been wrong?' She turned, hands on hips. Ayaz was about a foot taller than her but Rumi was more than a match for him.

'Never, my dearest one,' he replied, bending to kiss her on the temple. 'Now, are you inviting these good people in or what?'

'Oh! Come in! Come in!' Rumi practically dragged both me and Matt through the door, closing it behind us. 'And you must be Matt?' Rumi turned her large, dark eyes on him as he stood beside me in the small hallway, his upright bearing hinting at his previous career.

'It's a pleasure to meet you.' He smiled, extending a hand.

'Oh, none of that rubbish, give me a hug, you big lump.' Rumi grabbed him and he returned the embrace, laughing as he did so before stepping back and shaking Ayaz's hand. 'So you're the one that finally saw off that rat, Jasper,' Rumi said as we made our way through to the lounge in Rumi's small flat. Houseplants trailed their leaves from shelves as we passed, tickling our skin. Rumi had discovered a previously untapped love of gardening during the first lockdown and never looked back. With no outside space, this meant that pretty much every horizontal surface in the flat had been utilised as a place to put plants. The overall effect was a wonderful, tropical feel, especially mixed with the bright colours that Rumi liked to use.

The flat was rented so she hadn't been allowed to paint anything, but they'd done an amazing job of putting their stamp on it without making a mark on the place itself. I couldn't wait to see what she did when they finally moved into their own home in Norfolk. Although I had the feeling that, initially at least, Rumi's focus would be on the garden. The existing owners were downsizing and had planned to sell the greenhouse but, having witnessed Rumi's enthusiasm for the place, and heard about her newly discovered love for growing things, they'd offered to leave it for her, saying that they were thrilled the garden they had poured their time into would be looked after and their own love of gardening passed to a new generation. According to Ayaz, his wife had almost exploded with happiness on the spot.

'This is amazing!' Matt said, taking in the plants everywhere. Colourful chillies dotted the leaves of the various plants on the windowsills and a collection of herbs filled the one above the sink. Coriander butted up against basil, curry leaves snuggled up to the neighbouring lemongrass along with mint, dill and a couple of others I'd forgotten the name of. Both of them were amazing cooks and although Rumi hadn't grown up surrounded by great food as Ayaz had, his family had taken her in as one of their own and she'd spent many happy hours learning techniques and family recipes, which they had willingly shared as she'd developed her own skills. As Rumi had gained confidence, she'd experimented more and Ayaz's family had laughed, saying now she was the teacher. 'I love the tropical atmosphere in here,' Matt continued, touching a large, shiny green banana-y-looking leaf.

'Thanks.' Rumi gave him her biggest smile before turning to

me. 'He's a keeper.' She nodded at me and I gave her a steady look.

'I'm sure he is, but he's not mine to keep. I will pass the compliment on to his mum, though.' I glanced at Matt and rolled my eyes. 'Sorry. She wasn't exactly a fan of Jasper.'

'No one was a fan of Jasper,' Ayaz added. 'Anyone want tea or coffee?'

'Coffee would be great, thanks.' Matt smiled.

'Do we have time?' I asked him.

'Sure.'

'You're staying, aren't you?' Rumi asked.

'Umm, no. We have to head back to Wales.'

'Oh...' Rumi's face fell and I automatically gave her a hug.

'We'll get together again soon,' I promised. I wasn't exactly sure how but I'd find a way.

'It's just been quite hard to see you over the past couple of years...' She left the sentence to drift but we both knew what she meant.

'Jasper wasn't exactly a fan of Fleur associating with Rumi,' Ayaz filled Matt in. 'We're not the "right kind of people".'

'I'm really sorry about that.' I automatically apologised for what felt like the millionth time to my friends.

'Don't be daft,' Ayaz said, as usual. 'It wasn't your fault and you came when you could. You couldn't help that Jasper turned out to be an arse.'

'No. I suppose not.' Guilt nibbled at me. I should have made more effort to see Rumi and Ayaz. We'd spoken every day on messaging apps but even that had had to be done in secret. With the wonderful benefit that hindsight gave, I could see now that the people I should have been avoiding were Jasper and his friends. It was a mistake I wouldn't make again.

'I'm sure we could find a hotel with a couple of rooms for

this evening,' Matt said. 'I don't have anything I need to get back for early. It would be a shame for you not to take the opportunity to spend time with your friends as you're here.'

Rumi stared at Matt for a second then turned to me. 'Seriously. Marry him. Today if possible.'

* * *

'That was delicious,' Matt said as he placed his knife and fork together on the plate. 'I'm sure that'd go down a storm at the hotel. What do you think, Fleur?'

It took me a minute to realise he was asking for my opinion. My previous relationship had done a good job of conditioning me into just agreeing. Jasper would frame the sentence in the form of a question but, after the first couple of times I made the mistake of giving a viewpoint that contradicted his, it became clear that my purpose was, in fact, merely to back up his, always correct, beliefs. It wasn't a difficult habit to get into. It was one I'd been employing for much of my life in a variety of situations. It had all been part of the 'don't make waves' plan I'd lived by.

'Fleur?' Rumi prompted. Our eyes met and she got it. She knew.

'Umm... Yes. I mean. It was wonderful. But...' I looked at Matt, still unsure of this new chance to offer a truthful opinion. 'I don't know the clientele so I'm not really sure I can comment.'

'Would you order it?' Matt asked.

'In a heartbeat.'

'Then I think we have our answer.' He smiled at me but it was far outdone by the massive grin Rumi was now wearing. I widened my eyes at her, trying not to grin back, warning her not to make another 'marry him' comment. 'Now I just have to persuade your friends here to part with the recipe.'

'I'll email it to you,' Ayaz replied.

'Are you sure you don't mind?'

'Do I mind spreading the love of good Indian food? Definitely not. Fancy a beer?'

'Driving,' Matt replied, a hint of disappointment in his voice. We'd looked at the hotel availability but everything that wasn't booked was either horrendously expensive or looked like the sort of place you'd wipe your feet on the way out of.

'I've got an idea.'

'Brace yourselves,' Ayaz said, catching his wife's hand and kissing it as she tried to swat him.

'Stay here tonight. The kids are at the grandparents' for a sleepover. It's not ideal but at least you could both have a drink and feel refreshed in the morning.'

Ayaz looked over at Matt. 'It'd be great if you stayed but I do feel, in the spirit of honesty, that you need to see where you'd be sleeping before you commit yourself to anything.'

Rumi rolled her eyes and grabbed Matt's hand. 'He's exaggerating. Yes, it might be a little snug but still.' She opened the door to the kids' room to where a set of bunk beds stood in the corner, the ceiling above it draped with gossamer fine net and voiles, which drifted down and wrapped around the bedposts. The addition of fairy lights created the perfect princess setting for their little girl. It was a small room and the beds took up the majority of the space. To the side was a cheap chest of drawers a neighbour had been throwing out, which Rumi had repainted in the palest pink and one of Ayaz's siblings with a talent for art had drawn tiny fairies on, peeking out of the drawers and around corners. In contrast, the bottom bunk was dressed with a Marvel comic duvet cover and pillow and had little curtains hung in the same fabric so that their son, a gorgeous and luckily easy-going child, could get away from all the pink when he wanted to.

'Looks like my perfect room.' Matt grinned. 'But bagsy the bottom bunk,' he said, turning to me.

'I was going to choose the top one anyway. If it collapses under your weight I don't want to be under you!'

Rumi giggled and I realised how my words had sounded. I risked a glance at Matt, who was looking at Rumi, currently waggling her brows mischievously. Matt's smile continued to light up his face as he shook his head and joined in her laughter. I felt another of the tiny knots that I was made of unfurl.

As I folded my clothes and placed them on top of the chest of drawers, Rumi came in to tell me, yet again, just how great Matt was and how well he and her husband were getting on.

'Don't get excited,' I said, pulling one of her nighties over my head. 'We're not a thing. And we're not going to be a thing.'

'Why not?'

I clambered up to the top bunk and smacked my head on the ceiling. No wonder Matt was so quick to choose the bottom bunk.

'Because,' I said, rubbing my head, 'it's his family who've given me a job, and also because I spent most of the night that Jasper left wondering what I was going to do immediately and what I was doing with my life in general.'

'And what conclusion did you come to?' Rumi asked, taking a seat on the floor and looking up at me.

'That I didn't really know. That I seem to always lurch from one place to another. From one person to another. It never works and so that's maybe a sign that being in a couple is not meant for me.'

'Rubbish,' Rumi replied vehemently as she wiggled her toes, their nails painted scarlet to match her fingernails. 'I've never known anyone as loving as you. You've just met the wrong people, and given all that care and love to men who didn't deserve it. The right person is out there.' She glanced at the closed door, which led to the main living area. 'In fact, if you ask me, the right person is out *there*.'

I snuggled down before tipping myself carefully onto one side to look at her. 'Yes. Well, I didn't ask you.' I stuck my tongue out to punctuate the sentence.

Laughing, Rumi pushed herself off the floor. 'Yeah, but maybe you should. I told you from the start Jasper was an arse.'

I flopped onto my back.

'I know. Please don't lecture me. I know that was a big mistake but I...' I swallowed the rest of the sentence.

'Didn't want to be on your own?'

I pushed myself up on my elbows and whacked my head again. 'Bloody hell.' I rubbed it again. 'What do you mean?' Even I could hear the strands of self-protection twisting through my tone.

Rumi came to stand at the side of the bed, mounting a couple of rails of the bunk ladder so that she was at a level just below smacking her own head but could face me properly.

'Don't get defensive.'

'I'm not!' I said, defensively.

Rumi raised a brow.

'Fine. What?'

'It's natural for people to want someone to care about them. It's human nature. Neither of us got a good deal at the start and, if it wasn't for you, I still wouldn't have anyone.'

'Of course you would.'

'No,' she said, 'I wouldn't. I grew up with a determination that I was never going to let anyone close. If I didn't care about anyone and I didn't let anyone care about me, then emotion could be taken out of the equation. I would never feel abandoned again. To me that was the perfect solution.' She reached out and held my hand. 'And then this funny little baby came to the home and my childish rock of a heart cracked just a little.'

'You would always have found all this, Rumi,' I said as she squeezed my hand and I returned it.

'No, Fleur. I wouldn't. You helped make the cracks that let the light in. As you got older, everyone could see what a sweet kid you were.'

'Not everyone,' I said, pulling a face at her.

'Everyone that mattered. Would you really have wanted to go to a family who were picking kids just on how pretty they were?'

She had a point.

'And look at you now. Beautiful. Although I always thought you were anyway.'

Like an automaton, I pulled my hair so that it fell across my temple, hiding the now faded scar that had apparently been the catalyst for my arrival at the children's home. Time and treatment had healed it well, but the ugly red welts had turned more than a few potential adopters away in my early years. I'd grown up unsure and quiet and that hadn't helped either. I'd been accused of being sullen when in reality I was just trying to work out what people wanted me to be. But there were also complaints about the children who were more outgoing, and spoke their minds. It had seemed there was some magical balance that I failed to ever find.

Rumi reached out and pushed my hair back. 'You shouldn't hide this. It's a part of you. A part of your story.'

'I know.'

'Let me guess, Jasper wasn't a fan of having it on show.'

'It wasn't that. He just thought this hairstyle suited me better.'

My friend shook her head. 'When are you going to stop doing this?' We both looked round at the door as a burst of raucous laughter bounced around the small flat.

'Sounds like the boys are having a good time.'

'It does. It's lovely. I'm pretty sure Matt's the first non-weirdo you've ever brought home.'

'That's very judgemental of you,' I said, pulling a face at her. 'Just because someone is different from you doesn't make them weird.'

'Are you sure?' she asked, widening her eyes in mock innocence.

'I know. Shocker, right?'

'I had no idea!'

Rumi was the last person that needed to be reminded of this. Both her colour and sometimes her attitude had given people what they thought was the right to treat her differently. Her dial had been set to 'defensive' for a long time. I'd been one of the few privileged ones who'd been shown her true, caring, funny nature for a long time. It wasn't until she'd met Ayaz that she'd begun to drop the shields.

'Anyway, stop changing the subject.'

'I'm not. There is no subject.'

'Yes, there is. You always dating weirdos.'

'Maybe I'm the weirdo.'

'Well, yes, there is that.'

'Oi!' I said, giving her a gentle biff.

'Anyway, this one seems normal.'

'This one is also not a boyfriend.'

'He should be.'

'We've been over this.'

'Yes. And clearly you didn't listen. He's gorgeous, tall, fit, straight and has a decent job but, more than that, he's caring and funny and actually gives a shit about other people, unlike most of the men you've dated.'

'Don't sugar-coat it, will you?'

Rumi did a head tilt. 'You know me, right?'

'OK, yes, he seems really nice, but I just split up with Jasper and, right now, I'm wondering if I'm just better off forgetting about all that stuff.'

'Can I ask a question?'

'Since when do you ask?'

'True. So why did you put up with all these guys? None of them seemed to put you at the top of their priority list.'

'Could we not say "all these guys" – that makes it sound like I've been round half of London!'

'Fair enough. I apologise for my wording. But you still have to answer the question.'

I wriggled in discomfort and shuffled down the bed. Although it was bloody annoying not to be tall enough to reach the top shelf pretty much anywhere, my compact size was at least coming into its own right now. 'I guess we ought to let Matt in. I'm sure he's tired after driving today and he has to drive back up tomorrow.'

'In a minute.' Another bout of raucous laughter suggested that Matt wasn't standing at the other side of the door, desperate for sleep. 'Answer the question.' Rumi's voice was softer now. 'It made me so mad to see you moulding yourself into what others wanted you to be all the time.'

'Well, then. It's just as well I've decided to give up on the whole relationship thing, isn't it? I've spent years bending myself into shapes to fit into other people's lives and I don't. Whoever I meet, I don't fit. I didn't even fit in my own family...'

Rumi squished herself against me as best she could in light of the two different angles we were at. 'Hon, don't say that. We don't know the circumstances.'

'We know that I had boiling water spilled on me and was then abandoned. That hardly suggests there was a loving space for me there, does it?'

I tried not to sound bitter. I'd spent years trying to understand why I didn't have the same sort of family as the other kids at school, and then more years internalising the bitterness and confusion, but it had gradually dissipated, in large part thanks to the love and affection Rumi and the owner of the children's home had showed me. I knew I was lucky in a way. At least the home was a good one. We all knew things could have been so much worse. All that was left now was a pile of sadness in the corner of my mind that I tried to ignore by throwing a mental blanket over it and getting on with life.

'Anyway,' I said, smiling at her from the ninety-degree angle I was now at. 'As much as I love these deep and ruminating conversations with you—'

She grinned at my pun. 'No, you don't.'

'You're right. I don't,' I said, pushing myself back up, love and amusement lifting the corners of my mouth. 'And yet you insist on starting them.'

'Because you never finish them.'

'That should give you a clue as to how much I really, really don't want to have them.'

'If you just answered for once, I wouldn't have to ask any more.'

'I'm pretty sure you'd find something else annoying to start a conversation about.' Rumi opened her mouth to speak but I cut across her. 'And because you've kept me nattering, now I need another wee and have to get out and back before Matt comes in.'

'I don't know. He might appreciate the view.'

I narrowed my eyes at her and began trying to extricate myself from the bunk without adding to the bruises I'd acquired on the way in.

10

'On a scale of one to ten, how uncomfortable are you?' I whispered later that night once Matt and I were both wedged into the children's bunk beds.

'I'm indoors and nothing's going to creep into my boot overnight and give me a bite from hell so it's all good.'

'Put like that, I feel a bit ungrateful now.'

Hiss deep, quiet laugh drifted up from beneath me. 'Don't be. I'm no saint. I've also slept in beds that are big enough for a full grown adult, which, naturally, are more comfy.'

'OK. I don't feel so bad now.'

'But it's worth it, isn't it?'

I knew what he meant without the need to say more. 'Very much so. Thank you for this.'

'I didn't do anything.'

I shuffled onto my side and peered over the side of the bunk. The moon scattered beams on the carpet as it played hide and seek behind the scudding clouds. As we'd chatted earlier about their move to Norfolk Ayaz had mentioned that someone had shot out the streetlights outside the flat with an air rifle a few months ago and they were still awaiting replacements. On the plus side it did mean that the kids got to see moonlight now that there was less light pollution. In fact, their son had begun to take an interest in astronomy and that was something they were hoping would continue when they moved, once he had more opportunity to see the night sky in its natural beauty.

'Yes, you did. You helped me get the job at your parents' hotel.'

'That was just right time, right place.'

'Ha! That makes a change for me.'

'Sounds like the universe thought it was your turn, then.'

I peered at him for a moment, able to make out the shape of his face, if not the details. 'Do you believe in that?'

'What?'

'Fate. The universe providing and stuff.'

Matt shuffled, smacked a knee on the side of the bunk, swore, apologised and then replied. 'Mostly. I think life can put you in situations that force you to find something to believe in. For some people that's God, whichever of those they choose. For others it's fate and the universe.'

'Do you think that everything can be explained in that way?'

'Nope. I think whatever path you choose, there will still be circumstances that shake your faith. That make you want to scream at the sky and ask why.'

'And what happens then?'

'You scream at the sky and ask why and vent all the anger and pain you can and then you try and find a way to move on.'

I lay there in the dark thinking about that.

'Fleur?' Matt's gravelly tones were soft.

'Yes?'

'You OK up there?'

'Yes. Thank you.'

'Good.'

'And thank you for allowing me to come here tonight.'

'I didn't allow you anything, Fleur. But I'm glad we did. They're great people.'

On my lower days I wondered where I'd been hiding when luck was handed out, but Matt was right. I was lucky to have Rumi and her family in my life. I turned over and smacked an elbow. Although I was looking forward to a time when they could offer a bigger bed for overnight visits.

A short time later Matt's whispered words broke the surrounding silence. At least as silent as the surroundings get in the middle of an estate in London.

'What is it?'

'I didn't say anything.'

'I know. But your thinking is so loud it's keeping me awake.'

'Oh, rubbish.'

'Spit it out or neither of us will get any sleep.'

'I was just wondering if this is a bit weird.'

'What's that?' he asked in a patient tone. If he was annoyed he didn't betray it in his voice.

'The fact that I've really only just met you and now we're sharing a room.'

'Does it feel weird to you?'

'No. But maybe that's what's weird about it.'

Soft, melodic laughter drifted up to me.

'And how do you come by that conclusion?'

'I'm not entirely sure. But don't you think it should be?'

'Do you want it to be weird?'

'No!' I said, wriggling until I was leaning over the edge of my bed again so that I could meet Matt's gaze now that my own vision had adjusted to the low light of the room.

'What are you worrying about?' Matt asked gently, propping himself up on his elbows. 'If you feel uncomfortable, I'm happy to have the door open or go and sleep on the sofa. I don't mind. I totally get it. In fact, I probably should have offered earlier. Sorry.'

'No,' I said, quickly. 'It's not that. I don't feel threatened or uncomfortable at all.'

'OK. That's good.'

'It is,' I replied, unable to stop the smile that accompanied the words. 'I suppose I'm just not used to feeling this relaxed with people. It was the same with your mum.'

'I'm glad to hear you feel like that. Hopefully that means you will enjoy working with us.'

'With you?'

'Yes…' I could hear the confusion.

'I just… you said working with you, rather than for you.'

'We're a team there. That's how it works.'

I smiled in the moonlight. 'I like the sound of that.'

'Good. So, are you over the whole weird-that-it's-not-weird thing yet?'

'Not quite.'

He laughed again. 'OK. Is there anything I can do to help?'

'I don't think so. It's probably just me. It usually is.'

'Don't say that.'

'What?'

'You keep automatically taking the blame. Having been extremely lucky in my own family situation, I can't pretend to know what growing up the way you did is like, although Rumi gave me a quick overview earlier.'

'I knew she was up to something. Sorry about that. I'm sure that was the last thing you were interested in hearing about.'

'Not at all. And you don't need to keep apologising.'

'Oh...'

'OK. I don't like the sound of that "Oh". What are you thinking now?'

'It's just that... I know some people have a bit of a preconceived idea about people who come from certain backgrounds. I'm not saying you do,' I said, rushing on as Matt opened his mouth to say something. 'Your mum kindly gave me a job without knowing anything about me, but I can get a reference from the coffee shop I worked at and probably the place before that. I doubt Jasper will but—'

'Fleur. Stop.'

I snapped my mouth shut.

Matt shuffled until he was partly out of the bed too, his face directly beneath mine.

'You don't need to prove anything to anyone, and certainly not to me or my family. A person can have a fistful of glowing references but that doesn't mean I'd employ them. For us it's always been about the feeling you get from someone. For example, I could have told you within a few minutes that Jasper was going to annoy the... hell out of me.'

I giggled. 'I'm pretty sure I've heard any of the words you were going to substitute in that sentence so no need to spare my blushes.'

'Actually I was sparing my own.'

I laughed again.

'So?' He tilted his head, a silver moonbeam highlighting one side of his face as he did so. The expression was soft, a mixture of concern mixed with amusement.

'So...'

'Are we all good here now?'

I thought about it.

'Oh God, she needs to think about it. There must be more.'

I grabbed a cushion off my bed and aimed it at him. He caught it with a speed of reaction that reaffirmed the faith I'd had in him as a guide and I guessed that lightning reactions had probably also been a vital thing to cultivate in the military.

'Nice try.'

'Thanks again for bringing me down here. And the suitcase and stuff.'

'No need to thank me. I've enjoyed the trip and this way it means that hopefully you're able to get all settled in and feel at home quicker.'

'It would be nice to feel settled. I always kind of felt like a visitor at Jasper's even when I lived with him.'

The smile faded from the handsome face. 'Yeah. Unfortunately I can't say I'm shocked by that revelation.'

'No, I don't suppose you are. I think you're probably a far better judge of people than I am.'

'Or maybe we've just come at life from different angles.'

'Maybe.'

Matt watched me for a moment. 'I can see we're going to have to get you out in the mountains. It's great for clearing the head and slowing thoughts that won't stop whizzing.'

'You sound like you're speaking from experience.'

'I'm definitely speaking from experience.'

'I did enjoy the hike yesterday.'

'Good.'

'And I'm glad we didn't go up Crib Goch. I'm not such a fan of heights, between you and me.'

'Ah. Interesting, considering the original plan was to go up one of the most challenging peaks, but I assume that wasn't your idea. If you're interested, I can give you some local walking routes and, if I'm free and you want company, we can do a few treks. I'm sure you'll find your own favourites the longer you stay.'

'Mm-hmm.'

His face caught the light again, the expression serious. 'You're doing it again.'

'What?'

'Doubting yourself. I can tell. Believe me, there's enough people out there who want to tear others down. You've got to be your own champion, not your own enemy.'

'Easier said than done.'

'Or maybe it's just habit.'

I stayed silent.

'That's what I thought. Come on.' His hand reached up and for the briefest moment covered my own as it rested on the edge of the bunk. 'Try and slow those thoughts down and get some rest. You're going to need it once we start running you ragged in the restaurant.'

'Oh blimey,' I said, rolling myself back onto the bunk more securely.

'You'd better believe it,' Matt said, soft shuffling noises indicating that he too was attempting to get himself comfy again. Out of the two of us, I reckoned I had the better chance at that, but within minutes I could hear a steady, rhythmic breathing coming from below. I guess I'd been keeping him awake after all. Either that or he was one of those people who could conjure up sleep on a washing line if need be. There was something soothing about the almost metronomic sound and I closed my eyes, listening for a few minutes until I drifted off.

* * *

Rumi's scream made me choke on my breakfast tea and if Matt had antennae they'd have been on super alert right now. As it was, he was sitting even more straight than usual, looking towards the area the scream had come from. A second later, Rumi came barrelling out of their bedroom and ran straight towards me as I stood, ready to go to her.

'Whatever's the mat—Oof!' Rumi ran straight into my arms at full speed, tears streaming, her arms locked around my neck. I hugged her tightly for a moment before trying to stand her back. 'Rumi, what is it? What's happened? Are the kids OK?' It was then I saw her face was creased with happiness, not pain. Joy, not heartache.

'We've exchanged! The house! It's happening. It's really happening!' By this time we were both in tears and although I saw Ayaz's comical eye roll at Matt, I saw his own eyes shining. They'd waited so long for this moment and now it was here.

'Have you got a moving date yet?'

'Two weeks from today as there's no chain. I think I told you the people we're buying from are downsizing to a flat they already bought.'

'Oh my God, that's brilliant! I'm so excited for you all!' And I was. I could feel it radiating through me – all the thrill and unfettered joy of my friends' situation wrapped itself around all four of us.

'Congratulations, mate,' Matt said, shaking Ayaz's hand with his right and slapping him on the back with his left. The two had really connected yesterday and I loved being able to allow my happiness for them to show, knowing he understood and likely felt much the same.

'Obviously I'm miffed you won't be here to help us move but, as you've dumped that bloody awful Jasper, you have credits in the bank so I'll let you off.'

'Technically he dumped me.'

'Semantics,' Rumi said, with a wave of her bangled wrist, the thin metal rings tinkling together as she did so.

'If you want time off to come back and help, I'm sure we can work something out,' Matt said.

'No, no,' Rumi said, 'I'm just teasing her. Luckily I married a man who has about a thousand relatives so all the free labour is catered for.'

'I've got a brother too. That's what they're there for, right?' Matt nodded to Ayaz.

'Exactly. I mean, they have to come in useful at some point and make up for annoying the hell out of you growing up, don't they?'

'You'd hope so, wouldn't you?' Matt grinned back. I'd seen Matt and his brother swoop to back up his mum when Jasper had started kicking off in the hotel, and it was evident they were close.

Not for the first time, I wondered what that was like. Rumi had felt overwhelmed at meeting Ayaz's family initially but now she said that it felt as though they were as much her brothers and sisters as they were his. The light that shone in her eyes when she spoke about them was beautiful. For someone who had once claimed she didn't need, or want, anyone, my friend had found her true place – at the heart of a warm and loving family.

We said our goodbyes in good moods and with promises of seeing each other again as soon as we could.

'Traffic's looking OK so hopefully it won't be too bad a journey. We can stop off at some services for a bit of lunch and to stretch our legs. Sound good?'

'Absolutely. Which reminds me...' I hoiked my bag up onto my lap and reached into a small inside pocket, withdrawing some notes, which I tucked into the central storage compartment.

Matt frowned. 'What's that?'

'Petrol money.'

He shook his head. 'No need.'

'Yes, there is. I'd have had to spend money to get here on the train and then been lugging all my worldly goods around in bin bags that would have split within a few feet of the apartment anyway, because those things always do. You helped me avoid all that. I got a comfortable door-to-door journey, was able to leave the apartment with some dignity still intact, and got to see my friends. You gave up your own time to help someone you're already taking a chance on. So please. Accept the money. These things don't run on fairy dust and London's not exactly just around the corner.'

'Actually, you're wrong, there's a fairy-dust garage just off the motorway I was planning to head to.'

Matt's glance briefly connected with mine before concentrating back on the road. His grin said it all.

11

'You're doing great, love!' Bronwyn squeezed my shoulder as I took a five-minute breather on my first shift a couple of days later.

'I don't think table seven are very pleased with me, but I don't know what I did wrong.'

Bronwyn peered out at the restaurant then smiled back at me. 'Oh, don't worry about those two. They act like they're the grumpiest couple on the planet but they come back several times a year and always tip really well. I think that's just the way they are.'

'Oh, right,' I said, feeling relief slide down my spine. 'That's good to hear. I mean, about not having done anything wrong. Not about the tipping.'

'Sweetheart. You're in the hospitality business. It's OK to be pleased about the tipping when it happens.'

I gave an embarrassed smile and pushed myself up from the chair I'd perched on. 'Well, better get back to it.'

'Looks like table nine is ready to order. Don't take any truck from that lot. Right hooligans they are.'

I felt my throat close. Confrontation was my nemesis and having to deal with it on my first day at a new job wasn't exactly the start I was hoping for. I peered out and heard Bronwyn chuckling behind me before she pointed out the correct table – I was still getting used to the numbering system. At the table in question sat two tall, muscular men. Bronwyn's sons. Matt had his back to us, but the other saw his mum and gave a brief wave, his smile almost identical to his brother's other than the scar that ran across Matt's top lip. Bronwyn took my face between her hands. 'Oh, my goodness, your face! I'm so sorry, my lovely. Just my sense of humour.'

'It's fine.' I smiled, relaxing now I was part of the joke. 'I'm pretty sure I can handle them.'

Bronwyn grinned back. 'I don't doubt it for a moment.'

'Bit different from London, eh?' The rough-edged voice that was too sexy for comfort broke into my thoughts as I sat on a bench in the grounds of the hotel. Pink and white spring blooms decorated the trees and the early morning blue of the sky contrasted with the vibrant fresh green of the grass following the downpour the day before.

I looked up, stirred from my thoughts. 'You could say that.'

'How are you finding it?' Matt asked, taking a seat on the bench next to me, one large hand wrapped around a mug of coffee.

'Different,' I replied honestly.

'Good different?'

'Yes. I think so. I'm still getting used to the quiet. Everywhere I've lived and worked, everything I've ever known really, has always had a background of constant noise. It's a little unnerving to have that switched off.'

'I can understand that. I've got a mate who lives in Manchester, always has done. He came here for a weekend and we were sat looking up at the stars, chilling out with a few beers. As I was sitting there thinking how perfect it was, my mate pipes up, "How can you bear all this silence?" He needed the background noise to feel at home. I think people assume peace and quiet is the ultimate ideal for everyone, but it doesn't work like that, does it?'

'No, I suppose not.'

Matt shifted in his seat. 'So does that mean we're going to lose you back to the city?'

I turned my attention back to the ancient mountains striding across the landscape. 'No. I think you're stuck with me a little longer yet.'

He took a sip of his coffee. 'Glad to hear it.'

'You ready to go?' Andy, Matt's younger brother, asked as he appeared around the corner of the hotel, dressed ready for a day's hiking in a red jacket, black walking trousers and sturdy black leather hiking boots. 'The equipment is all in the truck.'

'Yep, just finishing this,' Matt replied, indicating his coffee mug as he drank the rest down.

'Hi, Fleur, how's you?' Andy asked. 'Hope Bigfoot here isn't bothering you.' Ignoring him, Matt put his coffee mug on the table next to the bench.

'I'm OK, thanks, Andy. No, not at the moment.'

'Yeah, I guess he's all right in small doses. I've probably come at just the right time. Get him out of the way before you're looking for a suitable boulder to nobble him with.'

Matt pushed himself up from the bench using one of the arms. Suddenly his hand went to his side and he bent again, resting the other hand on the bench. 'Oh no! I don't think I'm going to be able to do the hike with you today. I think I've just cracked a rib due to you being so utterly hilarious.' His face turned to mine, closer now that he was bent over. Mischief and amusement made his icy blue eyes twinkle, the skin beside them creasing into the regular laughter lines that showed there. I grinned back.

'Bigfoot...' I repeated, laughing more now.

Matt straightened and half turned to his brother. 'If that name sticks with Fleur, I'm going to be having words with you.'

Andy knocked his knees together in an over-exaggerated manner. 'Oh, no! Not words!'

Matt tipped his head to the sky. 'What did I do to deserve this?' When it was clear God wasn't going to make his thoughts known, Matt gave a dramatic sigh, checked his pockets for his phone and GPS tracker and moved towards his brother. 'Have a good day, Fleur.'

'Thanks.'

'See you, Fleur.' Andy waved and they tramped off together, Matt's height a couple of inches above his brother, laughter trailing behind them as they turned the corner and disappeared behind the hotel.

The pick-up rumbled into life and then that sound too dissipated into nothing, replaced instead with the sound of birds, the occasional chatty sheep and the soft rustle of a gentle breeze through the fruit trees that lined this part of the garden. Bronwyn had taken me on a tour of them and the kitchen garden when I started, explaining that they did their best to provide as much food for the hotel, and themselves, as possible.

Chickens roamed about a short distance away within a large caged-off area, which Matt had explained was dug deep into the ground as foxes would happily get into the enclosure if given the opportunity. I'd collected the eggs that morning, even though it was my day off. Bronwyn had told me I didn't have to, and to have a lie-in, but I'd never been one for lounging in bed and I'd quickly come to love the early morning feel of the fresh air in my lungs. I loved the job of collecting the eggs, often still warm from the nesting box, heading out woven basket in hand.

Even the fact I was carrying a wicker basket felt a little surreal. I'd never seen anyone using them apart from people in period dramas on the telly. And yet, here I was, wandering about between softly clucking hens, basket on my arm, filling it with eggs that in a short time would become my and the guests' breakfasts. Some days it felt as though I'd stepped back in time and I loved it. Matt had asked me if they were in danger of losing me back to London and I'd given a teasing answer, but the truth was that I'd never been happier.

I only hoped it would last. From experience, I had learned that just as I got comfortable and thought I was settled, something happened to tear that away and I'd have to start all over again. I loved this place and the people and I felt more relaxed here than I could remember feeling in a long time, if ever. And that was what worried me. *You know it can't last...* But wouldn't it be wonderful if, just this once, it did? I tipped my head to the sky as Matt had done a while earlier and sent out a silent wish – I wasn't sure who to, anyone would do – to ask if they could help me out.

* * *

'You've found a job for life there,' the man said as I gave a beagle a chin rub, having asked her owner if I could pet his dog.

'She's beautiful.'

'And doesn't she know it!' He laughed. 'Makes the most of it, flashing those big brown eyes at people for fusses and cuddles. And I'm the worst!' He had a booming laugh and ruddy cheeks that told of a life enjoyed outside. A brief thought of another pair of attractive eyes flashed into my head and I quickly shoved it out. The last thing I needed in my new life was to acquire a crush on Matt Morgan. Friends was good. Friends was perfect. That was all I needed and all I wanted. He and Andy were certainly popular with some of the female guests and Bronwyn chuckled that having produced good-looking sons had been a strategic business move.

'Something good had to come out of pushing two enormous babies out, at least!' she'd announced one afternoon as the family and I had sat around having coffee before re-laying the tables for dinner.

'Mum!' Andy had screwed his face up and his brother had pulled a similarly appalled expression, causing his mum and dad to laugh even more.

I pushed the thought of Matt's piercing blue, thick-lashed eyes out of my mind and concentrated back on the dog and what his owner was saying.

'This your first time up here?'

'Is it that obvious?'

He gave another uproarious laugh. 'Nope. I'm just here almost every day with this one and I've not seen you. Plus those boots look like they've not long been out of the box.'

I looked down to the hiking boots now adorning my feet.

'Maybe I'm just really good at cleaning boots,' I said, grinning.

The man chuckled. 'Where are you heading?'

Ordinarily I'd have been wary about telling a strange man where I was about to walk but there was such a feeling of camaraderie here among the walkers, I had no hesitation in explaining that I was heading down to see a memorial to a legend of a dog that some friends had told me about.

'Oh, old Beddgelert?'

'Yes. That's it.'

'Ah, that's a nice gentle stroll. If you want to go on a bit further you can follow the river. That's a lovely walk there. You can carry on all the way and come back up over the top or turn and come back the same way if you're not up for a longer one.'

'Oh, right, thanks. That's great.'

The dog gave a long, squeaky yawn. 'Looks like I'd better be getting this one home. We've done our six miles this morning so she's ready for a snooze. For a short while anyway.'

Six miles sounded a flippin' long way to me and I'd definitely be ready for a snooze too! I decided I'd just go to the memorial that Matt had told me about. Bearing in mind this was only the second time I'd ever worn hiking boots in my entire life, and I didn't have Matt's skills to rely on, I wasn't planning to overdo it. Although the river walk did sound tempting. In the meantime, spurred on by my love of dogs, I headed off, looking forward to reading about the legend of a much-adored pooch.

12

'That was awful!'

Matt looked up from where he was sitting on the step, unlacing his boots. 'Huh?'

'You told me to go and find Gelert's grave and read about the legend.'

'Oh, mate,' Andy replied, toeing off one boot with the other foot. 'You saw how gaga she went over that puppy the other day. You were asking for trouble there.'

Matt stood up and frowned over at Andy then down at me. 'What's the problem?'

'He died horribly!' I said, throwing my hands up. 'And for no reason! That's the problem!'

Matt swapped a look with his brother. 'It's just a legend.'

'That's not the point.'

He screwed his face up. 'Of course it's the point. You can't get upset about stuff that's not real. That's like crying because a dog dies in a film.' His broad shoulders shrugged and my eyes widened.

'I *do* cry if a dog dies in a film!'

'Why?'

'Because it's a dog!'

'What if people die in the film?'

'That depends on the character.'

'But any dog is a no-no.'

'Of course! Everyone normal thinks that.'

Andy let out a guffaw, gave me a wave and disappeared through the door to likely nab a coffee before heading off home.

'So that makes me abnormal?' Matt looked down at me and my indignation faced him for a moment before I considered that I had just insulted the son of my employer.

'Umm... no. That's not exactly what I was saying.'

'Are you sure?' he asked, features serious, no hint of amusement around his lips or showing in those icy, piercing eyes. 'Because that's exactly what it sounded like.'

'I... no... I was just... it's just not what I was expecting the story to be, that's all.' I met his gaze but it was taking all my willpower to do so. And then, like the sun emerging from behind a cloud, the smile broke on his face as he reached out one large hand and momentarily held mine. 'Don't look so worried. Believe me, I've been called that and far worse in my time. It's good that you said what you think to me. I want you to do that.'

'No, really. It's not...'

'However you're planning on finishing that sentence, don't. I want you to tell me what you think about stuff. We may not agree but that's not the point. You and Rumi don't always agree, I'm sure.'

'No, but that's different.'

'How?' He shoved his hands in his pockets, his whole body relaxed and sure. Unlike my nerves, which were currently so tight you could probably play Vivaldi's *Spring* on them.

'Because... because I've known her forever. It's different.'

'But you have to meet new people sometimes.'

'I know. And I do.'

'And do you just agree with them all?'

I remained silent.

'Yeah, that's what I thought.'

I drew myself up a little, not that it really made much difference, but mentally I felt it was worth making the effort.

'Don't say it like that. It makes me sound...'

'What?' His voice was steady. Questioning rather than sharp. Interested rather than accusatory.

'Weak.'

Matt studied me for a moment before taking my hand. 'Come with me,' he said, walking in his socks along the private paved patio area of the house side of the hotel. He stopped at the swing chair I'd admired but not yet dared to sit on. Bronwyn and Greg, Matt's parents, had been very insistent that I make myself entirely at home but, as someone who'd always felt as though I was on the outside looking in, I was taking a little time to relax into that directive entirely.

Matt steadied the swing so I could sit before sitting beside me. My feet dangled just slightly above the ground while his long legs stretched out, crossed at the ankles, heels resting on the ground.

'Sorry,' I said to break the silence. I'd realised now that Matt wasn't really cross with me but 'Sorry' was my default go-to and had calmed plenty of awkward situations in the past, even if, deep down, I didn't think that person deserved an apology.

Matt shook his head. 'You've got to stop doing that.'

'What?'

'Apologising for anything and everything.'

'I don't!'

'Yeah, Fleur, you do.'

I tightened the small knot my hands had made on my lap.

'Sometimes it's the easiest thing to do to avoid an argument or get out of a situation, I agree. But there are also times when you're right and not apologising is just fine.'

'I didn't mean to be rude to you.'

'You weren't.' He laughed, the sound gentle and melodic. 'You told me what you thought. I'm interested in your opinion. And by the way, I'm not your employer, my parents are, so you don't need to worry about that.'

'I'm sure they wouldn't be happy to know I'd called their son abnormal.' I risked a look under my lashes at him.

'To be honest, half the time they'd probably agree,' he replied, eliciting a small giggle from me.

Matt smiled at the sound. 'That's better. You've got to say what you think, Fleur. Otherwise how will people get to know the real you? You're too tactful and too kind to say anything that would intentionally upset anyone but it's OK to have opinions. To be you.'

'Whoever that is.' I'd meant it as a throwaway line, but Matt's gaze shifted from the distance back to me as the words came out.

'Maybe it's about time you found out.'

'It was just a joke,' I said, doing my best to laugh it off, but Matt's expression remained studious and fixed.

'Want to know what I think?'

'I'm not sure. Do I?'

'At least we're working on the saying-what-you-feel thing.'

'I guess.'

We sat in silence for a few moments before curiosity got the best of me. 'OK, fine. Tell me what you think.'

He shifted on the swing, setting it in motion, gently swaying back and forth as one long leg lazily moved. 'Sure you want to hear?'

I flicked him on the arm. 'Enough with the trailers, just bloody well tell me.'

He really did have a great smile.

'I think that maybe you tell yourself you're joking about not being sure who you are because it's a little too close to the truth for comfort.'

I gazed at the next field, over a dry stone wall that had deep blue flowers tumbling out in patches, somehow finding enough nutrition in their barren host. Lambs gambolled about, the odd one bleating loudly when it lost sight of its mum before charging off towards her once she was located.

'Are you mad at me now?'

'I'm still deciding.'

'Fair enough. At least you're not apologising.'

I shoved against him, his solid bulk steadfastly unmoving. I might as well have tried to jostle Mount Snowdon.

'Come on. Let's go and get a cuppa. I smelled baking when I was sat in the doorway.'

'I don't know where you put it all,' I said, allowing him to heave me up from the swing. Having served the two brothers in the restaurant, I was still astonished by the amount they could eat. But then I supposed they burned plenty of calories racing up and down mountains. My gentle walk today had got me plenty of steps. Having found the grave and read the sign that told of the legend, I'd decided to continue the walk down by the river as the man with the dog had suggested. The scenery was spectacular, the river roaring past and, at times, the walk more challenging than I had expected, but I had pushed on, feeling an unfamiliar sense of achievement. I had definitely been out of my comfort zone but I figured that could only be a good thing. And, with the season getting into full swing, there had been other walkers around so if I'd got stuck, hopefully someone would have helped me out.

That was something I'd noticed about the walking community. Everyone was ready to watch out and offer assistance to others. I came from a city where most people didn't even know their next-door neighbours, so this had been a surprise, but I was already loving the difference, even if I struggled to embrace it fully. Idle chat hadn't really been a feature of my life in London so it was something that would take a bit of getting used to, but I'd enjoyed the little exchange with the dog walker today and I was grateful that he'd suggested the longer route.

'So, apart from getting upset about something that isn't even real, did you enjoy your day?' Matt asked, handing me a slice of freshly baked malted chocolate cake.

'You have a heart of stone,' I said, pointing my fork at him before slicing off a small piece of the cake with it.

'Not the first person to say that,' he replied around a mouthful of cake before shovelling in another chunk.

'That sounds like a story.'

'Not a very interesting one, I'm afraid. So, how was the rest of the walk?' he asked again.

'It was good. I actually ended up going further, rather than just going back to the bus stop.'

'Oh?'

'Yes, I got chatting to a man with his dog.'

Matt quirked an eyebrow, still working on the cake. 'I hope you're not going around speaking to strange men.'

'Aside from you?'

He grinned.

'He told me about about the Fishermans' Walk alongside the river and gave me a couple of options that I could do if I wanted.'

'And did you?'

'I did. Not all the way because I wasn't entirely sure of the route and didn't want to get lost, but the bit I did was gorgeous.'

'Good.' Matt's face disappeared behind a large mug of tea.

I took a sip of my own, a question bouncing around in my brain.

'What?'

'Pardon?' I looked from where I'd been staring into the depths of my tea.

'You look like you want to ask something.'

'Oh! Umm... No, not really.'

'Not really means definitely. Come on, spit it out.'

Matt settled back in the chair, crossed muscular arms across his similarly defined chest and fixed his hypnotic gaze on me.

'What?' I said, self-consciously and habitually pulling my hair over the old scar. The neat bob I'd had, decided upon in a discussion between Jasper and a stylist at a top London salon, had already begun to grow out. I was no longer religiously straightening my natural wave and the whole look was far less corporate than the one I'd had when I arrived here. It was early days, of course, but so far I kind of liked it.

'If you have something to say, just say it.' Matt shrugged those broad shoulders, his tone conversational, rather than argumentative. 'Don't worry. It's pretty hard to offend me.'

'Yes, I can imagine, bearing in mind we've already established your heart of stone.'

'I'm regretting telling you to go there. I get the feeling I'm never going to hear the end of this.'

Andy wandered into the kitchen, catching the end of the conversation, glanced at me, then Matt, before turning away to poke about in the fridge, looking for something to graze on.

I pulled a face. OK. I sucked in a deep breath and, under the table, clasped my hands together.

'Just bloody say it, Fleur,' Matt said in a tone that was half exasperation and half amusement.

I gripped my hands together even tighter. 'I wondered why you didn't tell me about that particular route. It wasn't far from where I was going anyway and you must know it.'

'I do. You're right, and it's beautiful. But there's a few uneven parts and couple of areas that might be a scramble depending on how long your legs are. And then there's the rock that extends out over the water. That's not for everyone, and for someone who is not used to walking it might be too much. Not to mention I've no idea how good your navigational skills are and the last thing I need is for you to be getting lost.'

Andy turned back from the fridge munching on a stick of Peperami. He clapped his brother on his shoulder. 'Obviously none of those medals you've got in your bedside drawer are for tact,' he said as he threw me a smile and left the kitchen.

'I'm sorry if that sounds a bit harsh but you did ask.'

'Yes,' I said. 'I did.' Although I was now wondering whether that had been such a good idea. I thought I'd coped fairly well on the hike that we'd done with Jasper, considering I'd never attempted anything like that before, but I was obviously mistaken.

'You're very quiet over there.'

I dipped into my mental smile supply and stuck one on. That was an action I could do without trying. 'I'm fine. Just a little tired, I expect.'

'All that fresh air and exercise.'

'Yes,' I replied, my voice a little tighter than I had wanted it to be.

'That was a very loaded yes.'

'Not at all,' I said, trying harder this time with the smile.

Matt shook his head, then pushed his chair back and leant over, clearing the mugs and plates from the table.

'I can do that.'

'So can I.' He flicked the blue gaze at me and loaded the crockery into the dishwasher.

'OK. I'll leave you to it. Thanks for the cake.' Before he could reply, I grabbed the handle of the back door and walked out into the fresh air and towards the back paddock. As I headed towards it, I heard braying and watched as Delilah charged over, the noise continuing until I walked through the gate, closing it behind me, and gave her the fussing she wanted. When Bronwyn had first introduced me to their rescue donkeys, I'd been absolutely petrified. I didn't have a lot of experience of animals other than dogs. So when Bronwyn had led me into the field a short time after I'd moved in and three noisy creatures had begun hurtling towards us, I'd had one leg over the gate before Bronwyn had caught my hand and said one word.

'Wait.'

As much as I hadn't wanted to, I had. Partly because she'd still had hold of my hand. Then they had been upon us, Bronwyn had taken my hand and gently laid it on the head of the youngest donkey, a pale-coated creature named Delilah. Her loud braying had still unnerved me but as I'd followed Bronwyn's instructions and begun to stroke the young animal, I'd felt calm wind its way through my veins. Eventually I'd summoned up the courage to feed her a few treats from the flat of my hand, which she'd wolfed down, standing close, enjoying the fussing.

'She's just a babe, really. We got a call that she'd been left abandoned on a farm so Matt and his dad took the truck and trailer and went over to get her.'

'Why did they call you?'

'Because they knew we're daft enough to take her.' She'd grinned. 'She likes you,' Bronwyn had said, nodding her head at the little jennet.

'Do you think so?'

'Absolutely. She loves the attention, that's for sure, but she doesn't hang around for everyone. She's a bit like a small child. Easily distracted.'

'That seems to be true of people old and young these days.'

'Now there's a true word. But she looks like she'll happily stay there all day now.' The little donkey had closed her eyes, resting her rather heavy head on the arm that hadn't been stroking her. 'I think you've got a friend for life there. I'd better get on, but you can stay if you want.'

I had smiled briefly before turning my attention back to the animal.

13

From my experience, it took a lot more than a little attention to gain affection. I should know. I'd given everything I had to various relationships over the years and still nothing had worked out. Rumi was the only person I could really trust when it came to love and caring. We weren't sisters in blood but in everything else we were that and more. I'd witnessed plenty of sibling rivalry in my years in the hospitality industry and it wasn't pretty. But Bronwyn's sons seemed close. I supposed, when it came down to it, it depended on the character of each person. What I was learning, however, was that animals were much simpler to understand. If they were happy, they let you know, and if they weren't, they told you that too. Delilah nudged me and gave a small bray to illustrate my point.

'Oh, I'm sorry. Have you not had enough fussing?'

'That one's never had enough. You'll be there all night now.'

'I can think of worse places to be,' I replied as Matt leant on the fence and watched us.

The other two donkeys wandered over to see if he had brought any goodies for them. Discovering he hadn't, and having had a good scratch from Matt, they began munching at the grass nearby.

'It's been pointed out to me that I may have been too blunt with you.'

I glanced back at him briefly before returning my attention to my four-legged friend. 'Not at all. You were honest. I appreciate that.'

'Apparently I should have been a little more diplomatic in order to avoid hurting feelings.'

'I assume this advice is coming from Andy?'

'How did you guess?'

'Because he does seem the more social out of the two of you and I've noticed he's more the face of your business.'

'You're saying he's more tactful and suave than me.'

'Your words, not mine.' The truth was I was still disappointed at Matt's opinion of me and, although I was absolutely rubbish at confrontation, out here in the open field, with Delilah beside me, I felt a tiny bit braver. Perhaps I could adopt Delilah as my emotional-support animal. I stepped back as she did what donkeys sometimes had to do. If I did, I thought, I was definitely going to need to carry a shovel. Having done her business, Delilah then decided she wanted to have a play and set about nudging the other two into a game, leaving me to deal with my momentarily brave comment alone.

I could hear the smile in his voice even before I turned.

'As my brother pointed out, tact is not always my strong suit.'

'You don't say.'

The words came out before I really thought about them and I tentatively raised my gaze to meet Matt's.

For a second we just looked at each other. My natural instinct was to immediately back-pedal and try to assure Matt that I hadn't meant it in the way that it sounded. But the thing was – I did actually mean it in the way it sounded. I'd felt hurt by his lack of belief in me and I was annoyed with him.

Matt began to laugh.

'I have a feeling that that's the first time you've answered anyone back in a long while and for the record I'm sure I thoroughly deserved it.'

I moved to the gate, let myself out and checked that it was properly secured. I could feel the faint heat on my face but he was right. Again. Which was kind of annoying. I couldn't remember the last time I'd answered anyone back, apart from Rumi, of course, but that didn't count. She was in her own category of one. A category where I knew that I could say anything and everything and not be judged.

'It's good to see you coming out of your shell a little more. Even if it is at the expense of insulting me.'

'I wasn't insulting you,' I said, tipping my chin in defiance – also a new move for me. 'I was in fact agreeing with you. Tact definitely isn't one of your strong suits. At least not outside work.'

Delilah wandered over and shoved her nose through one of the gaps in the fence and I gave her another quick scratch before turning back to the house.

'Funny. She's never that excited to see me. I get a quick hello and that's it.'

'She's a female with good taste.'

'I think we've unleashed a monster.' He gave a low chuckle as I smiled down at my feet. 'Although there are probably plenty of people who would agree with you and her. My ex-wife being one.'

'You were married?'

'I was,' he said, falling into place beside me, his steps

adjusted for my shorter length of stride. 'Once. Long time ago now. Funnily enough, she mentioned my lack of tact more than once.'

'I suppose in the military you didn't always have to be that tactful.'

He gave a shrug. 'Depends on the situation, but not when you're training recruits et cetera, no. Tact is the last thing on your mind at that point. You're trying to toughen them up. Not that anything can prepare them, prepare anyone, really, for a theatre of war. But you do what you can and unfortunately that doesn't always leave a lot of allowance for niceties.'

'No, I imagine it doesn't.'

'But I'm working on it.' He glanced down.

'Glad to hear it. It's not always easy to change behaviour patterns that have been in place for a long time.'

'That's true. All we can do is try. So, in light of that and as an apology for being what my brother described as "a tactless arse", how would you feel about going down to the river when you're free and continuing that walk that you started on your own today?'

'With you?'

'If you can bear it.'

'I'll do my best. But don't forget, if you get all shouty Sergeant Majory on me, there's a handy river right there.'

'Ooh, she's getting feisty now.'

'It's probably about time, don't you think?'

'If it's part of who you really are, then I guess so.'

'You might find out you don't like who I really am.'

'One step at a time, eh?'

'I notice that wasn't a no.'

'I don't like to commit myself without knowing all the facts.'

'Of course you don't,' I replied, trying to hide the smile in my voice.

'I was on my way to check the chickens. Have you forgiven me enough to join me?'

'Only because I like the chickens.'

We walked in a comfortable silence towards the large coop. A couple of the hens had taken to laying eggs in unexpected places, so Bronwyn had sent Matt out to double-check that there were no rogue eggs left following collection this morning. We entered the enclosure and Matt secured the gate behind us as a dozen or more hens scuttled towards us on fluffy-bloomered legs to see if we had any scraps for them.

'Did you bring anything?' I asked.

'No, not this time.'

'No wonder the animals are never in a hurry to see you.'

'Ah, so now the truth comes out. Your gain their affection through bribery. Pure and simple.'

I turned out the pockets of my light jacket. 'Nope.' I smiled before looking down and seeing chickens all around me. A few wandered over to Matt and began to peck at the sturdy walking boots he was still wearing. One particularly brave soul began yanking the laces with her beak before he scooped her up and tucked her under his arm. I laughed as her momentarily indignant squawking settled into a relaxed and soft clucking as his free hand stroked the downy soft bronze-coloured feathers.

'Did you grow up here? I mean, in this house?'

'Yep,' he replied, still focused on the bird tucked under his arm, who was contentedly surveying her surroundings from this new elevated position.

'And have you always had animals here?'

'This was originally my grandparents' place. They were the ones that first started rescuing donkeys, so I'm sure they'd have loved you, bearing in mind you're as soppy about them as they were.'

'I'm not soppy, I'm just...' I gave a shrug of my shoulders. I wasn't sure what I was. But I did enjoy the company of animals. They didn't judge you and were pretty much always happy to see you even if you hadn't brought treats, as was now shown by the hen snuggling into Matt's muscular but gentle embrace.

'Don't take that the wrong way. I'm not saying it's a bad thing. I loved my grandparents to bits. And Mum and Dad are the same, and Andy too. I'm just not built that way.'

I gave the chicken under his arm another glance before raising my gaze to his. 'So you say.'

One corner of his mouth tipped into a half-smile. 'This is different.'

'Is that so?'

'Completely.'

'And how's that?'

'Because she'll probably be on the table Sunday. I'm just helping make her last few days pleasant.'

My smile morphed into horror. 'Your mum said you don't eat these!'

'Only if they stop laying.'

'Henrietta's still laying!'

Matt looked down at the chicken. 'Then I guess she's got some time left after all.' He bent to return the bird to the ground and, when he straightened, a bloody great grin was plastered across his face.

'Oh, ha ha. I suppose you think that's hilarious.'

'Amusing if not hilarious. You're so easy to get a rise out of. It's hard not to succumb.'

'Do try though, love.' Bronwyn's voice came from behind us and we headed out of the coop, a few extra eggs now resting in the basket Matt carried. 'Fleur is proving such a great addition. I won't be very impressed if she hands in her notice because you're just too annoying to put up with.' His mum looked at me. 'They were both brought up to be polite.'

'I'm polite.'

'When you want to be.'

'Especially when there's a pretty girl involved,' his brother called over as he began walking our way, hand in hand with a woman I didn't recognise.

Matt rolled his eyes. 'Hardly. Besides, Fleur's pretty so your theory doesn't exactly pan out there, mate.'

'Yeah, and has got the sense to have nothing to do with you.'

'If there's one thing I've learned it's never to get involved with anybody you work with. Far too messy and, on occasion, it can also leave you homeless.'

'What if it's meant to happen though?' The newcomer asked. She was dressed in a style that was best described as bohemian meets hippy, but really made it work. It certainly made a change from the local uniform of walking gear. Her long fair hair was braided into one thick plait that trailed over her shoulder.

'Anna, my love!' Bronwyn said as she pulled her into a tight hug. 'How was India?'

'Amazing! I had a meeting with my new supplier of organic cotton and toured their closed-loop system production facility, and we've also begun advertising in the local villages for people to do the block printing of the fabrics I'm designing, using natural dyes, which will help provide income to some more families in the immediate area. I'm so excited!'

'That sounds great, my darling. I'm glad it's working out.'

'It's early days and, of course, a tiny drop in the ocean

against the monster of fast fashion but it's something. Hi. I'm Anna.' She held out a hand. 'You must be Fleur.'

'I am. It's nice to meet you.' I paused. 'Umm... what did you mean about me being homeless being meant to happen?'

'Anna is a big believer in the whole fate thing,' Matt said in a tone that suggested his own beliefs didn't align with hers.

'Hello, Matt,' she said, giving him a huge hug, which he returned warmly.

'Well,' she said, turning back to me. 'From what I've heard, a specific sequence of events led you to here. Perhaps this is where you're meant to be.'

'Oh. I... I'm not sure I believe in the whole meant-to-be thing.'

'Lots of people don't until it happens to them,' she replied, apparently unoffended that she appeared to be in the minority with her beliefs. 'Have you ever been to India?' she asked.

I shook my head. 'No, I haven't travelled much at all, but it's somewhere I've always thought it would be interesting to go.'

'I think you'd love it. In fact, I'm sure of it. I get that feeling from you. If you're free some time it would be nice to get to know each other better over a coffee, and I can show you some pictures from my trip.'

'I'd love that!' I replied. Anna gave out an aura of calm and I would certainly be happy to benefit from that over a cuppa. I knew that Andy lived with his girlfriend but now, having met Anna, it was no wonder he was more chilled than his brother. Or maybe it was purely down to being different people with different experiences. Matt had been to war and Andy hadn't. It was impossible to think that hadn't left a mark on his psyche as well as his skin. As a group we headed back to the house, to the kitchen and the heart of the farmhouse.

Anna reached back her hand and took mine within her own.

'I'm so glad you're here,' she said, in a soft voice that had a gentle southern Welsh accent and a melodic roll to the words. 'I'm really looking forward to us getting to know each other. It would be lovely to have someone to spend time with when these two are talking about which crampon is superior.'

Andy cleared his throat.

She laughed a musical laugh and reached up on her toes to kiss his cheek, which seemed to satisfy him.

'You'd better wipe that dorky look off your face before any clients see you,' Matt teased.

Andy cocked his head at his brother. 'Not a romantic bone in his body.'

'I wouldn't be so sure of that,' Anna said as we all traipsed into the kitchen.

Matt gave an eye roll and closed the door behind us.

14

'So, I hear you and Anna went for coffee together?' Matt said as we laced up our boots, resting on the back of the pick-up. 'How was that?'

'Really good, thanks. She's lovely.'

'She is. Andy's been nuts about her since he met her.'

'Yes, I can imagine. He can barely take his eyes off her, can he?'

'Nope. Daft bugger. Almost as soppy as you with animals.'

I stepped away from the pick-up as Matt beeped it locked. 'It's clear who got all the romantic genes in the family.'

He gave a short laugh but there seemed little humour behind it. 'Yeah... afraid if you're looking for romance, you definitely need to turn in a different direction.'

'I assume that means you're not looking for it either.'

'Nope. Been there, done that, got the T-shirt and the solicitor's fees for the divorce.'

'Just because it didn't work out once doesn't mean it wouldn't again.' I pondered as we crunched down the gravel path towards the walk that Matt had planned for today.

'True. But I'm not really interested in all that any more. I spent a whole career looking out for people. Trying to make sure they were safe and then coming home and having to take care of somebody else? It proved too much of a strain. I just don't think I'm meant for that kind of relationship.'

'You make it sound like coming home was a chore!'

We strode along the path. In the distance the sound of the river rushing down between the rocks drifted on the warm air.

'Not a chore exactly, but Cally is not the most independent of women. She's beautiful, is an only, and very doted upon, child and grew up used to having things done for her. At first it was fine and I loved doing things for her. I was completely swept off my feet. But after my first tour, I was still trying to get my head around things I'd experienced and I couldn't really be the husband that I'd been before. Don't get me wrong, she did try. We both did. Neither of us wanted the marriage to end so we struggled on. But then I was deployed again and things just got worse. In the end we had to admit that the marriage wasn't working, and I knew a lot of that was down to me.'

'That sounds hard, but I don't think anybody who comes back from something like that is ever the same person. I don't see how they could be.'

Matt was silent and I looked up to see his gaze resting on me.

My fingers found the toggle on the end of my coat's hood tie and began fidgeting with it. 'What? Did I say something wrong?' A chill ran down my spine but my face was burning with heat.

'No,' he said, shaking his head. 'Not at all.'

'Why are you looking at me funny, then?'

The wide grin appeared from nowhere, chasing away the seriousness his face had held moments earlier. 'Define funny.'

'I can't now. You've changed your expression. But it was funny. Not ha ha funny, odd funny. Like I'd put my foot in it.'

'I can reassure you that you didn't.'

'So?'

He let out a sigh. 'For someone who only spoke when they were spoken to a short time ago, you're getting pretty chatty these days.'

'Are you complaining? I'm quite happy to spend the entire day in silence if that suits you better.'

He appeared to be thinking about it and I whacked him with the toggle I'd been fiddling with, causing him to laugh.

'No. I think I like this version of you.'

'Thanks. Although I still don't think I qualify as chatty just yet.'

'I hear you and Anna didn't stop talking the entire time when you went out.'

'She's easy to talk to.'

'And me?'

'Yeah, you're OK. It helps I know you don't have a romantic bone in your body. I have a record of falling for entirely inappropriate men when I get swept up in the initial romance of it all.'

'Fair enough. Plus Mum would kill me if I upset you, which I probably would before too long. As I said, romance isn't really my thing. I struggle with neediness.'

'I suppose that depends what you define as neediness. Some people just like being close and doing things together a lot. I don't think that's necessarily a bad thing.' *It might be rather nice...*

'Yeah. I guess you're right.'

'Yep. Well, don't worry, you're in no danger from me. Is this the way?' I said, pointing and marching off in the same direction before he'd even answered as his words churned around in my brain.

I concentrated on where I was putting my feet and was glad much of the trail was single file. We'd gone past the point where I'd stopped and turned back on my previous walk and I was now on unfamiliar ground, so Matt had now taken the lead. On our right the river rushed past, crashing over boulders, the clear, icy cold water polishing them smooth. In front of me Matt's bulk pushed on, striding up rocks that took me a little more effort plus the use of my hands to clamber over. He turned and offered me his hand a few times, but I waved it away and made my own determined effort to clear the obstacle under my own steam. The third time I waved him off, he stopped, turning to face me square-on.

'What's up with you?'

I frowned. 'Nothing. Why? I'm keeping up, aren't I?'

'You are. But it's OK to take a hand occasionally in tougher areas. You seemed happy to do that when I took you and your ex out.'

'Yes, and look where that got me. Him accusing me of flirting with you and ending up with no job and no boyfriend.'

'You have got a job. Arguably one that you enjoy more, from what you've said, and I was under the impression that you weren't exactly missing that idiot either.'

'That's not the point.'

Matt stretched his neck from side to side before his eyes focused back on me, pinning me in place like a laser. 'What exactly is the point, Fleur? You were absolutely fine and now you've gone into some weird mood.'

'I'm not in a weird mood.'

'Yeah. You are. If you're not enjoying this we can just turn back now.'

'I am enjoying it.'

'So why have you got a face like a slapped arse?'

'I assume you weren't in charge of any delicate negotiations when you were deployed!' I snapped.

'What's that supposed to mean?'

'Nothing,' I said, feeling the fight go out of me. As I made to go past him, his hand caught my wrist and I looked up. The blue eyes were still intense, studying me.

'I'm not going any further until I know what's going on.'

'Fine. I can go on ahead on my own anyway. I brought a map,' I said as I pulled it from my pocket and waved it triumphantly in his face. Deftly, and smoothly, he took the map out of my fingers and stuffed it in his own pocket.

'Oi! Give that back.'

'I will when you tell me why you've suddenly gone from relaxed to acting like you've got a stick up your backside.'

'Again with the diplomacy, I see.'

'Fleur.' It was just one word but it was loaded with meaning.

'I told you there's nothing.'

He continued his scrutiny for a few seconds then dragged his free hand across his forehead, a deep sigh escaping as he did so.

'Look,' he said, leading me carefully back to a large boulder, which he rested against before reaching out for my other hand so that he now held both loosely in front of him. 'If I've given you the wrong impression, I'm sorry.'

'The wrong impression of what?' I asked, genuinely confused.

'I was just being friendly. Trying to be helpful. It was a big deal what you did, moving from somewhere you'd known your whole life to somewhere completely different without knowing a soul. I'm sorry if you took things the wrong way or if I gave you an idea that I was interested in something more…'

I started to smile and removed my hands from his, which he released easily. 'You think I'm upset because I've got a crush on you?'

For the first time since I'd met him, Matt actually seemed unsure of himself, which only made me smile more.

'I just thought that maybe…'

'You thought that maybe you were so irresistible, poor little needy Fleur couldn't help but be drawn to you.'

'No. That's not what I meant. And I never called you needy.'

'Are you sure?'

'Yes. You've got it wrong.'

'Your words were pretty clear. I'm not quite sure how I could possibly have misunderstood.'

'OK, yes, but it's not what I meant.'

'What did you mean, then?'

He opened his mouth to say something then closed it again.

'Yes. That's what I thought. So, just to be clear – I do not have a crush on you. I've never had a crush on you, and I don't plan to have a crush on you. Apologies if that puts a bit of a dent in your ego but I'm pretty sure you can take it.'

'There's no need to be like that.'

'You insinuated I'm needy!' I snapped, the real reason for my upset and annoyance spilling out.

Clarity dawned over Matt's face and I turned away, watching the river power its way down the valley.

'I wasn't referring to you, Fleur.' His tone was softer now. I remained silent. Hot, embarrassed tears were threatening in my eyes and I didn't want Matt to see them. It would only reinforce his idea that I was far from the independent type.

The sound of voices alerted us to somebody else

coming along the path. Great, that was all I needed. I willed the tears back in as a group of walkers approached us.

'Here.' Matt handed me some tea from the flask he'd packed earlier. I took it, averting my face from both him and the oncoming group. As I drank, my red-rimmed eyes disappeared behind the metal cup. The other walkers marched past, exchanging hellos with Matt. Once they'd gone I lowered the cup.

'Thanks,' I said, having regained some stability, and handed the cup back.

'No problem.' He refilled the cup for himself and rested back on the boulder. 'Why don't we take a rest for a bit?'

'I'm not tired and I know you can't be. This walk is quite literally a stroll in the park for you,. I'm more capable than you think, you know.'

'I don't doubt it, but that doesn't mean it's not good to take a rest when you can.'

I gave a slightly overdramatic sigh and plopped down on a rock beside him. 'I can see you smiling.'

'Am I not allowed to smile now?'

'Not at my expense, no.'

'I can't help it if you amuse me.'

'Laughing at people isn't very nice, didn't you know that?'

'Being amused by someone and laughing at them are two very different things.'

I stared at the river, unconvinced, before sitting up straight. 'What was that?' I pointed at the river as another silvery streak leapt momentarily out of the water before disappearing back under the bubbling, churning surface.

'Salmon.'

'Really?'

'Yep. Plenty of them here. You sometimes see people perched on the rocks fishing for them.'

'Blimey. There's one way to get really fresh fish, I suppose.'

'That's for sure.'

'So they really do leap like that?'

'They do.'

'I mean, I've seen nature programmes and stuff but...'

'Yeah. It's different when you see it with your own eyes though, isn't it?'

'It is. Although I suppose you think it's probably a bit pathetic that I'm excited over a fish jumping out of the water for two seconds.'

'Oi.' Matt pushed himself up off the rock he'd been perched on, grabbing my sleeve as he gently pulled me back from the river edge where I'd been peering, the sunlight sparkling on its surface like diamonds in candlelight.

'It's fine. I'm not going to fall in.' I rolled my eyes at him.

'I know you're not. Because if you go in that means I have to go in and it's bloody cold.'

'I'm quite capable of keeping my feet on the ground.' I made to move away, stepped on a wet slab of stone and, as the universe laughed its arse off, my feet went up in the air and my bum made a beeline for a particularly damp piece of grass.

Matt's arm was around me before I hit the ground. 'Slippy there,' he said, waiting until he was sure my footing was secure before letting go.

I cleared my throat. 'So it would seem. Thank you.'

'You're welcome.'

'Although I reckon you made that bit purposely slippy somehow just to prove how *needy* I am.' I pulled a face at him as I said it.

With a swiftness that belied his size he hooked an arm

around my waist, pulling me close. 'Listen, you. I don't think you're needy and never have. You took something the wrong way and now you need to let it go.'

I gave a shrug and stared at the logo on his T-shirt. 'It's not like you'd be the first to say it anyway.'

'Oi.' His tone was soft, contrasting with that edge of gravel in his voice.

When I didn't look at him he repeated the word, this time with an accompanying squeeze. 'Look at me.'

I screwed up my nose. 'I'm not sure I want to.'

'Wow. That hideous, eh?'

'You have no idea.'

The rumble of laughter in his chest reverberated through mine as he held me and I tilted my head up to meet his gaze.

'Listen to me. Please. I don't think you're needy. I wasn't talking about you. Frankly I think you're bloody brave moving up here and starting a new life in the middle of nowhere. It takes real guts to do that, and I'm sorry if I touched a nerve. I know we don't know each other especially well but I hope you know that, tactless as I am, I would never purposely upset you.'

I paused. 'No. I do know that.' Now I did.

'Good. And just for the record, anyone who's accused you of being needy before obviously didn't take time to get to know the real you, which was a huge loss on their part.'

I watched him for a moment, the intense eyes focused on mine.

'You're being super nice to me. It's weird.'

'I know. You're right. It is weird. I'm going to stop now.'

'I think that's a good idea.'

He gave a short nod that made me think it might have harked back to his military days. His arms remained around me briefly as his eyes scanned the ground, making sure that my footing was secure this time.

'Come on, then, Bigfoot. Lead the way.'

'Right. That's absolutely the last time I'm nice to you.'

'Oh, big surprise.'

'Just keep up or I'm going to see to it you get a better look at those salmon.'

'Oh, ha ha.' A teeny bit of me decided it would be wise not to entirely put it past him, so I checked my footing and traipsed on as sunlight dappled the ground through the trees above and water, tinted copper from the minerals in the earth, quietly trickled down the banks, collecting into pools the colour of a shiny new penny.

15

'How you doing?' Matt asked as we got to the end of the trail, a gate onto a small road ahead of us.

'OK,' I replied, feeling a bit out of puff but not in a bad way. I swung my small rucksack round and pulled my water bottle from it, guzzling some down as Matt did the same before offering me a protein bar.

'Ooh! That's yum,' I said, peering at the wrapper as I took another bite.

'Yeah. I like these ones. You'll be pleased to know you took my favourite.'

I finished my mouthful and grinned. 'You're right. I am extremely pleased. I can see why it's your fave. We used to make things a bit like this at the café I worked at. They always went down well with the hipster crowd.'

'Ah, my people,' Matt replied, his expression serious.

'Yeah. I had you pinned as a hipster the moment I met you.' It was taking every ounce of energy I had to stop the muscles in my face from forming a huge smile.

'I know. It's pretty hard to hide,' Matt confirmed, looking the most un-hipster-like anyone possibly could, solid instead as any one of the boulders we'd clambered over during our walk rather than the slender, bespectacled, ironically bearded types I'd been used to serving our 'vegan nature bars' to. Then the grin began to show on his clean-shaven face, the lines around his eyes crinkling as it did so. 'Something tells me you don't believe me.'

'I've spent a lot of time observing people and you, my friend, most definitely don't fit into the hipster mould,' I said, finding a small rock to perch on.

'I'm probably going to regret asking this, but, in your experience, what mould do I fit into, then?'

I studied him for a few moments.

'That bad, eh?' he said, meeting my ponderous gaze.

'I don't have to tell you,' I teased.

'Of course you do. I can't not know now.'

'Are you sure you really want to?'

Now it was his turn to study me. I shifted under his gaze, feeling unused to the focus. The smile was softer this time.

'Yeah, I think I do.'

'OK. Then if you'd come in the coffee shop, I'd have said that you'd definitely been in the military because you have that stance. You never seem to slouch like the rest of us.'

'I'm not sure I'd agree with that.'

'Do you want to hear my trained observations or not?'

'Oh, so you're a trained observer now?'

'Absolutely. You'd be amazed how attuned you can get when you spend your childhood trying to suss out whether these are the people who'll finally pick you.' I hadn't meant to say anything so remotely personal and I suddenly found that my hiking boot needed adjustment and dropped my concentration to attend to it. 'Sorry. Just forget I said that.'

'No.'

My head snapped up. 'What?'

'I'm not going to forget it. You shared something private, which, from what I know of you, took a lot of guts.'

'Not really. It just came out.'

'Then I'm glad.'

'Well, I'm not,' I said, returning to my shoe. 'It makes me sound pathetic.'

'Wanting to be wanted is not pathetic, Fleur. Far from it and don't ever let anyone, including yourself, tell you any different. And that doesn't change whether you're a child or an adult. I am incredibly lucky to have two loving parents – and an irritating younger sibling – so I'm not even going to pretend to understand what your experience was like. But, if you ever do want to tell me more, I'll always be happy to listen. Don't ask me for advice, but listening I can do.'

'Thanks.' I said, toeing a stone with the tip of my boot and feeling annoyed that I'd accidentally ruined the playful mood that had previously surrounded us.

'So, come on, then. What else? I look like a soldier, apparently. Is that it?' Matt raised his brows in an enquiring manner. 'There's got to be more,' he said, stretching out his legs and bringing the playfulness back. 'I bloody hope there's more.' He narrowed his eyes at me momentarily. 'I think.'

'There is,' I said, relaxing again a little. 'You look serious a lot, so it'd be easy to think you were a bit of a grump.'

'There are those that would agree with that.'

'But then you have a great smile and the moment that happens your whole face transforms and true grumps don't do that.'

'Expert on them, are you?'

'I am, actually. Don't forget I've spent plenty of years in the hospitality industry so I've met more than my fair share of them. I also dated one or two, so, yes, I'd say I was somewhat of an expert on grumps.'

'So, anything other than military and potentially grumpy?'

'Ah!' I held up my finger. 'The appearance of grumpiness only. And yes. Good manners so you'd offer help to anyone that you saw needed it, but you don't suffer fools gladly, so the ever maddening propensity of people to watch videos and take calls on speaker in public would have you downing your coffee and leaving as quickly as possible. And, probably in your mind, crushing their phone under your boot as you left – to the cheers of pretty much everyone else in the place. Certainly you'd be getting free coffee from the staff for that.'

Matt rolled his lips, considering my words.

'Am I fired?' I said, only half joking.

There was that smile again. 'Nope. Do I get a go now?'

'A go?'

'Yep.

'You didn't say it was reciprocal.'

'Life's much fairer that way.'

'Since when has life been fair?' I asked, my attempt at a jovial tone shadowing the truth I felt about the question.

'That's very true. It most certainly isn't. Come on, you ready to head further on this walk and go up the hill or do you want to go back the way we came?' He pushed himself up from where he'd been sitting and grabbed his rucksack from the rock next to him.

'OK.'

'OK to which one?'

'OK to yes, you do get a go.' I plopped myself down, pulled my knees up to my chin and waited.

'Well, there's a defensive position if I ever saw one.'

'I'm not defensive,' I said, sounding more defensive than I'd planned.

'Come on.' He put out a hand to pull me up. 'I was just joking earlier. As has already been pointed out to you, tact is not listed on my CV as one of my attributes and I don't want to upset you. Especially not when there are large rocks and deep water nearby.'

'That doesn't bode well for your thoughts on me.' I felt the barriers clank into place loudly in my head.

A deep frown creased his forehead. 'What? I didn't say that and, for future reference, I would never say or think that.'

'So what are you scared of?'

Laughter bubbled up, the smile transforming the frown. 'I'm not scared. For one thing, you're small enough to be stuffed in my rucksack if need be. And scared is not the word. Cautious is more appropriate.'

'I'm a lot tougher than I look, Matt.'

'Now that I don't doubt. Actually that's one of the things on my list.'

'So tell me the rest.'

'You're not going to move until I do, are you?'

'Nope. And I'm not going in your rucksack either. You're going in that river before that happens.'

'Might be worth the challenge...' The grin flashed again.

I crossed my arms.

'OK, fine. So, as you rightly pointed out, you're tougher than you look, and also than you think you are. You're cautious of saying the wrong thing but have a natural ability to say the right thing anyway. Mum's already had a tonne of compliments about you. You're good at your job but you're always second-guessing yourself and not just in your job. You've let the Jaspers of this world make you feel like you're less than you are and now you believe it.'

I opened my mouth to argue but Matt got there first. 'Because actually you're way more than you think you are. And that's the truth you need to start believing.'

For a few moments the only sound was the river and rustle of breeze through the green canopy of leaves above us.

'Am I fired?' he asked as he screwed his face up, mimicking my own question.

'Immediately. Start packing the moment you get back.'

'One more thing.'

'Oh God, I think you found plenty. Thank you for the nice things you said, by the way. Go on, then, what is it?'

'It might be good to take some time to find out who you are. I mean, really.'

'I don't think there's much chance of that. I tried to find my mother once years ago but all I got was dead ends.'

'Oh... no, I didn't mean that, but if that's something you did want to pursue, perhaps we can try again.'

I knew he'd said it automatically, that it didn't mean anything, but I liked the idea that flitted in my brain for a moment of there being a 'we'. Not in a romantic sense. Matt wasn't my type. I wasn't even sure I had one. Possibly another thing I needed to find out about myself. But, as much as I hated to admit it, Matt was right about the fact I'd let people have their own way. I was the ultimate people pleaser and that was obviously coming in handy with work – I was thrilled that his parents had been getting compliments. In my job, I was happy to do what I could to ensure customers went away happy. It wasn't a chore. To most people, I supposed waitressing or making coffee wasn't the most aspirational career, but I loved it.

When Jasper had advised that he had the perfect position

in his firm for me, I'd been really sorry to leave my job. But the truth was, Jasper had been embarrassed to tell anyone that I worked in a coffee shop. It had been far easier, and far more socially acceptable, for him to say that I worked *for him*. But now, at the hotel, I felt as though I fitted in. Perhaps that was the first step. There were plenty more to go, that was for sure, but sometimes the first step was the biggest, the most difficult, and ironically enough, thanks to Jasper's dramatics, I'd taken it. I didn't have to be a people pleaser all the time. It was taking time but slowly I was discovering it was OK to have my own, true opinions.

'Maybe,' I said, looking up at Matt as he gazed down. His brow was creased in the faint frown he wore almost permanently but that disappeared entirely when he smiled that beautiful, even white smile.

'I'll take maybe,' he said, adjusting my far smaller pack on my back for me. 'Comfy?'

'Yes, thanks.'

'Now, back the way we came?'

I shook my head. 'No. I want to go on up there.' I pointed left towards the hill that sat atop the route we'd just taken.

'It's a tougher route. Steep climb to begin with but the views will repay you.'

'Don't think I'm up to it?' I asked, hands on hips, a rebellious smirk tilting the corners of my mouth.

'Fleur. I think you're up to anything you put your mind to.'

'Then lead on. But if you hear obscenely heavy breathing, or alternatively complete silence, just check behind you to make sure I'm not going for the Smurf look, won't you?'

'Deal.'

* * *

After another busy week in the restaurant I was looking
forward to spending the day nosing around the shops with
Anna. We'd really hit it off and it was lovely to have a friend I
could spend time with. Rumi would always be my bestie – we
still talked every day and when she'd called early this morning
she'd been amidst piles of boxes, still deciding what to put
where. She'd looked frazzled but thrilled. We hadn't been able
to chat long as they were trying to get the home office set up for
Ayaz as well as essentials for the kitchen so that he wasn't
working in total chaos when he started back tomorrow. She
hadn't stopped smiling the entire time and I'd promised to call
her tomorrow for a full video tour.

'Anyone in?' Anna's singsong tones accompanied the tap on
the door.

'Come in!' I said, buttoning up my third and final choice of
shirt. 'Hi! How's you?'

'Great, thanks,' she said, her wide bright smile backing up
the statement. She wore a maxi-length skirt with a watercolour
paisley design and a pale blue sleeveless top with laces up the
centre front that had a hint of Romany about it. Flat leather
sandals and an armful of bracelets completed the look. In her
hand was a straw hat that looked as though it had done a few
miles in its lifetime. Surrounded by wild mountains and rolling
valleys, her style definitely veered far from the average dress
code in these parts, but I'd soon discovered that this wasn't
attention seeking. Anna was the most authentic person I'd ever
met and a part of me wondered how that felt.

'That's a pretty blouse,' she said, taking a seat on the comfy
chair tucked in the corner by the window that gave out onto the
spectacular, soothing view. I'd spent a lot of time reading in that
chair since I'd moved in, now that I had the opportunity to get
back into that particular hobby again. Jasper had only really

approved of literary fiction – not that he read much himself, but his shelves displayed all the 'right' books. Despite my trying, they just weren't my thing and I preferred romance. Contemporary, historical, funny, I didn't mind – the only thing I demanded was a happy ending. Of course, romances weren't on his approved reading list and in the end I'd lost interest, but on a wander around the village here, I'd found the small, but clearly well-used library. A rush of excitement had washed over me as I'd looked around and then firmly ensconced myself in the romance section. I'd signed up for membership and come away with a big pile, which now sat on the table next to the window, close to the chair Anna currently occupied.

'Thanks,' I said, smoothing it down and picking a piece of lint off the black trousers I'd paired it with.

'You always look so smart and put together,' she said, smiling as I gave the back of me a quick check in the mirror and she pushed herself up from the chair, sensing we were ready to go.

'Oh, I'm not sure about that.'

'You do. Look at you.' Anna caught my arm and turned me back to the mirror. 'You look like you could conquer the world.'

I screwed my nose up. 'The trouble is, I've no interest in conquering the world. Far from it!'

'Oh,' Anna said, momentarily flummoxed by my reply.

I fiddled with the bracelet-length sleeve of my blouse again. The saleswoman in the swanky shop had told me that sleeve length was very stylish, and that may be. But to me they always felt like they were neither one thing nor the other.

'I don't think you can make it grow by yanking on it.' Anna laughed. 'Would you like to change into something else? You don't seem comfortable.'

I let out a loud sigh. 'I'm not,' I said, turning to her, finally saying it out loud as I pulled open the wardrobe door. Behind it hung other outfits of a similar ilk. Stylish. Expensive. Beautifully cut. But not me. They were what I'd been expected to wear in the life I'd been living. 'None of this is me but it's all I have. It suited my "previous life" but frankly my previous life didn't suit me either.'

Anna studied me for a few moments before tucking one side of my overgrown bob (Jasper would have had a fit!) back behind one of my ears.

'And how long were you living that life?'

'About two years.'

'When did you realise it didn't feel authentic?'

'Oh... pretty quickly,' I replied, avoiding her eye. I felt like a fraud and I had no idea why I was sharing this information with her. 'Anyway, we'd better get going if we're going to catch the train.'

'We have time,' Anna said, not even glancing at a clock to verify this.

'No, really, I'm just in a funny mood. I probably need caffeine,' I said, closing the wardrobe door and wishing I'd never said anything. I was beginning to think there was something in the air here. Since coming to Wales, I'd already said far too much to Matt and now Anna.

'Or you need a new wardrobe.'

'No, this one's lovely,' I said, leaning against the beautifully carved armoire that held most of my belongings. According to Bronwyn, a friend in the village who was downsizing had been about to consign it to the tip and was bemoaning the fact that nobody valued good furniture these days. With plans afoot in her head to make over the room we were now standing in from a general dumping ground to welcoming live-in quarters for staff, Bronwyn had taken it off his hands. Apparently it had taken her husband and both sons to manhandle the beast up the stairs and into the room.

'It is. Although you should have seen it when Bronwyn got it. It did look sad,' Anna said, tracing her slim fingers along a carving on the door.

'Really?'

'Yep. It was Matt who made it look like it does now.'

'Oh? I didn't know he was into stuff like that.' The truth was, apart from the obvious interest of hiking and climbing, I wasn't sure what else Matt was into. We'd talked on our walk but not really about anything like that.

'I'm not sure he was,' Anna said. 'He was grouching around the house because the snow was too deep to get much walking in, so Bronwyn told him there was some sandpaper and a pot of varnish waiting upstairs to be used. I don't think she thought he'd actually do much but this was the result. Much to her – and I think Matt's surprise. He's done a few other pieces for his own place now and we have a beautiful side table he restored that was their grandfather's. I think he finds it therapeutic, especially when the weather is awful.'

'A man of many talents.'

'That's what I hear,' Anna said, widening her eyes briefly before both of us burst into giggles.

'Don't say that. I won't be able to look him in the eye now! Come on,' I said, hustling her out of the room. 'We really are going to miss our train.'

16

'That looks amazing,' Anna said as I pulled back the curtain on the changing room to where she was sitting on a plush, emerald-green buttoned bench in a shop she'd told me was one of her favourites. Rather than the high street, Anna had brought me to an area of the city that was full of indie shops and boutiques.

'I don't have tonnes of money,' I'd said, when she'd suggested this shop, but she'd reassured me that many of their prices were similar to the high street, so long as I wasn't looking for £3 T-shirts.

'No, definitely not,' I'd said, having recently read a book on fast fashion that had been left in the hotel's 'take one, leave one' library in the sitting room. And Anna had been right. The shops we'd been into were filled with a variety of choices. I had no idea what my real style was but I needn't have worried as, just as Anna had promised, every time I'd tried the right garment on, I'd known.

'It's so you!' Anna said, excitedly clapping her hands, making the bangles on her arm clank together.

I looked down at the tie-waist skirt, the red and black irregular-print fabric swishing softly in the breeze drifting through from a fan positioned near the entrance to the dressing area. 'It looks great with your colouring, and the fit around your hips is fabulous.'

I took another look, twisting this way and that. Anna was right. The fit was perfect and, weirdly, it did feel like me, even though I was still in the process of finding out who that was. I knew who it wasn't. It wasn't the person that wore the tailored fitted clothes currently hanging in my wardrobe. Neither was it the goth I'd once been, again because that particular boyfriend had favoured the look, or the grunge look, or the fifties bombshell, although some toned-down elements of that style wouldn't be unwelcome. So, I knew who I wasn't. I also knew I wasn't as eclectic as Anna. The one thing I did envy about her, though, was her complete comfort in who she was and how she dressed.

'I like it,' I said, a small smile creeping onto my face.

'Bearing in mind for you that's the equivalent of spinning around singing "This Is Me", I think you should definitely get it.'

I grinned, gave one more swish and headed back into the changing room to get dressed back into clothes that were feeling more and more alien to me every day.

'You know,' Anna said as she took a sip from a massive double-handled mug of cappuccino, 'the clothes you have but don't feel comfortable in could be sold. There's various apps out there that specialise in that sort of thing. The clothes are good quality and could probably pay for your wardrobe refresh.'

I bit off my gingerbread man's leg and chewed as I thought. 'That's actually a good idea. Have you ever done it?'

'Not personally but I know friends from home have. Of course, there's Facebook and eBay, et cetera too. It just depends what you feel comfortable with.'

'I never use Facebook. I don't even have an account.'

'Let's look at some of the apps, then,' she said, pulling out her phone and tapping on the app store icon. A few seconds later a list of sites that claimed to help you make a mint from your wardrobe was displayed in front of us. 'This one is supposed to be good,' she said, pointing at the second one down. 'I know a friend sold a tonne of stuff on that and her style is more like yours than mine so that suggests they have a good audience for it.' She glanced at my bag. 'Your previous style, that is.'

'Do you think it could work?' I said, feeling a tremor of excitement. My salary here was very competitive and Bronwyn and Greg had suggested that, if I decided to stay, there could be a possibility of a promotion in time, if I was interested. With bed and board included, I was able to save more than I had before Jasper had always refused to take any rent from me and had actually got quite uppity about it when I'd tried to press it. But what I'd saved on rent I'd had to spend on the 'right' clothes. And they'd cost a bloody bomb! With the money I'd saved, I'd bought a little secondhand car which had given me freedom to explore further afield independently.

'I do. No harm in trying. My friend Nia styled her photos really well and took them in daylight and stuff, so I think making them look as attractive as possible really helps.'

'I could do that...' The cogs in my brain were starting to turn. 'Would you help me?' I said, turning my face from her phone to Anna.

'I thought you'd never ask!' she said, laughing as she took a bite of her chocolate muffin and rolled her eyes in delight.

* * *

'Wait. So you're selling all your clothes?' Matt said, his brows drawing together as we sat with Anna and Andy later that evening on the private patio, watching the sun go down behind the distant mountains.

'Sort of.'

He glanced at Andy then back at me. 'This is probably a stupid question, but what are you going to wear?'

'She's not selling everything,' Anna said, laughing and taking a dainty sip from a custom pink cocktail that Andy had presented her with. She hadn't even asked what was in it, just tasted it and made a sound of appreciation. I loved that he knew her so well, creating something special just for her that he was in little doubt she would enjoy.

'But you just said you were.'

'Only the stuff I don't feel comfortable in.'

'I thought that was pretty much everything you brought with you.'

The flush heated my chest and flared into my face. The fact I had a wardrobe full of clothes I didn't enjoy wearing seemed ridiculous. It made me feel silly and I didn't appreciate Matt pointing that out, even in front of people I was now lucky enough to be able to call good friends.

Anna gave him a shove. 'Remember that talk we had about tact?' She raised a brow.

Andy gave a snort. 'Told you, love. You're backing a losing horse with that one. Mum's been trying it for decades. Even she's realised her firstborn is beyond hope.'

Matt gave him a tight smile.

'Her second-born, however, is perfect.'

This time it was Matt's turn to scoff. 'A perfect muppet.'

'You're just jealous.'

'I always liked *The Muppets*,' I said, joining in the teasing.

'See?' Andy slung an arm around my shoulders. 'You just can't make me look bad, no matter how hard you try. It's impossible.'

'Although,' Anna added, 'you may have trouble getting that head back in through the door later.'

Andy gave a hearty laugh and pulled her gently from her seat, onto his lap. 'This is one of the many reasons I love you. You most definitely keep me grounded.'

Anna placed a hand against the dark stubble of his cheek and leant down to kiss him. I smiled at the tenderness and love so clear in the moment. It reminded me of Rumi and Ayaz. They too had moments like this when it seemed that, for an instant, the rest of the world receded and all that was left was the two of them. Matt turned his head towards where the burnt-orange disc of sun was now teetering on a mountain ridge.

'OK,' Andy said, giving Anna a squeeze. 'We'd better make a move.'

'I had so much fun today,' she said, hugging me as they prepared to leave. 'I hope you did too.'

'I really did,' I said. 'And thank you for the advice and for showing me all those great shops. I'd never have found them on my own.'

'Sometimes it's OK to accept a little help,' she said, and if I didn't know better, I could have sworn her glance swung momentarily to Matt. If it did, he either didn't notice or chose not to, instead wrapping her in an enormous hug.

'Glad you both had a good time today. You round for Sunday roast tomorrow?' he asked. 'Mum and Fleur have both got the weekend off so Mum's keen to do one if you're available.'

'Aren't you working?' she asked, taking in both the brothers with her question.

'When we found out Mum was doing a roast, we managed to juggle our schedules with a couple of the other guides, so we're off tomorrow too.'

'You didn't tell me that!' Anna said, giving her boyfriend a nudge.

'Sorry. I thought I had.'

She exchanged a 'men!' look with me. 'See you tomorrow, then!'

'Looking forward to it,' I said. And I really was. I looked down at the black and red skirt we'd bought, which Anna had insisted I change into the moment we'd got back. I'd paired it with a black designer vest top I'd bought for a ridiculous amount of money but, teamed with this, it felt different and at least it was a basic I could use to build into my new style. A style that was finally me.

We waved Anna and Andy off and then settled back to watch the rest of the sunset. Well, Matt did. I'd treated myself to a new book while we were shopping and was excited to start. I pulled it from the chair beside me and began the first page.

'Can you keep a secret?'

I looked up from my book.

'Without a doubt.' If there was one thing I'd learned growing up, it was how to keep a secret.

'Andy's proposing to Anna tomorrow.'

I dropped my book. With ninja reflexes, Matt caught it before its shiny new hardback spine hit the ground.

'Thanks,' I said, taking it back. 'Nice move, by the way.'

'Quick reactions have their uses in both my previous career and the current one.'

'Yes, I suppose so. So when is he proposing?'

'Tomorrow. At dinner.'

'Oh, wow! She's going to love that. It's easy to see how much a part of your family she is.'

Matt brought his gaze back from where it had returned to the last rays of sun sprawling across the landscape. 'Don't forget you're invited too.'

'Oh... Oh, no. I couldn't come now. It's... personal.'

'Fleur, Andy double-checked with me when we went to get the drinks tonight that you'd definitely be there. He wants you to be there and he knows Anna will too. She's always been a glass-half-full type of girl, but she dresses differently from the norm. She's open to more than the mainstream beliefs and that doesn't always sit well in rural places like this. We get plenty of visitors from all over so it's not as difficult as it could be for her but they're all transitory, even if they are regulars. But you're not transitory. You're someone she can call a friend, someone she can spend time with whenever. Like I say, Anna's always been an upbeat kind of person but Andy's mentioned before that she's felt lonely at times. That she felt out of place here.'

'Anna?'

'Mm-hmm.'

'But she seems so confident.'

'Looks can be deceiving. She's never doubted herself, that much is true. But she's not clicked with anyone, other than Andy, before.'

'You clearly think she's lovely.'

'OK, Andy and my family, Ms Pedantic.' He flashed a grin. 'But Andy said since you've been here, there's been a shift. She doesn't feel like she's the odd one out any more.'

'So you're saying we're both odd,' I said, laughter wrapping itself around my words. Andy was right. Matt really didn't have tact, even when he tried.

'In a good way.' He tilted his a little too wide but somehow perfect mouth into a smile.

'Oh, yes, that old nutmeg.'

Matt's smile widened, a breath of laughter escaping as he spoke. 'What?'

'The whole "in a good way",' I said, doing the actions for emphasis.

'No, no,' he said, waving one large hand. 'What did you call it?'

'That old nutmeg. You know.'

'No,' he said, really laughing now. 'I know "that old chestnut" but never that old nutmeg.'

'Ha, if you think I'm falling for that, you're sadly mistaken.' The owner of the children's home I'd grown up in had always used this phrase and Rumi and I, both being long-term residents of the place, had naturally picked it up. Matt could tease all he liked. Chestnut indeed.

'Don't get me wrong,' he said, the smile still in place. 'Personally, I think it's a much better phrase, but chestnut is the traditional one.'

'Oh, it is not!'

Matt pulled his phone out of his pocket and brought up a search engine, entering both the phrases. Mine brought up nothing, whereas the other explained the definition and history of the phrase.

I lifted my eyes from the screen. 'Oh God, I've been saying it wrong all these years. People must think I'm a total idiot!'

'Not at all!' Matt wrapped his hands around my own, which were currently covering my face as I thought about all the times I'd said it. 'Hey, Fleur. It's a great phrase. I'm definitely using it from now on.'

'Now you're just making fun.'

'No. I'm not. I promise. You're all totally right in the fact that I'm not the most tactful person around. It's not intentional. It's just the way I am and I don't set out to try to hurt feelings, and believe me I've had to back-pedal and explain that more times than I care to remember. I guess I'm not as sensitive as some others. In the life I had, you had to grow a thick skin pretty damn quickly or you wouldn't make it. It's hard to shed that. I know you won't believe me, but I am trying.'

'I do believe you,' I said, meeting his eyes and seeing nothing but truth written there.

'Good. And another truth is I love that phrase. It's fun and out of the ordinary. Like you.'

I giggled, grateful for him trying to lighten the atmosphere. 'I think you've gone a bit too far the other way now.'

'What?'

'I don't think I'm either of those things.'

'Yes. You are.'

'Isn't being ordinary, normal, what everyone wants to be?'

'Is that what you want to be? And for that matter, what's normal?'

'Honestly,' I said, still looking into those deep blue pools, 'I have no idea what I want to be. I've spent so much of my life trying to be what other people want me to be, I don't actually know what I want.'

'There's no rush. By the way, you seem pretty comfy in that outfit. It's the first time since I've met you, other than when you're wearing walking gear, that I haven't seen you pulling or fiddling with your clothing. I'm no fashion expert... obviously.' he added as I giggled. 'But to me, that says quite a lot.'

'I wasn't aware I even did that.' I felt the smile breaking nervously on my face. 'I do love it.'

'It's pretty. You look nice in it.' He held up a hand. 'And yes, before you say anything, I'm aware compliments are something I need to work on too. My ex-wife still despairs of me when we meet up.'

'Oh. You still see her?'

'As a friend. Thankfully we managed to come out of our marriage with a mature approach and a wish for each other to find the person that could make them happy. Which she has, thank goodness. God knows, I wasn't that person and she deserved better.'

'I'm sure you tried.'

'Yes. I did. But you can't change who you are.'

'No. Although we can try and improve aspects of ourselves.'

'That's very true. And I'm trying. Maybe you could help?'

'In what way?'

'Steer me in the right direction if something I say is coming out wrong?'

'What makes you think I'd know the right thing to say?'

He shrugged strong, broad shoulders. 'I trust you.'

'You hardly know me.'

'I've assessed people in far less time than that with a lot more riding on it.'

'You've been assessing me?' I said, grinning.

He dragged a hand down his face. 'That's come out wrong too. See? I need help.'

'Oh, you need help? That old nutmeg!' My grin widened.

'Exactly!' he said, the joy in his face matching mine. 'And I really don't want to say the wrong thing tomorrow or in the best man's speech.'

'I don't think you need to worry about the speech just yet. I'm sure it will be a while before they get married.'

'Don't count on it. Andy's hoping to do it here at the end of the summer. The hotel's licensed to do weddings. We just haven't been promoting it yet as Mum and Dad are busy enough as it is. I think they've considered working with a planner but it's something on the list that they haven't got to yet.'

I tapped one finger on my chin, pondering what he'd just said. 'If that's really something they're interested in pursuing, I might know someone who could help.'

'Really?'

'Yeah. She's lovely and absolutely brilliant at her job. She's pretty in demand but she used to come in the café a lot before the pandemic and we got quite friendly. I follow her on Insta and we've chatted a bit on there. She's actually hoping to come out and do some walking here with her new husband now that I've sung the praises of the place.'

'It definitely sounds like something worth looking into, if she's interested.'

'I can give her an overview and just see what she says.'

'Sounds great. Thanks, Fleur.'

'You're welcome. I mean, it might not work out—'

'Even if it doesn't, you're invested and willing to try. That means a lot.'

'And in the meantime, you can practise being tactful.'

'Without sounding like I'm taking the pee.'

'Ideally.'

'That's a hard target.'

'I have faith in you.'

'That may be misplaced. I have a long record to upend.'

'One step at a time.'

* * *

The next day, in the gorgeous, airy dining room that looked out onto the magical landscape beyond it, a soft breeze entering through the bifold doors which had been opened to their fullest extent, no one at the table had dry eyes. Except Matt. He was thrilled though. That much was clear from the wide smile and the huge hug he'd given Andy and Anna but he just didn't do tears, apparently, no matter how sad or happy he was.

17

'So, you're definitely having the wedding at the hotel?' I asked Anna as we slumped down into a battered old sofa in a coffee shop after several hours of trawling the shops for more clothes for me and a wedding dress for Anna. Her idea about selling some of my clothes online had been brilliant and I was now left only with a few basics from my previous sartorial life that I could match with the style I was now creating for myself. It turned out I liked a far softer look than anything I'd gone with before, but more classic than Anna's wonderful bohemian look.

'Yep. It's such a beautiful backdrop for the photos – assuming it doesn't rain!' she said, laughing.

'It wouldn't dare! Not with Andy and Matt on the case.'

Anna grinned, a moustache of cappuccino delicately framing the cupid's bow of her upper lip. 'Let's hope. That's assuming I ever get a dress!'

'You will. There's still three more places to visit according to this list,' I said, turning the piece of paper Anna had laid on the table around to face me. For someone who appeared to be what some people unkindly called 'airy fairy', when it came to this wedding, Anna's organisation could have edged out Marie Kondo. Bronwyn had already insisted on doing as much of the food as she could, with anything that needed to be cooked on the day in the capable hands of a close friend who often came to the rescue when Bronwyn and Greg were particularly swamped or wanted to take a bit of time off.

'I know.' She forced a smile onto her face. 'I'm sure there will be something there.'

'I think the perfect dress is just around the corner.'

'Do you?' Anna seemed unusually concerned.

I paused for a moment. 'I really do,' I said, reaching over for her hand. 'You know I don't believe in all the destiny stuff that you do, but I do have a good feeling about this.' Anna watched me for a moment and then flung her arms around me, pulling me into a massive hug. 'I'm so glad you ended up here. I know you say you don't believe in fate but I really do think you're supposed to be here. Of all the places you could have booked...'

'Actually I didn't have anything to do with any of the arrangements. That was all my ex.'

'That makes me believe it even more, then. You're supposed to be here, Fleur. I know it. You'll see.'

I took a sip of my tea. 'If you say so.'

'I do,' Anna said. 'And not least to help me navigate through all the arrangements of this wedding.'

'You know Bronwyn will do everything she can to help. She adores you. The whole family do. I'm pretty sure even Matt would have come wedding dress shopping if you'd been left with no other option!'

Laughter bubbled up from my friend, soon infecting me. 'Bless him. I think you're right. But could you imagine? I'm sure he's probably had days on deployment he'd choose to repeat rather than spend a day traipsing in and out of wedding dress shops!'

'But he'd still do it. You're as much a sister to him as Andy is a brother.'

'I know. I love him to bits. I'm so lucky.'

The waitress put down two toasties on the table and we began tucking in. After a few chews, I decided to ask the question that had been circling my brain for a while.

'Are your parents coming?'

'I haven't actually asked them yet.' Anna looked up as she finished the first half of her sarnie. 'Honestly, I don't know if I want them to. I didn't fit into the mould they had ready for me and all they ever do when I do see them is criticise. Being doctors and stuck in their ways, they think all the natural stuff I'm interested in is rubbish. And of course, to them, being a textile designer isn't a real job. I'm sure they'd just find plenty to pick holes in about the wedding too and every single choice we've made.'

'Have they seen the size of your fiancé?' I said with a grin, doing my best to return the smile to my friend's face.

'They have. I'm sure that stopped Dad saying more than he did. Of course, the fact Andy "roams around hills for a living" didn't exactly make him the best choice in their eyes. I always knew if the man I chose wasn't a doctor or a barrister parental approval was out of the question.'

'How long since you last spoke to them?'

'About a year now.'

'Have you heard from them at all?'

'I've had a couple of messages but I don't really have anything to say to them. We're just too different, I think. I will never fit into their ideal of the perfect daughter.'

'Andy thinks you're perfect.'

'He does. God knows how I've managed to swing that one so long!' she said, her smile now finally back in place.

'Stop being so modest and finish that,' I said, pointing at the other half of the sandwich. 'If fate is real, your parents will be there if they're supposed to be, but in the meantime, we have a wedding dress to buy!'

'Oh, Matt, she looked so beautiful in all of them!' I said, clambering over a rock, and stepping on a mossy bit. My foot slipped and my face smacked into the moss. 'Ow!'

'I'm sure she did,' he said, not looking back. 'You all right?'

'Yep,' I said, pushing myself up and finding a different place to put my foot this time, and managing to traverse the boulder cleanly, although I could do without the throbbing nose. 'But she still hasn't found the one yet.'

'Has she decided to invite her parents?' Matt asked as I placed my feet in his footsteps as we tramped along a ridge. I still wasn't ready for scrambling up the huge mountains yet but my stamina, bravery and enjoyment had increased in the months since I'd moved to Wales.

'Undecided still, apparently.'

'Shame. They're missing out on a great girl.'

'She said she doesn't fit in with their image of what she should be and I have a bit of experience of that with Jasper.'

From behind, I could see Matt's muscles tense. 'Yeah. Well, it was obvious to everyone he was a complete—'

'Yes. Thank you.'

'You're not defending him now, are you?'

'Of course not. I was just pointing out that I don't need you reminding me.'

He shrugged. 'Just can't see what you saw in him. You're not materialistic so it wasn't his money.'

'No. Definitely not. He was charming to start with. Can we change the subject now, please?'

'You're the one that brought him up.'

I let out a sigh. 'Got out the wrong side of someone's bed today, did you?'

'Funny.'

'What's up with you? If you wanted to change plans, you could have just said so. I wouldn't have minded.'

'We'd arranged something. If I say I'm going to do something, I do it.'

'Well, there's no point if you're resenting every moment of it.'

He stopped suddenly and turned. 'I'm not resenting every mome— Bloody hell!' Matt reached out for me. 'Why didn't you tell me to stop?' With long strides, he led me to a fluffy hillock and perched me on it before crouching down in front of me, slipping his pack off as he did so.

'Matt! What are you doing?' I said, going to stand up again.

He placed a hand lightly on my arm as he rummaged with his free one in a pocket of his rucksack. 'Fleur, just sit there a moment. Your face is cut. Why didn't you tell me? You don't have to cope with everything alone now. Don't you realise that?' he said as he drew out a small first-aid kit. 'Oh, shit. What did I say this time?'

'Nothing,' I said, swiping at my nose and suddenly noticing that it was covered in blood. 'Oh!' I'd realised I'd probably collected a bruise from my slip and I'd been intermittently and automatically wiping my nose anyway from the mild hayfever I suffered from. I pulled my hanky from my pocket. It looked like I'd mopped up a small bloodbath.

'Here.' Matt handed me a clean tissue and I wiped my eyes in frustration as he dabbed at my face with some gauze pads that stung when he applied them.

'Ouch.'

'Sorry,' he said, his tone soft, and sounding genuinely pained. 'You should have told me it was hurting. I'm sorry if I was grumpy. I just have a few things on my mind.'

'Honestly, you didn't have to come today. I don't mind you changing plans if there's something else you'd rather do.'

'There's nothing else I'd rather do, Fleur. It's not that. I didn't mean to upset you.'

'You didn't. Ouch.'

'Sorry. Then it's more painful than you let on.'

'It's not that either.'

He looked up at me through thick lashes, concern creasing his face. 'What is it, then?'

'Nothing.'

He let out a sigh and returned the first-aid kit to the ruck-sack. I pulled out my phone and used the selfie camera to see the result. 'Oh. Nice. Well done, Fleur.'

'Sorry. Best I can do out in the field.'

'No, I didn't mean it like that. I just...'

'It's just scrapes. They will heal pretty quickly. You obviously gave your nose a bit of a bash but it's stopped bleeding now. Just sit there for a few minutes. While we're waiting you can tell me what you're upset about.'

'Or we could just take in the view.'

Matt turned his head, studied me for a moment then turned back to the view and took a seat leaning against the hillock I was sitting on.

'It's more comfy down here. You can rest against it. Here.'

He held out his hand and made sure I managed the tiny distance without incident.

'Thanks,' I said, letting go. 'I'm pretty sure I could have coped though.' I grinned.

'I don't know. I can see I'm going to have to keep a closer eye on you. When we get back, I'm going to see about fitting wing mirrors to my pack so I can make sure you're not up to any more acrobatics.'

'It could have happened to anyone,' I said, a hint of defensiveness in my tone.

'I know. It could. You're absolutely right. I just don't like it happening to you. And certainly not on my watch.'

'It's not your job to keep me safe, Matt.'

'Of course it is.'

'No. You're off duty. I'm not a client.'

'No, you're a... friend. Which means it's even more important. Not to mention Anna would kill me if something happened to her bestie.'

We sat watching the changing clouds throwing shadows that morphed continually as they scudded across the sky in the warm westerly breeze.

'That was one of the nicest things anyone has ever said to me.' After several companionable minutes of silence, my almost whispered words broke the spell.

Matt turned his head, close to mine now that we were sitting close on the grass. He didn't ask anything. He didn't speak. Just waited, somehow knowing I would continue when I was ready.

'What you said about not having to cope with things alone any more.'

He slid an arm around me and gave me the slightest hug. I'd

noticed he was far less tactile than Andy, other than with his family and Anna, so I appreciated the gesture even more.

'Don't forget it.'

I shook my head. I knew that I wouldn't. Ever.

* * *

'OK, this is the one. I can feel it in my bones.'

'You said that last time,' Anna said, enthusiasm fading from her voice.

'Yes, I know. But this is it!' I forced all the certainty I could into my voice. Anna was right. I had said that before to try and buoy her up, but this was different. There was something about this tiny boutique, one that hadn't even been on our list but that we'd discovered having exhausted all the ones Anna had written down. Tucked away in a tiny street, it looked stylish, the window chic but welcoming. A complete contrast to one of the places we'd been to where the proprietress had made no attempt to hide the fact that apparently we weren't the 'right type' of people for her shop. Sneaking a surreptitious look, it had seemed that the other potential clients oozed wealth, from the Birkin bag slung casually over the mother-of-the-bride's arm to the teetering, embellished stilettos of the bride, complete with red soles. Anna was actually wearing a dress far more exclusive than any of them – unique, in fact, in that it had been made up from her own design in less than twenty-four hours by an Indian dressmaker on a decades-old Singer machine and was impeccably sewn. But it didn't have a 'name' so consequently meant nothing to the people who fitted into the particular world of that boutique, unlike this one which was still stylish and elegant but the whole vibe couldn't have been more different.

'Hi! How are you?' The owner had come out from behind the pale pink painted desk. 'Oh wow, what a beautiful dress,' she said, looking at Anna.

Anna's smile broke and the sense of renewed hope that accompanied it was almost palpable.

'Thank you. I got it in India.'

'Don't they make the most wonderful things? The skills some of those tailors and seamstresses have.' She shook her head. 'Incredible.'

Anna beamed a smile. This was definitely the place.

18

An hour and a half and two glasses of champagne each later, Anna had The Dress. Elegant but relaxed, stylish but dreamy, it suited her, and her personality perfectly. Emma, the owner, had picked it out first after Anna had taken a look and declared them all to be absolutely beautiful and that she had no idea where to start.

'I mean, they're all just so gorgeous,' Anna said, swishing to and fro and watching herself in the mirror, a wide smile lighting her face. 'But this is it. I know it. I can *feel* it.' She turned to me. 'But what do you think?'

'I think your face says it all. That's the biggest smile I've seen and – I don't know – it just looks like "you". Does that make sense?' I asked, turning to Emma. Once upon a time I'd have never asked such a question. I'd have kept the thoughts to myself but, since moving to Wales, and with the support I'd found here, something inside me was changing. I was still shy, but each day seemed to bring with it the tiniest sliver more of confidence. And a belief that perhaps my point of view was valid, just as Rumi had always tried to tell me, and that it was OK if I didn't always agree with what others said. This time, however, I was in full agreement.

'Andy is so going to cry when he sees you.'

'Probably,' she said, taking hold of each of our hands as Emma and I assisted her down from the little dais she'd been standing on. 'He makes out he's this tough outdoorsy guy, but he's really quite a softy underneath.' She handed me her glass before heading towards the changing room, then turned back, pointing at me. 'But you can't tell him I told you that.'

I drew a cross across my heart with my finger and Anna gave another grin before pulling the heavy velvet changing-room curtain closed.

'So, I'll see you in a few weeks' time for us to check those alterations,' Emma stated as she handed Anna the bag that contained a headdress she'd fallen in love with that suited the dress perfectly. Bronwyn was lending her her own wedding veil for the 'something borrowed'.

We waved goodbye to Emma and headed towards the railway station.

'Are you working tonight?'

'Yeah,' I said, checking my watch. 'That second glass of champagne probably wasn't such a great idea.'

'Oh, but wasn't it all so lovely? Especially after that horrid place earlier.'

'Just forget about that shop,' I said, linking my arm through my friend's. 'They don't deserve to have you wear one of their dresses anyway. It's their loss.'

Anna squeezed my arm. 'I'm not sure I could have afforded one of them anyway. Did you see the prices?'

'Yeah. And frankly, I thought Emma's designs were far prettier.'

'Me too. Although I guess we're biased.'

'Maybe a little. But the important thing is you have a dress!'

'Oh gosh, I'm so relieved.'

Hearing the announcement for our train, we grabbed each other's hand and ran the last few yards to the correct station platform, laughing as we did so before finding a seat in the carriage and flopping down.

'You sure you're going to be all right tonight?'

'Yep. I've got time to have a meal when I get in and that will soak up any remaining alcohol floating around. I've been known to drink plenty of others under the table on more than one occasion so I'm fine.'

'Really?'

'Yup. Won more than my share of bets during some misspent moments in my youth.'

Anna gave me a grin then almost immediately dropped off to sleep on my shoulder. Good job we'd not placed the same bet. I'd have won by miles!

* * *

'Another round over here when you get time, Fleur?' Matt leant back in his chair a little as he sat with a group of about seven others, the majority I couldn't help noticing were young, female and attractive. It was pretty obvious that more than one of them were a little smitten with him and also obvious that he didn't mind in the slightest, and was, in fact, rather enjoying the attention.

'Yep. Give me a minute.'

'No problem.' He flashed a smile and then turned back to the table.

'Someone's enjoying himself,' Bronwyn said as she helped me prepare the drinks for Matt's table.

'Looks like it. Are they clients?'

'Yes. He took them out hiking today. I forget where. Although I don't think they'd care where he led them.' She gave a wink.

'No, he does look to be rather popular with them.'

'Ah, well. It's nice to see him smile.'

I had to agree on that front. Matt Morgan possessed what was probably the best smile I'd ever seen.

Pulling a pint to add to the tray, I glanced over at his mum.

'He had some difficulty adjusting back into civilian life when he came out of the forces, and with his marriage having broken up too – well… he wasn't the happiest of boys.' We both looked over to where he was now, surrounded by the bevy of young things vying for his attention while at the same time trying to seem cool about it.

'He looks pretty happy right now.'

She gave a chuckle. 'He does that. It's taken a while but he's finding himself again now, slowly but surely.'

'Seems like this is a good spot for doing that.'

Bronwyn placed the last drink on the tray. 'Let's hope, eh?' She gave my shoulder a quick squeeze. 'You OK with that?'

'Yep, fine. I'll come back for that other one in a sec if you don't mind serving that chap?' I said, nodding at the bar.

'Good girl.'

'Here we go,' I said, placing the drinks in front of the correct people.

'Thanks, Fleur,' Matt said as most of the group were too involved in their own conversations or in their conversations with Matt to offer much thanks of their own.

'Yours is just coming. Back in a sec.'

'No problem.' He looked up, relaxed with his company and the help of a few beers. 'How are you?'

'Busy,' I said, flashing him a grin before turning back to the bar to collect the second tray with the last few remaining drinks on.

'Is that your girlfriend?' one of the girls said, her voice trailing behind me. Funny how alcohol completely knackered all volume control.

'No,' Matt said as I turned round with his beer and a couple of other glasses. 'Fleur has far more sense than to go out with the likes of me.'

The girl that had asked the question gave me a cool smile before moving her chair even closer to Matt's. Any closer and she'd be on his lap and, the way she was going, probably would be before the night was out.

'I don't think there's anything wrong with you in the slightest.' False lashes fluttered as she looked up at him from beneath their thickness.

'That's probably because you don't know me very well,' Matt said as I cleared the empties from the table.

The girl beside him adopted a sultry tone. 'There are ways to fix that...'

I took the empty glass from Matt as she said it. Our fingertips brushed and his eyes met mine. Behind him, his would-be seductress glared.

'Thanks.'

'All part of the service,' I said, taking the tray back to the kitchen to be washed.

* * *

The next morning the group from the night before were sitting in a corner, several of them, including the woman who'd been wrapping herself around Matt yesterday evening, looking a little worse for wear. There was no sign of Matt.

'What can I get you?' I asked with a smile as I approached the table, notepad in hand.

'Full Welsh for all of them,' a deep, gravelly voice said from behind me, amusement laced through the tone. The woman turned a subtle shade of green and shook her head. 'Got to fuel up for the hike today.'

'I don't think I'll be going,' his admirer croaked out.

'Oh? That's a shame. You'll miss some great views.'

She shot him a look that said the only view she was interested in was the inside of her own eyelids.

'Can I get you anything else? A juice or croissant? Or just toast?' I asked, and she looked up. 'Some toast would be great, thanks,' she said, the faintest glimmer of a smile showing on her face.

'No problem. I'll bring it over shortly.'

'Looks like you're a lot less popular with somebody this morning than you were last night,' I said as Matt followed me into the kitchen to drop off the order. He put his own in with a laugh and jokey exchange with Dave, the chef.

'Not for the first time.'

'You've met her before?'

'No,' he said, snagging some juice from the fridge. 'Never. I just meant it's not the first time someone half-cut has found me less attractive the following morning.'

'I don't believe that for a second,' I said, straightening my apron and peering out of the door, seeing if there were any more new guests to attend to.

Matt shrugged.

'He's fine until he opens his mouth,' the chef said, looking over from his station. 'All the women think he's this rugged-explorer romance-hero type and then he opens his gob, poof!' He flexed his hands. 'Explodes the whole myth.'

'Now, that I do believe,' I said.

'Oh, ha ha.'

'So, what did you say to this one?'

'Nothing,' Matt replied, trying to steal one of the sausages being cooked to perfection and getting a whack on his knuckles with a pair of tongs for his trouble. 'Ow!'

'Don't mess with the food.'

'I wasn't. I was going to test it.'

'It doesn't need testing. It's superb.'

Matt wiggled his head in an 'ooh, get you' manner but Dave just shrugged. 'I know my skills. So, were yours not up to scratch?' The chef cocked his head out towards the restaurant. 'Is that why she's pissed off with you?'

'My skills are just fine, thanks. And no.'

'So why?'

'Who knows?'

Dave pointed his tongs at him. 'You do. I've known you since we were at school and all your covert training doesn't fool me. What did you do?'

'Nothing. That's why she's pissed off.'

'You... turned her down?' Dave's eyebrows rose until they touched the brim of his white chef's hat.

'Not my type,' Matt said with a shrug, twiddling a fork.

'You're single and she's pretty and available. What's the problem?' Dave reached back to the fridge and grabbed another paper-wrapped parcel of bacon that had been delivered yesterday by a local farmer. 'Oi!' he snapped as Matt took a bite from the end of the sausage he'd snagged with his fork when Dave's back was turned. Matt gave him a look, then headed out of the kitchen.

'Explains why she's in a mood if he turned her down,' Dave said as he plated up a couple of covers for me. 'Our Matt has quite the reputation in the bedroom department.'

'Umm, way more than I need to know! Thanks.' With that, I backed out of the swing door and took the steaming, delicious-smelling breakfasts to an older couple laughing together as they sat at the window table. They'd been here a week now and every morning and every evening they chatted and laughed. It was easy to see Andy and Anna being the same as the years passed. I hoped that they always looked at each other the way the older couple looked at each other now. As for his brother though, who knew? But what Matt Morgan did with his time was no concern of mine.

'Seriously?' Rumi asked when I was barely through the door. 'You still haven't got together with him? He's perfect for you!'

'If this is setting the tone for the whole trip I'm going to leave now,' I replied, although I suspected the huge grin on my face at the delight of finally getting to Norfolk to see my oldest friend likely put a large dent in that particular threat.

'You wouldn't dare. Besides, the kids wouldn't let you.' With perfect timing Rumi's two children came haring down the hall and slammed into me with arms outstretched and I revelled in their hugs, not realising quite how much I had missed the feel of their little arms clinging to me until I was once again enveloped within them.

* * *

'So, is there really nothing going on between you and Matt?' Rumi asked again later that week as we sat on two deckchairs, watching the sky darkening slowly over the large garden, already stuffed with vegetables, plants, fruit bushes and flowers.

'No. How on earth have you managed to fill this place so much, by the way? You've barely been here five minutes.'

Rumi rolled her head against the heavy twill of the deckchair to look over at me. 'I will answer the question, despite the very unsubtle change of subject, purely because I'm too excited about this place not to, but don't think I won't be coming back around to the original discussion again soon.'

'Oh, I didn't doubt it, just hoped in vain. So?'

'The couple that sold the house left a tonne of seedlings and stuff in the greenhouse, knowing that I was enthusiastic about learning to garden and growing our own fruit and veg She'd obviously put the word out too as the neighbours have all been lovely, popping round with excess plants and seeds and offering advice if I want it.' She looked over at me. 'Sometimes I wake up and can't really believe we get to have all this. I lie there in the morning, before the kids wake up, and all I can hear is the soft sounds of nature. There's no traffic, no sirens, no screaming and shouting. It's just... perfect.'

I reached out and Rumi automatically did the same. There were no words needed between us when it came to moments like this. We knew each other too well for platitudes. The joining of our hands said more than enough.

'So. About Matt.'

'Oh my God...' I said, laughter swamping my words. 'When are you going to give it a rest?'

'When you marry him, of course.'

'Oh, right. So, when are you breeding those flying pigs?'

'I know what I saw.'

'And what did you see?'

'Ease.'

'Huh?'

'You. At ease with someone. Which is a rare thing. You weren't at ease properly with Jasper, or Marcus or any of the others.'

'There weren't *that* many!'

'No, because you latched onto them for dear life and moulded yourself into whatever you thought they wanted you to be and stuck with them far longer than they deserved – if they even deserved you in the first place.'

My hands were back on my lap now and clasped close together. Rumi had never been one to sugar-coat the truth but right now it was far more bitter than I'd expected.

'Are you pissed off at me?'

'No,' I said, my voice neutral.

'You're not saying anything.'

'I'm not sure what you want me to say. You're allowed your opinion, even if I don't agree.'

'I'm not wrong though, am I?' Rumi said.

'I think you are, but we've had this argument before and I don't want to argue with you now.'

'We can discuss things without arguing.'

'It's kind of hard not to argue when your best friend just called you a sap.'

'I did not!' Rumi sat up. At least she tried to. The deckchair had other ideas and she flailed around for a few seconds in indignation. Getting a grip on the sides of my own chair, I pushed up and stood in front of her, offering my hand, which she took, and together we manoeuvred her upright. 'Bloody things! Ayaz had this thing in his mind that he wanted to sit in a deckchair in his own garden with a beer and look out across the fields. He failed to mention the damn things can bite your hands off when you try and open or close them and are impossible to get out of.'

'I managed all right.' I gave a small shrug as punctuation.

Rumi looked at me. 'I'm not sure which is worse – you leaving me in the chair or this smug face staring back at me.'

'The chair's right there. Just say the word.'

Rumi pulled a face then reached out to take my hands again, holding them out in front of her. 'You know I wouldn't do or say anything to hurt you for the world, don't you?'

I looked down at our hands. A spoken answer was unnecessary.

'And I would never, ever even think you a sap, as you put it.' Her voice was stronger this time and I raised my gaze to meet hers, now shining with tears. 'I would never do that and I'm sorry if that's how it sounded to you. It just makes me so mad when people take advantage of your gentle nature. You're a people pleaser and there have been some that have used that to their advantage.'

'Yep. I know. You might have said so one or two times.'

'More like one or two hundred. But Matt's not like that, is he?'

I tipped my head back and groaned at the stars now twinkling in the wide expanse of deep blue sky.

'Listen to me,' she said, resisting my attempt to free my hands at the mention of Matt.

'Do I have a choice?' I said, looking at her now.

'No,' she said, her wide smile breaking, sensing the tension draining from my own body. 'That's the kind of man you need.'

'I don't *need* a man.'

'No. You don't. I couldn't agree more. But you want one. You want someone to spend your life with. Am I wrong?'

'No, but it's looking like that's not on the cards for me and, actually, I'm kind of getting used to the idea.'

'Really?'

'Yeah. I like having time to myself, reading when I want, watching what I want. Doing nothing if I want.'

'That's really good. But you do know the right person wouldn't stop you doing any of those things, don't you?'

I inhaled deeply. 'Honestly, Rumi, I'm not sure it's possible. You and Ayaz are special and I don't think many people end up that well suited.'

'We still have to work on things,' she said, shrugging one shoulder. 'Like the fact he adores these stupid bloody chairs.' She gave one a slight kick to illustrate her point and it collapsed, almost trapping her foot in it. 'See? Bloody death traps.'

'Slight exaggeration.'

'I'm just saying don't give up. You have too much to offer to give up on a dream you've had since you were a child.'

'Childhood dreams rarely come true.'

Rumi looked around. 'But sometimes they do.'

I gave her a hug. 'And I couldn't be more thrilled. You know that, and nobody deserves all this more than you two. But Matt Morgan is most definitely not my dream man.'

'I don't know. Looked pretty dreamy to me.'

'And to half of the women he meets through his job.'

'Oh, really?'

'Yep.'

'Hmm. Anyone long-term?'

Picking up the collapsed deck chair and folding the other up without drama, I took one in each hand and began walking back to the patio where a mature grapevine, combined with old-fashioned roses and clematis (according to Rumi – I hadn't a clue) scrambled up a pergola. Once there I set them up as Rumi watched me, a slight look of awe on her face.

'No, I don't think so. He was married once but it didn't work out.'

'Recently?'

'No, some time ago, from what he said. When he was in the forces. I get the impression he's comfortable doing what he wants now too. No one seems to expect him to settle down again and I've no desire to be anyone's next notch in a bedpost. Not to mention it would be super awkward. He might be good-looking—'

'And helpful. Remember he drove you all the way down to London when Jasper left you in the lurch.'

'And helpful... when he wants to be,' I added, determined not to add too much shine to Rumi's already highly polished opinion of him. 'But I'm actually really enjoying this new job and... well, new life, I guess. I'm not going to deny he's attractive but I'm not about to give up all that for him.'

'Wow.'

'Wow what?'

'I like this new Fleur!'

'She's not new. I just think she's been hidden but I'm finding out more about her every day.'

'And what have you discovered?'

I thought for a moment before taking a white rose between my fingers, its petals now almost luminous in the moonlight, and bent to inhale the sweet scent.

'I discovered I quite like her.'

Rumi grinned. 'Now that sounds like something we should celebrate. One of the neighbours dropped round a bottle of something fizzy as a housewarming gift but we haven't opened it yet. He makes it himself so I've no idea what it's like.'

'Only one way to find out!'

19

'Oh my God!' Anna's hearty laugh made me smile despite the samba competition my skull was currently playing host to. Rumi's neighbour's gift had been duly followed by another neighbour's home-made rhubarb gin, which, although delicious, should have come with a danger warning. 'It looks like you had a good night!'

'Shhh!' I put my finger up to my lips and simultaneously tried to find the volume control on the side of my phone.

'Sorry,' she said, whispering theatrically. 'You having a good time?'

'Yeah, lovely thanks. Although...'

'What?'

I felt a bit daft saying it, but Anna and I had talked a lot and I felt almost as relaxed discussing things with her now as I did with Rumi. 'I miss... being in Wales.' Calling it home still didn't seem right, although I struggled to think of anywhere but there as home now.

'See, mate? I told you she wouldn't forget you.' Andy stuck his head in and waved and I felt my face grow warm as Matt followed him, glancing at the phone and giving me a brief hand raise.

'Apologies for my brother. It's his day off from being the village idiot but he likes to keep his skills up. You enjoying yourself?'

'Yes, thanks. It's been lovely. The week has gone quickly though.'

'Always does when you're having a good time. Still on the three-ten train tomorrow?'

'Yes.'

'OK.'

'But I was thinking, I can get the bus. I looked up the times and I wouldn't have to wait long.'

'It's fine. I'll pick you up as arranged. It's a long bus journey after a long train one so...' He gave a shrug and a smile before giving another wave and disappearing from view.

''Bye, love.' Andy dropped a kiss on Anna's temple, before flashing a grin at me and following his brother out of sight.

'Sorry about that,' Anna said. 'They were outside a minute ago.'

'Not a problem.'

'What?' she asked.

'Nothing,' I said, adding an innocent shrug.

'Rubbish. I know you well enough now to know when something's bothering you. You may as well tell me. I can be quite persistent if I want to be. Just ask Andy.'

'Oh, I believe you, and I've had enough interrogation here this week, thank you,' I said, laughter in my voice.

'It's not interrogation. It's loving enquiry,' Rumi called across the room, knowing I'd made the comment for her benefit.

'I just didn't want you thinking that when I said about

missing being there that I meant Matt. It's just that Andy's comment...'

'Oh, ignore him. You know what those two are like. If they see an opportunity to wind the other one up, they're going to take it.'

'But you don't...'

'No. I don't. That doesn't mean it wouldn't make me ecstatically happy should you two get together.'

Rumi was beside me like a shot, shoving her head in the phone camera's view. 'That's what I said! I've only met him once, but the two of them looked so good together and seemed so relaxed. And believe me, our Fleur here is not generally the relaxed type, at least she wasn't before she moved there. I'm Rumi, by the way.'

Anna was smiling widely. 'Anna. I've heard so much about you. It's lovely to meet you. Hopefully at some point we'll get to see you in person too.'

'Definitely. The pictures Fleur showed us are unbelievably beautiful. The kids, of course, want to go to that place... what did you call it?' She turned to me.

'Fairy Glen.'

'That's it.'

'Oh, it's lovely. So peaceful and you can really see how it got its name. I'm sure you'll all love it.'

'Can't wait. But in the meantime, do you really think Matt is interested in Fleur or was that purely his brother winding him up?'

Anna gave me a wary look.

'It's fine. Believe me, my ego is going to survive Matt not suddenly realising that I'm the woman of his dreams.'

'I didn't say that...'

Rumi practically leapt through the phone. 'What?'

I grabbed her top and pulled her back. 'Excuse my friend. She gets a little overexcited about non-existent situations.'

'He does like her. You,' Anna said, turning her head from Rumi to me.

'I knew it!' Rumi punched the air.

'She doesn't mean like that, Rumi.'

'No, I don't. Well, I do.'

'What?'

'What?'

'He has been asking about you.'

Rumi's eyes were now like saucers and, despite my better judgement, I couldn't help asking Anna what she meant.

'Just, you know, general stuff.'

'See?'

'General stuff doesn't mean anything, Rumi. And that's a good thing.' Sense kicked in. 'His brother's just winding him up because he's all loved up himself. Right, Anna?'

'Umm, yeah. I'm sure. Those two certainly know how to push each other's buttons. And Andy knows Matt's quite protective of you so—'

'Protective?' I said, frowning. 'Rumi. Close your mouth, you're catching flies.'

Rumi snapped her mouth closed before immediately turning to me and mouthing, *Protective!* With a huge bloody great grin on her face. I knew I should have taken Anna's call in the guest room.

'Yeah, you know.'

'No. I don't.'

Anna was looking uncomfortable now, clearly thinking that this was old news to me, rather than breaking. Rumi was hanging on every word. Sense pushed its way to the forefront of my mind and I took control of the conversation.

'I think what Anna means is that he's like that with people he knows. He was up like a rocket when Jasper started at his mum, and I'm sure he'd walk through fire for Anna too. I'm lucky enough to be considered part of the household so I get included in that field of protection too.'

I looked back to Anna for confirmation. She was nodding, although something about it seemed a little forced, her eyes not quite meeting mine. 'Anyway, I was just saying hi and to let you know that there was a woman in here yesterday asking about you.'

'About me?'

'Yeah.'

'Did she say who she was?'

'No. Bronwyn asked if there was a message but she said no.'

'Oh.'

'Maybe it was someone from the café?' Rumi suggested. 'You did say Nish rang you to see if you'd managed to find something, so he knows you're up there.'

'Hmm. I don't think he'd tell people exactly where I was though.'

'No, but you said there's that board with everyone's photo on. If they saw that?' Rumi shrugged. 'It's a popular place for people to visit. Not unfeasible to run into someone you know.'

'Yeah. I guess.'

'She said she'd catch up another time so she might be back.'

'Is she a regular, then?' I asked Anna.

'Not that any of the family recognised.'

'Weird.'

'I shouldn't worry about it,' Rumi said. 'So, what was Matt asking about Fleur?' she added, attempting a sudden swerve back to the original topic.

'Bye, Anna!' I said quickly as she laughed and got the message, waving before I hung up and put down my phone.

'Oi! That's enough.'

'Protective about you, eh?' Rumi waggled her eyebrows.

'If you don't give it a rest, I'm going to be using you to compost your own vegetables!'

'I wonder if that works...' Rumi pondered, apparently seriously.

'Do not google that.'

'Too late,' she said, typing away.

'You know that's going to look really bad should the police ever get hold of your phone?'

She waggled my phone at me. 'That's why I used yours.'

'Thanks.'

20

I did my best to ignore the unexpected rush of warmth that zipped through my body as I exited the station to find Matt resting against the pick-up, long legs crossed at the ankles. He looked up and saw me, a smile creased the previously serious face and I automatically returned it as he made his way towards me.

'Hello, stranger,' he said, wrapping me in the kind of hug that made you want to stay there forever.

'Aww,' I said, looking up, feeling uncharacteristically mischievous. 'Did you miss me?'

'Annoyingly, yes, I did,' he said, pulling back and taking my case. 'You've done a good job of getting under everyone's skin.'

'I sound like a splinter.'

'In a good way,' he elaborated.

'I see. Still not enrolled in those tact lessons, then.'

He shook his head as he opened the door for me and took my hand to assist me in. I didn't really need it, but the chivalry was warmly appreciated. 'Lost cause, I'm afraid.'

'No one's a lost cause,' I said, looking back at him on a more even level now that I was up in the cab of the pick-up. 'What? You're looking at me funny.'

'Not funny. Just with curiosity.'

'I see. First I'm a splinter and now I'm a museum exhibit.'

'It's all right. I've no plans to have you stuffed just yet.'

'Ha ha. So? What's with the look?'

Matt didn't answer but walked round to the driver's side, slid behind the wheel and shut the door.

'Do you truly believe that?' he asked.

'About nobody being a lost cause?'

'Yeah,' he said, glancing at me briefly as we pulled out onto the main road back towards the hotel and home. It had taken me a while to think of this place like that. But now it was the only way I could think of it. I was going home.

'I do.'

He gave a brief nod to acknowledge he'd heard me then continued driving in silence.

'Well, I enjoyed that deep conversation.'

His warm laugh filled the cab. 'Fair point. OK. So have you always felt that way?'

'No,' I answered honestly. 'Not at all. Quite the opposite, in fact. I thought I was a lost cause throughout my childhood and that continued into adulthood. Unless something happens to change your perspective, those ingrained beliefs can be hard to dislodge.'

'I'd agree.'

'So do you believe in lost causes?' I asked.

'Yeah. I do think there's such a thing but I'm not sure there's always a way out.'

'Really?'

'You seem surprised.'

'I am,' I said. 'I suppose I thought that with your background and with what you do now, belief that things can always get better would be sort of essential.'

He thought about that for a moment. 'Maybe, but I think a belief in circumstances and in people can be separated. You're absolutely right, though. Sometimes you have to hold onto the belief that there's a way out, that things will get better, otherwise you can end up in a worse situation.'

'So why can't that be applied to people?'

'Because people are complicated and can sometimes be more resistant to change than the toughest landscape.'

I studied the strong, dark profile for a moment. He was clean-shaven, dressed casually and, when he'd hugged me, I'd got a whiff of something woody with a fresh, earthy undertone. 'Are we talking about you?'

'Nah. Just chatting.'

'Fibber.'

He laughed again. 'You've definitely come out of your shell, haven't you? You wouldn't say boo to a goose when you first got here.'

'No, I know.' My thoughts drifted back to the woman I'd been. So eager to please everyone, looking for something I'd never find. The only time I'd ever felt even remotely authentic was when I was with Rumi and eventually her family.

'I've put my foot in it again, haven't I?'

This time it was my turn to laugh. 'No. For once.' I flashed him a grin, which he returned, the frown of moments before clearing from his face. 'You're right. I do feel like that. Unfortunately for you.'

'Why would it be unfortunate?'

'Because I no longer agree with every word you say.'

'Then you're a wiser woman too.'

'I like to think so. Although I'm sure you have plenty of women just dying to tell you how wise you are about *everything*.' I leant over and batted my lashes at him as we waited for an elderly chap to cross the road with a walker, each step slow and deliberate. Halfway through, he paused and gave a wave of thanks. Matt returned it before turning his head, the piercing eyes looking down at me.

'And what makes you think that?'

'I have eyes!' I said, chuckling as I sat back up straight. 'Not to mention your reputation.'

'You shouldn't believe everything you hear. And things aren't always as they seem.'

'So that wasn't you surrounded by a group of fit-looking twenty-somethings the night before I left for Norfolk?' I tapped my chin. 'Hmm, funny. It looked *just* like you...'

'I'm beginning to think I liked the other version of you better.'

'No, you don't,' I said, unsure where my confidence to banter with Matt further had come from but enjoying it all the same.

'No, you're right. I don't. She was lovely but I could tell there was someone even more interesting beneath the surface.'

I rested my head back against the headrest and took in the dramatic peaks and valleys I'd missed during my trip, Matt's words drifting around in my mind.

* * *

We pulled into the driveway and Matt steered the vehicle carefully to the family's private area. He set the handbrake and turned off the engine.

'You've gone very quiet,' he said. 'If I've upset you on the drive home, Mum's going to kill me. Not to mention Dad, Andy and Anna.'

'Oh! No.' I laid my hand on his forearm and felt the corded muscles beneath the dark hair. And yes, I probably left it there just a little bit longer than was needed. Sometimes a girl had to grab her thrills when she could. 'I'm not upset.'

'Phew!' he said, comically wiping his brow with his other arm.

'I'm just... surprised, I suppose.'

'Why?'

'I don't know...' Heat crept up my face. I might have gained some confidence in myself but I still had some way to go yet. 'I suppose I just didn't think you thought... well, anything really. I mean, what you said about there being someone more interesting beneath the surface.'

'Like I said, things aren't always what they appear to be.'

'No, I suppose not,' I replied, meeting his gaze and wondering what else about Matt wasn't what it appeared to be.

'So,' he said once we'd got out. 'How are Rumi and the family settling into their new place?'

'Oh my God. They totally love it! It's everything they wanted and more. You can see the joy on their faces every day. I mean, there's stuff they'd like to do to it to make it their own but they're already so at home.'

'That's great. Did she manage to plant some veggies like she wanted?'

'Did she? They're practically self-sufficient already.

Everyone has been so kind and helpful. I think that surprised her at first.'

'Kind of like it did with you here?'

'Yes, I suppose so. Like we were saying, sometimes you get this idea in your head and it can be hard to shift.'

'They sound happy.'

'They are. Over the moon.'

'And I'm sure they were thrilled to see you.'

'Yeah, it was lovely. Although, I have to say, not as thrilled as they'd have been if I'd brought you along too.'

'Really?'

'Oh yeah. Seriously,' I said as I made to swing my case out of the truck's storage area. 'Ever since you gave me a lift to grab my stuff from Jasper, Rumi's decided you're the best thing since sliced bread. And you made a friend for life with your praise of Ayaz's food.'

'Well, that's nice to know,' Matt said, reaching over me to get the luggage. 'I hope they take up the offer of coming here sometime.'

'I know they want to. We were talking about it when I was over there actually. Although you might regret the offer in time!'

We began walking towards the house and Matt's face creased lightly into a confused frown. 'Why on earth would I regret it?'

I scrunched one side of my face up. 'Like I said, Rumi thinks you're wonderful. I did try and put her right, of course, but she was having none of it.'

'Glad to hear you at least made an effort but, so far, I'm not seeing the problem.'

'Well, let's just say she hasn't exactly been a fan of most of the previous men in my life. Not that you're "in my life" in that way!' I added hastily.

Matt rested his hand on the door handle. 'But she's under the impression that would be a good idea.'

'Umm... yes.' A thought zipped into my brain. 'But I've never suggested I want that!'

He twisted the handle. 'The absolute horror in your voice whilst making that statement assures me that's true. Not that I'd have thought any different, but good to have the clarification.'

'Oh, come on,' I said, giving a rock-hard biceps a poke. 'You're not going to try and convince me I've wounded your ego. I've worked here too long to believe that.'

'There she is!' Bronwyn and Greg came through into the kitchen, Bronwyn's arms outstretched, ready to envelop me in a big hug. This family really did do great hugs.

'I'll take this up to your room,' Matt said.

'Thanks,' I said, over his mum's shoulder. 'And thanks for picking me up.'

'Any time.' With that he disappeared out of the door and I got caught up in telling his family about my trip as Greg busied himself making us all mugs of tea and Bronwyn popped a plate of freshly made ginger biscuits in the middle of the table.

'It's been ever so strange without you here,' she said, taking a seat next to me and giving me a squeeze. 'We all really missed you, didn't we, love?'

'We did that,' her husband agreed and I felt a rush of warmth and affection for these people who'd taken me into their home, their hearts.

'Didn't we, son?' he said as Matt returned to the kitchen.

'What's that?'

'We were just saying we missed Fleur when she was away.'

'Oh, right. Yeah. Anna's been quite lost without you. Andy just messaged to say they're on their way round.'

'I've missed her too.'

'I'm sure she'll be glad to hear that. As will Andy. He's getting all the wedding talk at the moment.'

'It is his wedding too.' I gave a shrug. 'Maybe he actually enjoys talking about it.'

Matt snagged a biscuit, took a chair next to me and gave a shrug in answer. I turned back to his mum. 'I'm sure you're excited, at least.' I threw Matt a look as I spoke. He pulled a face and waggled his head.

'Oh, we can't wait. I mean, Anna's been like one of our own since Andy brought her her home to meet us. Which is just as well, considering how much interest her own parents show in her.'

'They're the ones missing out.' Matt's gravel-edged statement was quiet but certain.

'They are. I can't understand it,' Bronwyn said.

'She's lucky to have you all to help fill that void,' I said, really meaning it.

'I think we're lucky to have her. She makes Andy so happy and she's got a good heart. No parent could ask anything more for their child. And you can stop rolling your eyes over there. Don't think I can't see you.'

In my peripheral vision, I'd seen that she'd been absolutely right but the fact that Matt was sitting the other side of me and his mum likely couldn't see him, yet had still nailed it, made me smile. He turned his head and grinned. 'I swear there's hidden cameras in here.'

'Oh, no such thing,' she said, pushing her chair back and peering out of the window as the sound of a car arriving caught her attention. 'I just know my boys.'

'Aren't you a fan of them getting married?' I asked, confused at his reaction. I knew he adored Anna. In a different way from his brother obviously, but I'd spent a lifetime people watching and Matt, I knew, would walk through fire for that girl.

'Of course,' he said, a deep frown creasing the tanned forehead. 'She's a great girl. And the fact that she's prepared to put up with that lump for better or worse? Well, that shows she's got more stamina than some of the blokes I served with, which is saying something.'

'I heard that,' his brother said, coming in from the lobby and flicking his brother, not lightly, on the ear.

'Oi!' Matt said, rubbing his ear and failing to hide the grin. 'I was complimenting your fiancée!'

'Thank you,' Anna said, wrapping her arms around his neck from behind and plonking a kiss on his cheek as he laid one large hand on her delicate hands where they joined to accept the hug.

'Yeah, by insulting me.'

'I don't know what you're talking about,' Matt said as Anna stepped back and hugged me tightly, laughing at their banter.

His brother leant in for another flick and the speed that Matt moved took us all by surprise. For a big bloke, he could certainly shift! Within a second he had his baby brother in a headlock and was about to tweak his ear.

'Don't you dare,' Bronwyn warned.

'What?' Matt looked over at her as his brother tried to squirm free, with little success, and instead resorted to thumping Matt on the arm. 'He started it!'

'I don't care who started it. Put him down.'

Matt obeyed and Andy stood straight. 'I told you I was her favourite.'

'It's only because she feels guilty for dropping you on your head when you were a baby.'

I rested back against the window ledge, part of the group but also a little apart from it at the same time. If things had been different, would I have had this for myself? The fun, the banter, the teasing, the love. Or would it have been more like Anna's fate of not being able to match the expectations of demanding parents?

21

'You're deep in thought,' Matt said, leaving the others to their conversation to join me at the window.

'Not really,' I lied.

'OK. Now we've got that fib out of the way, is it anything you want to talk about?'

I turned to face him, tilting my head to meet his eyes.

'Like I said, I'm good at reading people,' he said in answer to my unasked question. 'So? Anything I can help with? Did something happen when you were away?'

I held the unmistakeably sexy blue gaze for a while. 'No. Nothing. I had a lovely time. But I did miss this place. As much as I loved seeing Rumi and the gang, I was looking forward to getting back.'

'Like coming home?'

I studied my socks, suddenly feeling silly.

'Hey.'

'Hmm?' I answered in the most casual way I could as I began examining my fingernails.

Matt said nothing and after a few seconds I looked up. He

was watching me, evidently waiting for me to fill the silence. A tactic that clearly worked.

'What's up?' I asked.

'Nothing.'

He let out a sigh, signalling that he knew that was yet another fib. Pushing himself from the ledge, he held out his hand.

'Where are we going?'

'Just somewhere else.' His eyes focused on mine and I put my hand in his, feeling the warmth of his as it closed around my cool one. He headed out of the door and led me around to the wooden garden swing that nestled between pots of flowers, the little fountain in the wildlife pond next to it bubbling gently. Sitting down and stilling the swing's movement with one muscled leg, Matt gently encouraged me to follow him, my hand still in his.

'So, what's really up? Whatever you say stays between us if that's what you want. You can trust me.'

Whatever else I felt, whatever feelings tumbled confusedly as I found my place in this new life, I knew one thing for sure, and that was that Matt was someone I could trust. I'd known that the first time I'd met him for the hike. I'd trusted him to take us alongside ridgelines that dropped away, sheer and high, and I trusted him now. And yet, something still held me back. A lifetime of keeping thoughts to myself. An ingrained feeling that the people who should have been there had chosen not to be.

'What did I do wrong?' The question fell out of my mouth.

Matt's dark brows drew together. 'When?'

'I'm sorry,' I said, moving to get up, horrified that the words had been spoken aloud. The only person I'd ever talked to about my history was Rumi and even that was rare. And yet here I was, about to blab away to a man I'd only known for a few months and wasn't even dating.

'Stop,' he said, gently but still commanding.

'I can't,' I said. 'I forgot I have to...' I turned, meeting Matt's gaze. It was obvious that he knew I didn't 'have to' do anything.

'I'm sorry,' I repeated.

'For what?' he asked.

'I... just... I don't usually... I mean...'

Matt's smile was soft. 'I'm going to need a few more verbs.'

A giggle bubbled up as my brain didn't know whether to send instructions to laugh or cry. 'Sorry.'

He shook his head, wrapping a strong arm around me and giving a gentle squeeze as I settled back on the swing. 'Stop apologising.'

I opened my mouth, looked at him, grinned and closed it again.

His own smile widened. 'That's better.'

'There's clearly something going on, judging by your question. I'm not trying to force you to tell me something if you don't want to, but I can't stand seeing that look you get on your face sometimes and if I can help, I'd really like to.'

'What look?'

'One I've seen in all sorts of places on all sorts of faces.'

'And what does it say?' I wasn't entirely sure I wanted to know. Right now I felt the most exposed I'd felt in a long time. Part of me wanted to run but something kept me pinned in place. I wasn't sure if it was the calming effect that these views had had on me from the first moment, or if it was the man sitting next to me now, studying my face. For once I didn't automatically reach up to ensure the scar was hidden or look away – my usual go-to actions. Something was different here. I was different here. Maybe that was the problem.

'It can say a lot of things.'

'And what does it say when you look at me?' I asked. On that first hike, I'd felt that Matt had almost sensed my thoughts. When I'd hesitated, he'd known when to encourage me, and when to remain silent. Just as I'd felt the tension building as Jasper had said or done something disrespectful or smug, Matt would say something funny or point out a local spot of interest and I would feel the strain dissipate.

'It's like you're lost.'

My face suddenly felt aflame and I shoved myself off the swing. Matt's thigh muscle tensed as I did so, stilling it once again. I'd looked after myself pretty well since I'd been unceremoniously kicked out of the care system at eighteen. Yes, all right, I'd made a few dodgy decisions when it came to relationships but so did lots of people and some of them probably had good role models!

'And now when I look at you, you look mad as hell.'

Unlike Matt, my voice had not retained the calm tone of before. 'That's because I am!'

'OK.'

'OK? OK? You say I look lost and pathetic and then all you can say is OK?' I turned to storm off but Matt's hand circled my wrist as he stood up from the swing.

'Remind me when I called you pathetic.'

'Just now!'

'No. I said that sometimes you looked lost.'

'Exactly!'

His broad chest expanded beneath the navy T-shirt that fitted in all the right places and Matt let out one long breath.

'Fleur. You asked me what I saw when I looked at you. Looking lost is not the same as looking pathetic.'

'It sounds it.'

'Well, it's not!' His tone was stronger now. 'And that certainly isn't what I meant. You are far from pathetic. Jesus, you split up with someone, lost your home and your job in one fell swoop and yet you picked yourself straight up and took on a job far from everything and everyone you knew and just got on with it. That's guts right there.'

My breath slowed as I turned his words over in my head. 'It wasn't like I had much choice.'

'Yes, you did. You could have gone back to him. That was what he wanted. That woman was there at his apartment purely to try and make you jealous, make you realise what you're missing. But you didn't fall for it. You kept your head high and walked back out on him. Which I, for one, am incredibly glad of.'

'You are?'

'Absolutely. His loss, our gain.'

I swallowed. 'Thank you.'

He shrugged. 'Just the truth. Plus you can do far better than him.'

I let out a small laugh. 'Probably.'

'No doubt about it. Jesus, Jasper's an arsehole. The only reason I didn't let him trip off a ridgeline that day was because I liked you and I thought you'd be upset.'

'Well, I'm glad you didn't as it probably wouldn't have done your business reputation much good.'

'Interesting to note that you are more concerned about how it would have affected our business than the demise of your boyfriend.'

'Very funny.'

Matt let loose that grin and I felt the last remnants of my anger carry away on the gentle breeze. 'You going to sit back down?'

I looked down to where his hand still loosely circled my wrist. His own gaze followed and he immediately let go. My skin felt cold at the loss of his touch.

'OK.'

He held the chain as I retook my seat before joining me.

'So, what did you mean?' I asked. The door had been opened now so I decided I might as well see what was behind it.

'Sometimes I look at you and it seems like you're on the outside looking in. Like you're holding yourself back that little bit, just in case.'

'Just in case of what?'

'That's a question only you can answer.'

My throat suddenly felt raw as a surge of tears threatened to spill. Matt's comments were shockingly accurate. Even Rumi couldn't read me as he could.

'But whatever the answer is, I need you to know that I'm here for you. We all are. You're not lost, Fleur. If you want to let go, you can. We won't let you fall. I won't let you fall.'

His echo of the phrase he'd spoken that first day we met when I'd hesitated at a craggy spot made me look up.

'I promise,' he said, just as he had back then. I'd trusted him then and I trusted him now.

This time I replied. 'I know.' And then I sat back in the swing, Matt beside me, and let go just that little bit more.

* * *

'That's the woman that was asking about you before.' Win, an older waitress who'd been with the hotel years, pointed out an elegant woman sitting on her own at a table for two near the window.

I studied her for a few moments but couldn't place her at all. 'I don't recognise her. I'm usually pretty good with faces but I served a lot of people over the years at the café.'

'Can't remember everyone,' Win agreed before heading over to take an order from a couple who'd joined us this afternoon. The woman was in my section of the restaurant so I'd speak to her shortly. It did bug me that I didn't recall her. At the coffee shop, the others would tease me that I would be great for a police sketch artist if we ever got robbed as I had what they liked to call a 'freaky' memory for faces. I preferred to consider it a talent.

'Hello, you.' The deep voice close to my ear sent a flutter through places flutterings had no business being.

'Hello,' I said, turning around to face Matt. 'How was work today?'

'Hard to call it work on a beautiful day like this – but it was good. Thanks. Nice family.'

'That's good. You here for food or purely for the pleasure of seeing me?'

'Can it be both?' Matt grinned.

'Oh, go and find a seat. You're not fooling me. I'll take your order in a few minutes.'

'Thanks.'

I watched him go for a couple of seconds. Maybe I should take up more vigorous hiking because it certainly had done amazing things for Matt's bum. Or maybe he was just endowed with a great bum anyway. Either way it was—

'You all right, love?' Bronwyn said.

'Oh! Yes,' I said, scrabbling for the pencil I'd dropped when her question jolted me from my trance. 'Sorry.'

'Nothing to apologise for. We're all allowed a bit of a daydream from time to time.'

I gave her a quick smile and hurried off to take the mystery woman's order.

'Hi, can I get you anything to drink?'

The woman looked up and stared at me for a few moments before answering with a smile. 'Yes, please. A glass of white wine would be lovely. Whatever you suggest.' The French accent was soft and lilting but still distinct.

'The house white is actually very good, or I can get you the full wine list.'

'No, thank you. The house one will be fine.'

A few minutes later I'd returned with the drink and asked if she was ready to order.

'Is there anything you recommend?' she asked, glancing briefly at the menu before focusing her pale blue eyes back on me.

'To be honest, everything's good. We're lucky to have a great chef here so I think you'll enjoy whatever you choose.'

'It seems a very popular restaurant.' She looked around, her eyes momentarily lingering on Matt, who had glanced over and, catching my eye, gave me a smile. To be fair, a lot of people's gazes caught on Matt when he was in here. Tonight he was sitting on his own at a small corner table, a book propped up against the condiments. The woman's age was hard to pin down and I hadn't missed him cast a glance back. It was understandable. My first thought when I saw her was that she might have been a ballet dancer. She had that elegant long neck and her hair was pulled chicly into a bun. Her skin was like porcelain with just a few lines that only seemed to add to her beauty. Once upon a time, I'd have felt intimidated by such a woman but now, as my own true personality and style had had the freedom and confidence to grow, I felt a lot more comfortable in my own skin, and less worried about others' judgements and opinions of me.

'Yes, we're open to the public as well as hotel guests so it's always quite full.'

'It obviously keeps you busy.'

'It does, but that's OK. It's a lovely place to work so I don't mind.'

'Have you been here long?' she asked.

'Not really, I just started this year. So,' I said, eager to direct the topic of conversation away from me. 'So, did anything take your fancy?' *Apart from Matt.*

She chose the lemon sole and I scooted off to drop the order into the kitchen and then back out to my other tables.

'Think you've got an admirer over there,' I said as I readied myself to take Matt's request.

'Huh?'

I pointed subtly with my pencil towards the elegant woman whose gaze had lingered on him earlier.

'Ah. No. I don't think so.'

'Coming over all modest? That's not like you.'

He gave me a tight smile. 'You know, I think I liked you better when you wouldn't come out of that shell of yours.'

'Too bad.'

He gave a half-smile that was far too sexy for my liking before turning back to the menu. 'I'll have the steak, please.' There was no need for him to tell me how he liked it. Medium rare it would be.

'Thanks,' I said, taking the menu back from him. 'How's the book?'

'Good, thanks.'

'I'm not sure I've ever seen you reading much before.'

'No, I sort of got out of the habit.'

'Being the centre of attention for all the fit women you dine with can really suck up the time.'

He gave a small sweep of his hand to show his table for one.

'I suppose everyone needs a rest from being adored.'

'Yep. Definitely preferred you before.'

I gave him a wink and spun on my heel to see to a nearby table on my way to the kitchen, his laughter following me as I did so.

22

By the end of the evening, only one table was still occupied. 'Is there anything else I can get you?' I asked the mystery woman.

'No, I'm fine, thank you. Am I holding you up from finishing your shift?'

'Oh no, that's fine.' I waved her concern away. She was, actually, but I didn't mind. It wasn't as if I had a long commute. Matt was sitting at the bar chatting to his dad, who'd been serving behind it. Bronwyn and Greg had begun stepping back from the day-to-day chores of running the hotel, relying instead on trusted staff, but Roddy the regular barman had got a puncture on his way to work so he'd had stepped in, falling easily back into the rhythm of many years past.

'Actually, I wonder if I could speak to you about something.'

'Me?'

She nodded.

'Umm... was there something you were unhappy about with the service or the meal?'

'Oh! No, no, no. It was all perfect.' She had a lovely smile, although right now there seemed something else behind it. A sense of unease.

'OK…' I wasn't sure what else she could need to talk to me about.

'It's a little more… personal.'

I glanced round at Matt, catching his eye. He gave the smallest tilt of his head in question. I took a deep breath and turned back to the woman. I could do this on my own. Thinking I needed someone else all the time had led to some poor life decisions and, honestly, how bad could this be?

'I'm not sure I understand.'

She looked around. 'Is there somewhere a little more… private we could go?'

The tension had already tightened my throat and knotted my stomach. Right now I was in a place I felt comfortable in. Gathering my new-found inner strength, I decided I wasn't about to be danced around by this stranger. It was here or nothing.

'We're actually closed now so it's fine here.'

I saw her eyes dart to Matt and his dad, ostensibly deep in conversation although I had a feeling that Matt had one ear on that and the rest of his Spidey senses tuned in my direction.

The woman studied me for a moment and there was something in her look, a sudden flash of insecurity, that I recognised. It was a feeling I knew well.

Relenting, I indicated a room to the side. 'There's a little snug area through there that we can go to if that's better?'

A tiny knot of the tension on her face softened as she gave a small smile. 'Yes, that would be lovely.' She stood from her chair, tucking it carefully back in, and nodding a thank you at Greg.

'Thank you,' he called. 'Have a good evening.'

I indicated the way to the snug and went to follow her.

'Fleur?' Matt had one long leg straightened from the stool, as though ready to stand.

'I can handle it.'

He met my eyes. 'I know. But if you want us, you know where we are.'

The woman walked ahead of me, her head high, back straight and a gentle sway to her slim hips. I had a similar build but most definitely not the elegance. She took a seat, perfectly manicured hands resting in her lap. I perched on the sofa opposite.

'Thank you for agreeing to speak with me.'

I wasn't quite sure what to say so I remained silent.

'I know it all seems quite strange. I can see your boyfriend has concerns. He clearly is protective of you.'

'My boyfriend?'

'The man sitting at the bar?'

'Oh. Right. Just a friend. He's like that with everyone.'

One dark, exquisitely shaped eyebrow rose the tiniest amount.

'What is it that you wanted to talk about?' I asked, moving the conversation on. I'd done my shift and ideally would be heading to bed right now. The last thing I felt like doing was having a chat about an imaginary love life with a complete stranger.

She clasped her hands together in her lap and twisted them a couple of times. Then, with a deep breath, she laid them back in her lap and looked up at me.

'I'm not really sure where to start.' She gave me an awkward smile. I waited. If she didn't know, then I sure as heck didn't. 'You grew up in a children's home, I understand.'

Every fibre in my body tensed and I felt as if I'd been

plugged into the mains. Who the hell was this woman? My hands gripped into fists at my sides as I quickly stood up.

'I really don't think that's any of your business.'

The woman remained seated but now there were tears in her eyes. 'As I said, I don't really know where to start. Perhaps it is better just to tell you outright.'

'Tell me what?'

I saw her swallow. 'Fleur… I'm your mother.'

For a moment there was just silence, each of us staring at the other. And then, in a split second, I had a thousand clanging bells in my head as the words the woman had said rang out. I sat down heavily then opened my mouth to speak but no words formed. I closed it again.

'I'm sorry to spring it on you like that. I did think about writing a letter.' Her words were rushed, as if she felt a need to fill the gaping silence that hung in the cosy room. 'But then I thought it would be better in person, but now…'

My mind focused on just two words as a whole slew of emotions raged inside me, each competing for top spot.

'You're sorry?' I stood back up sharply.

'Yes.'

'For coming to my place of work and just casually blabbing that you're my mother?'

Anger was definitely winning at the moment, kicking and punching all the other emotions out of the way.

'Yes.'

The laugh that escaped me was strangulated and bitter. 'Well, it's a shame you're not sorry for abandoning me as a baby.'

'Oh, Fleur!' She stood and made to reach out to me but I stepped back. Her hands dropped to her sides as the tears that had filled her eyes spilled down over her high cheekbones.

Cheekbones that I now realised I'd inherited from her. 'I know you won't understand, can't understand, and I wouldn't expect you to. But I've been sorry every day since I gave you up. I've never stopped wishing everything had been so, so different. I did everything I could to keep you. You have to know that.'

I stared back at her. 'Am I meant to feel sorry for you now?' The cold voice I heard sounded nothing like my own. I'd dreamt so many times of my parents coming to find me over the years, and the images that had played in my head had been joyful. Full of tears, yes, but those had been happy tears as the terrible misunderstanding that had led to me being separated from them had been explained along with how they had vowed never to stop looking for me. But as I grew older, reality took the place of dreams and I realised that no one was coming for me. That I'd not been wanted. Given away. And now this woman wanted me to feel sorry for her?

'No, Fleur. I don't. I just want you to understand—'

'Understand? You gave me away! How am I supposed to understand that? That you chose to hand over your own child? And you didn't even have the guts to do it properly. You abandoned me in a hospital! Just left me there!' Hot, angry tears streamed down my face unchecked as I yelled at her.

'Fleur?'

I turned to see Matt and his dad at the entrance to the snug, concern shrouding both their faces. The moment he saw my face, Matt strode towards me, his arms wrapping tight around me. 'What the hell is going on?'

'Matt, Greg,' I said, the tone still cold. 'Meet my mother.' I looked up at him. 'Also, I think I'm going to be sick.'

'Sit down,' Matt said softly and I obeyed, mostly to stop the sense that the world around me was spinning out of control. His hands, slightly rough to the touch, cupped my face. 'Breathe. In...

out... in... out.' As I followed the instructions, the spiralling feeling began to dissipate, the nausea subsiding. As my breathing slowed, Matt lowered his hands to wrap around my own. 'OK?'

I nodded.

'Do you want me to stay?'

As I said no, inside my brain was screaming at me. The truth was I did but I also knew I needed to do this alone. Now that my confidence had grown and I realised I didn't need back up, it didn't stop me wanting Matt there. Not because I didn't think I could handle it but because it felt so right. And that was exactly the reason I had to say no.

'OK. I'll be next door when you're done.'

'Thanks.'

He gave a brief nod, glanced at the woman opposite with an unreadable expression then walked away back to his dad, who was still waiting at the door. They closed it behind them.

'They are nice people here.'

'Yep.'

'And you live here?'

'I have a feeling you already know the answer to that question. How did you find me?'

'It's taken a lot of work and far longer than I had hoped.'

'I suppose that can happen when you walk off and abandon your baby decades earlier.'

Her head tilted down and a brief flash of remorse surged through me. It was a shock to realise I'd been storing all that bitterness inside me all these years, but now it was spilling out, flowing directly towards the person I held responsible for all the heartache and bad experiences I'd had over the years. The loneliness, the insecurity. Right now, I couldn't see anything but searing, white-hot pain.

'You have every right to be angry, Fleur, but, with your permission, I'd like to tell you the circumstances. I know it can't change things and may not affect how you feel. If that's the case, I will leave and promise I will not contact you again. But it's important that you know, despite how it looks, you were never not wanted. I knew from the moment I fell pregnant that I wanted you and when I held you in my arms that first time…' She mopped her tears, a smile shining through them. 'You were so beautiful. Absolutely perfect. And I knew I would do everything in my power to give you a good life.'

Words of recrimination hovered on my tongue but I swallowed them back. I certainly wasn't going to rush into her arms, but there was something about her words, her expression, that told me it was the truth. Her tears told the heartbreak but the smile was pure remembered joy. I needed to know the whole story. As Matt had said when I'd hesitated on parts of the hike that first day – one step at a time. Just concentrate on your next step. I took the next step.

'Would you like a drink?' I asked.

It was as though she sensed a truce. 'That would be lovely, thank you.'

'Tea, coffee?'

'Perhaps a brandy for each of us would be a good idea, no?' Her smile was hesitant, but I met and returned a small reflection of it, the gesture causing a visible release of tension in her face.

'That's not a bad idea. I'll be back in a minute.' I headed out of the door and closed it behind me, walking towards the closed bar where Matt and his dad were still sitting talking. As the door to the snug opened, their conversation ceased as both men turned towards me. Neither spoke.

'Would it be OK to get a couple of brandies? I can settle up with you tomorrow.'

'Nothing to settle up,' Greg said, sliding off the bar stool. 'I'll get them for you.'

'Thanks.'

'You all right?' Matt asked as his father busied himself with glasses and optics.

'Honestly? I'm not sure. Everything feels a bit surreal at the moment.'

'I'd say I can imagine, but I can't. But you know what I mean.'

'I do, thanks. And sorry about earlier. I didn't mean to disturb anyone. I just kind of lost it for a few moments.'

Matt laughed, his brows high in disbelief. 'Bloody hell, Fleur. I think you're more than justified in causing all the disturbance you like when you receive news like that.'

'Still...'

'Still, nothing. There's nothing to apologise for.'

'Here you go, love. Do you want me to bring them in?'

'No, I've got it,' I said, lifting the tray, noticing that Greg had used their own beautiful glasses rather than the restaurant ones. As I did so, the contents swayed and danced, the crystal delicately clinking together under my shaking hands. Quickly I returned the tray to the counter.

'I'll bring it in.' Matt stepped off the stool, expertly lifting the tray with one hand and following me back through the door. Lifting one glass, he put it in front of where I'd now taken a seat and the other opposite me.

'Thank you.'

Matt looked down at the woman, gave a small nod of acceptance and turned away. As he did so, he caught my eye and I knew he wouldn't be going anywhere tonight until I was done.

The door closed behind him, the ensuing silence broken only by the promised rain that had started and was now pummelling the windows as a strong wind blew across the mountains and valleys.

'Cheers,' I said, lifting my glass. Inner me cringed. I rubbed my forehead at the ridiculousness of such a phrase in this particular circumstance. It had just come out and I wished to God I could take it back. But across from me, my mother seemed to appreciate the banality of the statement as the silence broke, and lifted her own glass.

'Cheers!' she returned, holding her glass up. I saw the hesitancy in the movement. The flicker of hope.

I tapped my glass lightly against hers and took a good swig. She'd been right. Tea was just the thing in most situations, but this particular one definitely called for strong alcohol. The brandy warmed its way down my throat and gave me the courage I needed to ask my next question.

'So,' I said, 'perhaps you can start at the beginning?'

23

She took another sip of the drink and let the glass rest in her hands, gently swirling the liquid inside before she spoke.

'My name is Elodie and when I was seventeen, the ballet company I had just been accepted into was doing a world tour. I was so excited. I grew up in a very rural area and had never travelled so this was beyond my wildest dreams.' The pale eyes sparkled with remembered joy. 'Have you travelled much?'

I shook my head. 'No.'

Her smile faded for a moment before continuing with her story. 'The tour was almost over and the last location was London. The first night a few of us were still on a high from the show and we went for a drink at one of the bars near the theatre. As we were talking, a man approached us. He apologised for intruding but said he wanted to say how much he had enjoyed the performance. The others invited him and his friend to join us, which he did, and I was seated next to him.'

I shifted in my chair, unsure which way this story was going to go.

'We ended up talking the rest of the night, until the bar

closed. I'd not had many boyfriends, only one really and that hadn't been serious. I was always too busy putting everything I had into ballet and following my dream of becoming a prima ballerina. But something about this man was different from the boys I'd met before. He was a little older, only five years, but that seemed a lot to me back then. He was sophisticated, and intelligent and funny. He made me laugh like no one else ever had, or ever has since.'

I had a million questions already but I bit them back, caught between wanting to ask them and desperate to hear the rest.

'We saw each other every moment we could after that and even though I'd never been in love before, I knew I was with Ralph and I knew it was the same for him.' She pronounced it 'Rafe'. 'I was due to return to France in a few weeks but I think we both pushed that out of our minds. It was almost as if we didn't think about it, we could pretend we wouldn't have to deal with it. Do you understand?'

I nodded.

'A couple of weeks before I was due to leave, the inevitable happened. It wasn't planned, but one thing led to another, and hormones and lust helped it along.' She put a hand to her face. 'I feel a little awkward saying this to you.'

'I'm hardly a child. I know how it is.'

'Yes. Yes, of course.' She gave a tight, embarrassed smile. 'Well. The time for me to leave came and we decided that we would try and make it work. A long-distance relationship. And we tried. We really did. But it wasn't so easy back then. Not that it's easy now but the communication possibilities were less and, the day before I left, Ralph was offered a prestigious academic position in America. The added time difference made things that much harder. I knew he loved me and I was desperate to be with him but I wanted my career too. He was loving his new job and I was getting more and more exhausted trying to stay up so that we could talk on the phone and the same went for him. It wasn't working. As much as we wanted it to, it just wasn't. And then I found out I was pregnant with you.'

'Did you tell him?'

She took another sip of the brandy before meeting my eyes, her own filled with tears now. 'No. I should have, I know. But I knew Ralph. I knew he'd do the right thing. He'd be on the first plane back and proposing.'

'But you wanted your career more than him or me?'

'Oh, no! No, you mustn't think that!'

I scratched the back of my neck and fiddled with my hair for a moment, my chest tight with confusion.

She tilted her head. 'Of course, I can see that it might look that way. But please, let me explain.'

I downed the last of my drink and waited for her to continue.

'I loved Ralph so much. I don't know if you have ever been in love, but that feeling when you want the thing that is best for them, even if it means breaking your own heart?'

I didn't know. And from the pain that showed in her face at the memories she spoke of, I didn't think I wanted to.

Having placed her glass on the table, her perfectly manicured hands were now wrapped around her body. 'There was nothing that would have made me happier than to have married Ralph and raised a family with him. But the last time I spoke to him, it was clear that his job was working out incredibly well for him and was going to be a springboard for bigger and better things. Suddenly having me and a child to care for... it would have taken him away from the things he'd worked so hard for.' She gave one of those shrugs that the French did so well.

'What happened then?'

'I told him it was over. That the time differences were too much and affecting my performances.'

'Was he upset?'

'Terribly! He was devastated. He said he would find another job.'

'He might have done.'

'Yes. He might. But the one he was doing was exactly what he'd planned for. What he'd hoped for and, every time we spoke, his enthusiasm for the studies just bubbled over. I couldn't stand in the way of that.'

'So you ended it without telling him about me?'

'Yes.'

I shook my head, trying to keep my tumbled emotions in some sort of order, but one thought kept fighting its way to the top, determined to be heard.

'He might have wanted me!'

Elodie's face creased and her eyes filled again. When she spoke her voice was hoarse. 'That's exactly why I couldn't tell him. It's not an excuse, I know. But I was only seventeen and had no one to talk to about any of it. I couldn't tell my parents that I was pregnant, and I couldn't tell anyone in the company, although obviously I was going to have to tell them eventually.'

'Why couldn't you tell your parents?'

'They were very strict and traditional, and they'd supported me from a small child when I'd told them I wanted to become a prima ballerina. When I was accepted by the Paris Opera Ballet, they were so proud. Telling them I was pregnant outside marriage and would lose my place in the company... it just wasn't an option.'

'People have children outside marriage all the time! More often than not, these days.'

'But it wasn't these days,' Elodie countered. 'And the village I came from was very reserved. Both my parents had been born and raised there and the old way of life was still held to be the "right" way.'

'So... what happened?'

'I hid my pregnancy for as long as I could then approached the director of the company.'

'Were you fired?'

'No. Actually they were very understanding. I was told that they would hold my place for me for six months after the baby was born and then I would be able to come back. But they would not be able to make any extra allowances after that. It was up to me to find a reliable babysitter, et cetera. I was thrilled but, as I couldn't dance, I had to find myself another job in the meantime and I would interview potential babysitters.'

'So what went wrong? How come you changed your mind?'

'I never changed my mind,' she said, gripping her hands into fists. 'Not once.'

I met her gaze, realising suddenly that I was looking back at my own eyes, that same shade of pale blue. The blue of the early morning sky in summer, Matt had called them once, after Anna had been trying to decide their particular shade. We'd all been surprised by Matt's poetic comment, no one more so than himself. He'd downed the rest of his pint and then asked his brother a question about the rugby.

'I found a job as an assistant to an interior designer. She was from a similar background to me and also a fan of the ballet. I loved going with her to houses and making notes about how she thought the space could be transformed into what the clients wanted. And she was wonderful to me. I was lucky to have quite an easy pregnancy, not affected by morning sickness, and generally felt very well. I think being so young worked in my favour in that respect at least. Her own assistant had had to take some long-term sick leave so she was happy to hire me for the interim period.'

'And then after the grace period with the ballet company was up?'

'I absolutely hated having to leave you. You were such a good baby, so happy and smiley. But I'd found someone I felt I could trust you with when I was working, that I could afford and I really thought it was all going to work out.'

'So what happened?'

'The woman I hired turned out to be someone who wasn't as reliable as she promised. Some days she failed to turn up and I was eventually put on a warning with the company. Although I loved ballet, I loved you more, so I went back to the interior designer I'd been working for to see if there was any chance of continuing with her and finding someone else to look after you. However, her previous assistant had now returned to work.'

'So that was it?'

'No. I looked for other people and then thought I had someone. The company was going on a tour and she was happy to do that but it seems she was more interested in the travel than her responsibilities. The first night she had you, she spilled boiling water on you.' Her voice broke as she spoke and automatically I pulled my hair over my temple.

'She wasn't at the apartment I had rented when I finished work and I was frantic, trying to find her. Eventually she returned and told me you were at the hospital.'

'But you didn't come to get me.'

'I rushed there and found you. They'd treated the burn and

there you were, so tiny with all these bandages…' A sob escaped and I felt the rest of the ice I'd encased my heart in beginning to melt as a swathe of emotions rushed through me. Part of me still wanted to hold everything against her but, as she told her story, it was obvious that she'd wanted me. I tried to imagine what I'd have done if I'd fallen into the same situation at seventeen with no one to call on.

'Hang on,' I said, doing my best to keep my voice even as I got up and crossed the room.

Matt's head turned as the door opened. 'Hey.' His dad had obviously gone to bed.

'Hi. Are there any tissues?'

'Yeah. Mum's got some stashed in one of the cupboards,' he said, ducking under the bar and reappearing with a square box, a white tissue peeking out of the top. 'How's it going?'

I puffed out my cheeks and blew out the air slowly. 'Can I get back to you on that?'

'Sure,' he said, handing over the tissues.

'You OK?'

'I think so.'

His eyes dropped to the box.

'They're not for me.' I gave a shrug as I tilted my head up to meet his eyes. 'Not right now anyway.'

His gaze softened as his arms reached out and wrapped around me and I sank into the comfort of the embrace and the warmth of his hard body. 'Just remember, you're not on your own.'

'I know. Thanks.' As much as I felt I could have stayed there longer, I had to get back to my mother. 'I'd better go.'

'Yep. I'll be here when you're done.'

I glanced over at the grandfather clock that stood in the corner. 'It's late, you should go home.'

'I can wait.'

'You don't have to.'

'I know.'

'OK, thank you. But don't blame me if you're tired and cranky in the morning.'

'I promise.'

* * *

'Here,' I said, offering Elodie the tissues.

'Oh! Thank you.' She took one and delicately dabbed at her eyes before blowing her nose daintily. Whoever my father was, I was guessing he blew his nose like a foghorn. I had to have inherited it from somewhere. I waited until she seemed more composed before asking the next question.

'Once you were at the hospital, what happened then?'

Her features tensed as she reached out for another tissue. I noticed the shake in her hand. Either she was a brilliant actor or I had to believe that giving up her child really had broken her heart.

'I looked down at my beautiful child, swathed in bandages, an IV in your tiny, pudgy hand, and I realised in that moment that I wasn't a good mother. I felt like I didn't deserve you. I didn't have the capability to look after you and continue my career, but neither could I find a job that let me keep you with me. If I'd been older I would have found some way to teach instead but no one was going to send their child to someone who was barely more than a child herself. I realised that you deserved more, much more, than I could give you. And then I did the hardest thing I have ever, and will ever, do in my entire life. I got up and walked away. It felt like my world had exploded and there was nothing there any more. You'd been my everything but I couldn't keep you safe. As I left, all I felt was darkness. Like the light in my life had been switched off.' She looked up at me. 'You were such a darling baby, I thought you'd be found a good family straight away.'

'I wasn't.'

'No. When I found that out I cried for weeks... months.' She put out a hand. 'And I don't say that to ask for sympathy. I just... it made me feel like I'd given up my baby for nothing. That I should have tried harder.'

'It sounds like you did what you could.'

'I don't expect you to forgive me, Fleur. And I'm sorry that I've upset you coming here.'

I breathed out a sigh. 'It was always going to be a shock.'

She made a silent nod of agreement.

'So, what made you decide to start looking for me?'

'I've been looking for you for years.'

'You have?'

'Yes. But when the babysitter took you to hospital, her writing on the forms was so bad they had no idea what your surname was. When I saw her, and found out you were in hospital, she reeked of alcohol, which I think is how the accident happened in the first place although she denied it. Anyway, so when I looked for you, there was no trace of Fleur Auclair. That was my maiden name.'

'My surname is French.'

She smiled sadly. 'That makes sense. The flowery blanket that went everywhere with you had French words embroidered on it, and, of course, your name, Fleur, so I can see why they gave you the name French.'

'So my real surname is Auclair?'

'Yes. Or you'd be entitled to use your father's name.'

'Which is what?'

'Richard...' She pronounced it with a French accent, softening the last few letters. 'It means brave. It seems appropriate... We tracked down one of the nurses from the hospital and she remembered you. She said you were so brave during the surgeries and care you needed for the burn.' Her eyes moved to my temple then she cleared her throat. 'But the change of name meant that it was harder to find you.'

I rolled the names around in my head but they both sounded alien.

'Does he know about me now?'

'Yes,' she said.

'And how did that go down?' I asked.

'Not well.'

I tensed and Elodie rushed to correct herself, her slim hand reaching out to touch mine. 'I'm sorry,' she said, drawing it back and lacing her hands together on her lap. 'I misspoke. He was absolutely thrilled about you.' I felt a fluttering inside me but couldn't pin it down as nerves or excitement, or joy. Perhaps it was a mix. 'He was angry that I hadn't told him. That he'd missed out on having a daughter.' She paused. 'Having you.'

24

The lump in my throat seemed to be expanding until it blocked my voice completely. Elodie looked at her watch. 'Oh, my goodness, is it that late? I am so sorry. You must be exhausted.'

'I'm OK,' I said, but a glance at the woman opposite me told me that I wasn't the only one who'd been drained of emotion tonight. I didn't know whether I forgave her yet. Everything was still turning and tossing around in my mind. And now there was my father to discuss.

'You should rest.' Her smile was gentle yet hesitant.

'Where are you staying? Do you live near here?'

She shook her head. 'No. We live in Cambridgeshire but we're staying just down the road.'

I frowned. 'We?'

There was a pause before she answered. 'Your father and I.'

'I... but... you're both here?'

'Yes. But we felt it would be better for just one of us to speak to you first.'

'But how...?'

'We found each other again after far too many years apart.'

She twisted a ring on her hand before looking at me again. 'Finding you...' I heard her swallow. 'It would make our family complete again. Just as it should have been so many years ago.' Her hands reached out for mine and I let her take them. 'I could say sorry to you both until the end of time and it still wouldn't be enough. I thought I was doing the right thing but now I know I should have just told Ralph. It was his decision to make. You are his child too.'

There was still a mass of emotions flip-flopping around my body but I kept coming back to the fact that, at the time Elodie had been required to make such life-changing decisions for all of us, she had been just seventeen years old and effectively alone. The anger still coursed but it was tempered with a modicum of understanding. And now there was a fresh wash of feeling that, whilst my mother sat in front of me, somewhere not too far away, my father was waiting.

Elodie checked her watch. 'You ought to get to bed.'

I nodded although I didn't think there was much chance of my brain slowing down enough for sleep any time soon.

Elodie stood and smoothed down the fabric of her grass-green dress. For a moment we both just stood there, wondering what the next step was. Did we shake hands? Hug? High-five? Somehow I didn't think Elodie was the type of woman to high-five.

'Thank you for coming today.' I broke the silence.

'Thank you for listening. And again, I am so—'

'You don't have to keep apologising. It was a difficult situation.' I let out a deep sigh. 'Impossible even. Yes, of course I wish it had been different. But you did what you could. What you thought was best. I'm not going to pretend it isn't going to take time to process but at least I know now that it wasn't because you didn't care.' Grabbing the tissue box, I held it out to her and she gratefully pulled two or three out and put them to work.

'Thank you for your understanding, Fleur.' She tilted her head slightly and studied me. 'You have your father's mouth.'

'I expect he probably wants it back now.' God knew what possessed me to spout such a flippant comment at such a time and my hand immediately flew to my face, my eyes wide with embarrassment.

Opposite me, Elodie's eyes had also widened but then they began to shine, the corners of them creasing as laughter burst out. Tears once again streamed down her face. I opened my mouth to apologise but her hand reached for mine and she clasped it within her own before bringing it to her lips and gently kissing it. 'I'm afraid you may have inherited his penchant for bad jokes too, for which I am even more sorry.' We stood there together for a moment before my own laughter bubbled up. Tears mixed with laughter, joy mixed with pain and regret and when she reached for me, I let her and allowed myself to be wrapped up in my mother's embrace for the first time I could remember.

Matt walked towards us as the door to the snug opened and we exited, both faces tear-stained but smiling. 'Hi.' I gave a brief wave.

'Hello,' he returned, the gravel edge of his voice even rougher – and sexier – now tiredness was thrown into the mix.

I glanced at the clock in the darkened room. 'You should have gone home ages ago.'

He sent me a glance that said. *We both know that was never going to happen.*

'I'll leave you in peace now. Get some rest.' Elodie laid a hand gently on my cheek for just a second, as though her motherly instincts had automatically kicked in. I caught it as she pulled it back, holding the slim cool hand between my own stickily warm ones.

'I'll take you home.'

'No, my love. I'll call a taxi.'

'No need,' Matt said, grabbing his keys from the bar.

'Elodie, this is Matt.' I saw the interest in her eyes as she looked at me. 'He's a good friend,' I said purposefully. Elodie gave me a small conspiratorial smile. 'His family own the hotel. Matt, this is Elodie...'

'Richard.' She filled in for me.

'Elodie Richard. My mother.'

Matt put out his right hand, swamping my mother's one within it as they shook. 'Pleased to meet you.'

'You're married now?' My yawn was cut off midway.

Elodie turned back to face me. 'Yes, I thought I said.'

I shook my head. She wore several rings but it was only now, as emotions subsided, that I noticed the solitaire diamond and platinum band on the third finger of her left hand.

'There's so much we need to catch up on. But yes, we married shortly after we met again. As we should have done so many years before.' Her gaze dropped to the floor and Matt and I exchanged a look and could only guess at all the thoughts and, undoubtedly, guilt that currently coursed through her mind.

'What's done is done,' I said, breaking her train of thought and causing her to look back up. 'It's what we do now that matters.'

'That is true. And I must thank you, and your family, Matt. I understand that you were kind enough to offer Fleur both employment and a home when she was put in a predicament earlier this year?'

'How do you know all this?' I asked, frowning.

'I think it's going to take a while to get totally caught up, for both of you,' Matt added.

'I think so too,' Elodie replied before answering my question. 'Our quest to find you led us to Jasper Hamilton-Grey.'

'Oh.'

'Yes. Unfortunately he was less than helpful but luckily his PA was more than happy to fill us in on what had happened.'

'I always liked her.'

'She liked you very much too and did send her regards, should we be lucky enough to find you.'

'I'm glad she was there but also kind of sorry that she's still stuck with him.'

'Actually she said she was handing in her notice that afternoon. She's got a far better offer.'

'Oh, good!'

'It seems you did too.' Elodie's expression was innocent but I was pretty sure she wasn't just talking about the job.

'It's a lovely place, yes,' I replied at the same time as trying to stifle another massive yawn.

'I'll run you back, Elodie. I assume you're staying locally?'

'Yes, at The Fiddle and Flute.'

'Good choice. Sally does a great breakfast.'

Elodie smiled. 'She does indeed. It's the best part of the day for my husband.'

Her husband. My dad...

'I'll ring you tomorrow, then?'

'Please,' she replied, the flicker in her smile showing that she was aware how overwhelming this evening had been for me and wasn't entirely sure if I would keep my word. But I knew I would. I couldn't guess at the relationship we might have, going forward. It was a lot to get my head around and would take time. But I had questions. So many questions and I needed to know, to see, who my father was. The man whose smile I'd inherited, along with a love of corny jokes. But right now, my body just wanted its bed. The adrenaline of earlier was throttling back and leaving nothing but weariness and exhaustion in its wake.

'Are you sure you don't mind taking her back?' I tilted my tired gaze up to Matt's face.

'Not at all,' he replied, his words gentle. 'I'm going to go home after that. I'll catch up with you tomorrow.'

I nodded and automatically gave him a hug, loving the feel of his strong arms around me, the warm breath on my neck. Bloody hell, I really did need to get some sleep before my overtired mind started darting off in directions it had no place going.

Elodie turned. 'Goodbye, Fleur.' Her voice cracked on my name and I reached down for her hands. 'I'm sorry. I just... the last time I said that...'

'But I'm here now,' I said, dredging up strength that I didn't know I had. 'And we'll see each other again soon.'

'We will, won't we?'

'Yes,' I said, the same strength filling my words. 'I promise.'

* * *

'Where are you off to?' Matt's deep tones broke into my thoughts and I made a squeak of surprise as I stood from lacing my boots. 'Sorry, didn't mean to startle you.'

'Fibber.'

'OK, fine, but that squeak you make is so funny.' I stuck out my tongue. 'So where you off to?'

'Just walking.'

'Want some company?'

'Don't you have clients?'

'Hal wanted to swap dates with me so I'm free now.'

'Well, I'd have said yes but, as you took the pee out of me, I don't think I do.'

'OK,' Matt said, adjusting the small rucksack on his back. 'So where are we going?'

I gave a snort of derision. 'It's a good job your parents are lovely.'

'I'm lovely,' he said, falling into step with me.

'If you say so.'

He really was but there was no way on earth I was telling him.

'Sleep OK?' Matt asked.

'Better than I thought I would, to be honest. I guess it was probably more exhaustion than anything else.'

'I know you were mucking about, but if you really do want to be on your own today—'

'I don't.' Everything I'd thought I'd known about my earliest years had been entirely turned on its head and right now I wasn't sure about a lot of things, but the one thing I knew was that Matt's company was appreciated.

Matt looked across at me. 'OK.'

'Thanks for taking Elodie home last night.' I still wasn't in a place where I could call her 'Mum' or even 'Mother'. I wasn't sure I ever would be but – one step at a time.

'You're welcome.'

'I'm meeting them for dinner tomorrow night.'

'That's good.'

'Do you think so?'

'Don't you?'

'I asked you first.'

His lips tilted up as he turned his head back towards me.

I shrugged. 'Well, I did.'

'It's kind of a big question, Fleur, and the only one who can answer it is you.'

'I know but I'm asking your opinion. You must have one. You have one on every other topic.'

He huffed out a laugh. 'Did you ring Elodie this morning to arrange the dinner?'

'No. I messaged her. It seemed less difficult.'

'Understandable. But when you decided you were going to contact her, how did you feel? Did you *want* to contact her or was it something you were doing because you felt obliged to do so?'

I sucked my top lip in and rolled it back and forwards a little with my teeth as I pondered his question. 'I think I wanted to.'

'You think?'

'No, I did. Definitely. It felt weird, that's for certain. But I was excited too. And nervous. Oh, I don't know.' I shoved my hands in my pockets. Matt reached over and gently removed my right hand, the one nearest him, from its resting place. 'Remember. Hands free to protect yourself if you fall.'

'As you've invaded my walk, the least you can do is catch me if I fall.'

'If I'm around, I'll always catch you, Fleur. But it's wise to get into good habits.'

I pulled out my left hand with much show and huffing, which my companion ignored as we trudged on, the gravel and shale path making a satisfying crunching noise beneath our boots. I waved my hands in front of his face. 'Happy now?'

'Ecstatic.' There was a curve to his mouth and a glint of amusement in his eyes as he replied.

'Can I ask you a favour?'

'Of course.'

'Will you come with me?'

'Where?'

'To dinner.'

'With your parents?'

'Yes.'

'I'm not sure that's a great idea.'

'Why not?'

He stopped walking and waited for me to come back the few extra steps I'd taken before I'd noticed. 'Because this is personal, Fleur. This is time for you all to try and build the bond you've missed out on.'

'I think it's going to take more than steak and chips to do that.'

'It's a start.'

I didn't reply.

'You can do this, Fleur. You're stronger than you think. Far, far stronger.'

'I know. But...'

'But what?'

I tilted my head to meet his gaze. Those blue eyes that could send a look as soft as melting chocolate or as hard as polished steel. 'What if I want you to come? I know I don't *need* you there, but I *want* you there.'

His Adam's apple bobbed as he looked back at me. 'Then I can't say no.'

'Thank you. I'll message her later and get them to change the reservation to four people.'

'They might prefer to see you on your own, of course.'

'I'm pretty sure the ball's in my court to do what I want with after all these years.'

'Fair point. What time shall I pick you up?'

'Seven would be good, thanks.'

'Done. Now, come on. Let's get some fresh air in those lungs.'

'That's another way of saying I'm going to take you on a shattering walk that will leave you with jelly legs for the rest of the afternoon, isn't it?'

25

'I'm glad you drove,' I said, getting out of Matt's car as he opened the door for me. 'My legs are all wobbly. Maybe Elodie's approach of telling me who she was without giving me time to prepare was the better way of doing it after all. What you don't know, you can't worry about, right?'

Matt's warm, strong hands rested on my upper arms. 'Fleur. There's nothing to worry about here. Nothing at all. I promise. And I know it probably doesn't help but I'm guessing they're sitting in there just as nervous as you.'

'You're right. It doesn't help.'

A lopsided smile flashed on his face before he stood back, one hand having slid down my arm and caught my own hand within it. 'Did I tell you how absolutely stunning you look this evening?'

Shivers of pleasure trickled down my spine. I no longer needed a man's approval to make me feel worthy but when the words came from Matt, I couldn't help the spark of delight that ran through me and the smile I returned.

'No. But if you want to, I won't mind.'

'OK,' he said. 'Fleur, you look absolutely stunning.'

'Thank you.'

'Ready to go in?'

I blew out some air. 'Not really, but I guess I'm going to have to at some point.'

'Now's as good a time as any.'

'I suppose. Matt?'

'Mm-hmm?'

'Thanks for doing this?'

'What? Taking out a gorgeous woman and getting free food? Of course. There's no downside from what I see.'

'Oh! I told my mother that you'd offered to pay.'

'Right.' He turned away.

'Where are you going?'

'Back to the car. Have you seen the prices of this place?'

'Get your arse back here.'

'Oooh, stroppy Fleur.'

'That's right. And don't make me bring her out again.'

'Shame. I kind of like her. That stern look conjures up all sorts of things...' He gave a mischievous brow waggle.

'Oi! Stop conjuring and keep your mind on the job, matey.'

'Which is?'

'I don't know but it definitely doesn't involve you thinking about whatever it is that's brought that look to your eyes.'

'I don't think you want to know what I'm picturing right now.'

'I'm pretty sure I don't either.' Actually I was dying to know but a glance at my watch told me we were already a few minutes late. And somehow, I knew that if I got Matt to tell me, we might never get into the restaurant. On the plus side, he had at least distracted me from my nerves.

'Good evening,' the perky, pretty blonde in a fitted floral

satin jacket greeted us as we stepped through the entry way. 'Is it a table for two?'

'Err... no... I'm, err, I mean we are umm... meeting someone?'

'I see,' she replied, wide, laser-white smile still in place. 'If I could just take the name of your party, and I'll get someone to show you to the table.'

'Yes... it's umm, Richard. I think.'

Her smile didn't flicker as she replied. 'I'll just check for you. Ah yes, the rest of your party is already here. Excuse me for one second.' She turned and headed into the main restaurant on four-inch heels so thin they practically defied physics.

'Well, I hope you're suitably impressed by my eloquence,' I said, running a hand back over my hair in an attempt to smooth the wisps that the light breeze had dislodged.

Matt's hand found mine and squeezed it lightly. 'It's natural to be nervous. Don't worry about it.'

'I was babbling like a baboon,' I whispered back. 'I expect she's gone off to ask security to remove us.' I'd mistakenly thought this second meeting wouldn't be so bad. I mean, at least I'd met my mother, but, as it was, my nerves felt like exposed wires, sparking and crackling as they made contact with my thoughts.

Matt's chuckle rippled through me. 'You weren't. And security can try.'

'Good point. At least while they're both trying to move you, I can sneak in.'

'Ah, now comes the truth of why you invited me this evening.'

The ghost of a smile forced its way through my nerves. 'Rumbled.'

He grinned back. My hand was still wrapped within his own and his thumb moved lightly back and forth over my skin.

'Good evening,' the young waiter who appeared with the return of the perky blonde greeter addressed us. 'If you'd like to follow me, I'll show you to your table.'

'Thank you,' I replied, before glancing back to thank the woman, catching her giving Matt a surreptitious once-over.

We followed the man towards the far end of the restaurant to what was, from its position, obviously considered a prime table.

'I think I'm going to be sick,' I whispered.

'No, you're not,' Matt whispered back. 'Just remember to breathe.'

'Bloody hell, I knew there was something else on my to-do list.'

There was that low, deep chuckle again, turning down the power on my flickering nerves. I was so thankful for his company, and his ease despite being plonked in the middle of what could be quite an awkward, emotional meeting.

'Here we are.' The waiter went to pull out my chair but the man next to my mother at the table was already out of his seat.

'I can do that.' He was softly spoken with a kind smile and no distinguishable accent.

The waiter nodded, smiled and left us.

'Hello, Fleur.' Elodie extended both her hands and I took them, grateful that she hadn't expected a familial kiss or a hug. She smiled and I could see in her eyes that she wanted all that. Maybe I did too but right now there was still too much time, too much pain, too much of everything between us and I couldn't forget all that just yet. Considering all I'd longed for for so many years was to be part of a family, to be wanted, to have everything I felt I'd missed out on, I realised the irony that I was now the one holding back.

'Hi, Elodie. It's nice to see you again.' And I meant it. 'You know my friend, Matt. He was kind enough to drive tonight.'

'It's a pleasure to see you again, Matt.'

'Nice to see you too.' He shook my mother's proffered hand firmly but gently.

'May I introduce my husband, Ralph Richard?'

Matt took the man's hand as my hands were currently tucked firmly into my dress pockets. They didn't advertise dresses with pockets as perfect for those awkward moments when you met the father you never knew but it was definitely something they should consider.

'Pleased to meet you, Mr Richard.'

'Ralph, please,' he replied, pronouncing it without the l, just as Elodie had.

'Ralph,' Matt repeated with a crisp nod.

'Hello, Fleur.' His voice cracked as he spoke my name and his hazel eyes filled with tears. 'Sorry.' He shook his head, busying himself suddenly with trying to extricate a handkerchief from his pocket, which seemed unwilling to be pressed into service. Elodie tapped his arm and handed him a tissue before placing her hand protectively over his forearm as he mopped at his eyes and gave his nose a wipe for good measure.

'It's fine,' I said, my heart already softening towards the man who hadn't even known I existed. I felt a twist in my stomach and switched my gaze to my mother. This was her fault. But as I saw his pain reflected on her own face, I knew that anything I held against her couldn't begin to measure up to the regret she already felt for hurting this man in her naïve and inexperienced belief that she was doing the best thing for him.

'Here, let me get your chair,' Ralph said, hastily shoving the tissue into his trouser pocket.

'Thank you,' I said as he positioned the chair for me and placed my napkin on my lap. 'You could probably get a job here if you wanted.' I snapped my mouth shut before opening it again immediately to apologise. 'Sorry. I have a habit of saying daft things when I'm nervous.'

'Me too!' he said, a joyful tone to his words, lightness replacing the pain his face had shown moments before, seemingly thrilled to find a similarity so soon. 'It's led to some interesting job interviews, I have to say.'

I giggled then and he followed suit, both of us releasing tension so that a palpable sense of relief extended around the table. 'I'd like to hear about some of those.'

'And I'd love to tell you.' His eyes filled again. 'Oh, bloody hell. Silly old fool.' He spoke almost to himself as one hand reached for the tissue again, the other resting on the table. Instinctively I covered it with my own and his head lifted, gaze connecting with mine. I didn't have any words but it seemed I didn't need any. Tentatively he placed his other, now free, hand over mine and let the tears flow unchecked onto the crisp white linen of the tablecloth.

* * *

'How you doing?' Matt asked as we drove home several hours later. I'd left my parents with the promise to see them again before long. They were heading home to Cambridgeshire in the morning as my father had lectures to give. Finding out he was a fellow of Christ's College, Cambridge had been a bit of a surprise but I'd immediately pictured him engrossed in some subject, piles of books and papers around as his alert, inquisitive eyes alighted on new and interesting information. When I'd alluded to this, my mother had laughed and told me I'd read him exactly right.

'I'm afraid we had to come to the decision that Elodie would stay away from my home study for her own mental well-being. Instead, when I'm at home, we meet for coffee in the kitchen so that she doesn't have to see the mess.'

'But I suppose you know where everything is, despite how it seems to others?'

'Good God, no! Not a bloody clue. I spend half my life trying to find something I knew I had yesterday.'

'I'm OK, thanks. Better than I thought I would be, if you really want to know.' I replied.

His hand went briefly to my knee before returning to the steering wheel. 'I always really want to know. And good, I'm glad.'

'I hope you weren't bored.'

'Not at all. They're interesting people.'

'They are, aren't they?'

Silence settled over us again for the next couple of minutes but it was the comfortable sort. The type you didn't feel you need to fill and could merely enjoy the peace it brought.

'Thanks again for coming. I do appreciate it.'

'Thanks for inviting me. It was a pretty big thing you did tonight and I'm privileged you felt comfortable enough to want me with you.'

'It helped having you there.'

'Then I'm here the next time too.'

I stared out of the windscreen, his words echoing around my brain. Was he? Could he really make that promise? We were just friends and there was every chance that at some point he wouldn't be there. That someone else would need him first. I accepted that. I knew how it worked. People left. Sometimes, like tonight, they came back into your life, but I had the feeling that was very much the exception rather than the rule.

'You shouldn't make promises you can't keep.'

'I don't.'

I looked at him, and, briefly, he took his eyes off the road to look back. In the low light of the car, I could make out the planes of his face, the set of his jaw and the determination in his eyes and knew that he meant what he said.

26

Turning my head, I checked out the back of my pale yellow bridesmaid dress in the mirror, making sure I hadn't got it tucked in my pants. As Rumi had opted for a traditional Indian wedding this was my first experience of being a bridesmaid, and I didn't want the key memory of it to be flashing my knickers to the gathering following my last-minute nervous wee.

'Right, that's better,' I said, returning to the spare bedroom in the Morgans' farmhouse that had been commandeered as Bride Central for the morning. 'You sure you don't need one?'

Anna shook her head. 'No, I'm fine, thanks.'

I reached up and adjusted one of the late summer flowers that Anna had made her headdress with. The crown of flora looked perfect on her and complemented the ethereal design of the dress she'd chosen. Pale ivory silk swished softly, the shape on her slim frame created by the two ties at the waist, which I'd knotted into a draping bow behind her. 'You look amazing.'

Her smile, enhanced by the light make-up done for both of us by an old schoolfriend of Andy's in the village, was radiant.

'How are you so calm?' I laughed, shoving my hands into the in-seam pockets in my dress – a genius design.

'I have no idea.' She giggled back. 'I thought I'd be super nervous but I feel totally calm. I guess it's just meant to be.'

'I think you're right,' I said, pulling a tissue from said pocket and dabbing my eye gently, fearful of ruining the make-up.

'Oh, no! You can't start that.' Anna laughed. 'You'll set me off!'

'Sorry. Sorry!' I laughed, turning away and making a concerted effort to pull myself together. 'I'm just so happy for you both and this is just...' I gave her a shrug. 'All so wonderful.'

Anna reached out and took my hands in hers. 'I know the route wasn't ideal but I'm so glad you ended up here. You know how much I feel like this is where you're meant to be.'

I wasn't sure if that was true, but I did know that, since moving to Wales, I was the happiest I'd ever been. Here I had the space, both figuratively and literally, to discover who I really was, and who I wanted to be, rather than who other people wanted me to be.

'Knock, knock.' Greg's voice preceded him poking his head around the half-open door.

'Come in!' Anna said, smiling widely.

'How are my girls?'

At this both of us smiled and I had to have some serious internal words with my eyes, warning them not to fill up again. The simple phrase went straight to my heart. Maybe Anna was right. Maybe this was where I was supposed to be.

'All ready?' he asked. 'Wow.' Greg looked from one of us to the other. 'You both look so beautiful.'

'No-o-o-o!' Anna laughed as Greg began to well up. 'I've already told Fleur she can't cry!'

'A manly man like me crying?' Greg said, puffing out his

barrel chest. 'I don't know what she's talking about, do you, Fleur? Never heard such rubbish.'

I giggled and the nervousness I'd felt earlier finally dissipated. All I felt now was joy and excitement.

'Shall we get this show on the road, then? That boy down there will be thinking you aren't coming.'

'I'm ready if you are,' I said, turning to Anna.

'More than ready.'

'OK, then, let's go.'

I positioned myself behind Anna and gathered up the gossamer train that fell in delicate folds from the shoulders of her dress like angel wings and followed behind as Anna took Greg's arm. Proudly he led her down the stairs and to the garden where the guests, and Andy, were waiting.

* * *

'Anna must have used one of her spells to get this weather,' Matt said, having made his way through a throng of people gathered outside the marquee, all enjoying the Indian summer.

'Oh, shoosh,' I said, batting him on the arm. 'Just because she's a little more bohemian than you doesn't mean she's a witch.'

'I've never said she's a bad witch. She's like one of those white witches. Wiccans.'

'It's a good job she isn't – you'd probably have been turned into a toad long ago.'

'There are those that would argue I already am one.'

I pulled a face, signifying that I could see how that might be possible.

'Oi!' His long fingers pinched gently at my waist.

'You still shouldn't say that though. You know some people

around here haven't accepted her because she dresses and thinks a little differently.'

'And she brightens up the place by doing so. If I do hear anyone saying anything against her, they can explain it to me.'

'Ooh, I love it when you're masterful!' My hand slapped up to my mouth as soon as the words had left it. 'I'm sorry. I don't know where that came from.' I glugged a swig of champagne and let my gaze dance everywhere but in front of me, where Matt stood. Suddenly I was aware of him moving closer, his body as close to mine as to almost, but not quite, touch.

'What are you doing?' I asked as he bent over.

He looked at me without moving his head, meaning that I was now dangerously close to that sexy mouth.

'Peering into that glass of fizz as I'm pretty sure that's where that comment came from. I'm looking to see if there are any more.'

'There aren't.' I replied with more conviction than I felt.

He waited until I met his eyes. 'Shame,' he replied. The rough-edged voice was low and teasing. I gave him a snooty look and did my best to hide the fact that my drink wasn't the only thing fizzing right now.

'Hello, my loves!' Bronwyn popped out through the crowd and walked, a teensy bit unsteadily, towards us, her arms out for a joint hug. 'Bloody ground's all uneven,' she said, looking down momentarily as Matt shot me a grin. 'Oh, you both looked so lovely up there, supporting Andy and Anna. Now, give me a hug.' Her arms were already wrapping around us and Matt's back curved as he dipped to a height comfortable enough to accept his mum's hug without her dangling off the ground. As she pulled us both close, Matt's arm curved around my waist, bringing us all closer.

'Such a handsome boy,' she said, standing back and

reaching up to her eldest son's face, catching his chin between her thumb and forefinger.

'Mum...'

'Aww, am I embarrassing you?' She gave a hearty laugh. 'A big, brave lad like you.'

'Mum,' he forced out between lips that were now squidged together into a chubby cupid's bow as Bronwyn laughed and finally let go. Matt moved his jaw left and right a couple of times following his mum's grip on it.

'Ah, Fleur already knows you're a handsome boy, don't you, love?'

I swallowed my mouthful of champagne and pretended to study my companion. Had my body been in charge of my mouth, God knew what my answer would have been, but as I wrangled back control, I fixed a disinterested look on my face and lifted my hand, tilting it one way then the other.

Bronwyn's laugh rang out again as she hooked an arm around mine, Matt snatching my glass out of my hand moments before his mum's ebullience tipped the rest of its contents down my gown.

'I'm so glad you came to stay with us, love. Aren't you, Matt?'

'Depends on the day,' he replied.

'Oh, don't you listen to a word of it. I've never seen him happier since you came, I swear. Who are you looking for?' she asked as her eldest peered over the top of her head.

'Dad,' he said. 'I was just wondering if he knows his wife's three sheets to the wind.'

'And I'll be four or five if I please. Thank you very much.'

Matt was too busy laughing to avoid the ensuing clip round the ear. 'Ow!'

'Ha! Good shot, Mum. What's my older but substantially uglier brother been up to this time?'

'Being a cheeky so-and-so and suggesting his own mother is drunk.'

'It wasn't a suggestion,' Matt replied, moving me swiftly in front of him as he finished the sentence.

'Oi! I'm not shielding you.'

His arms were linked around my shoulders, his body pressed close to the back of mine and I could feel the deep rumble of his laugh in his chest.

'Too late,' he said as his mum pretended to swipe at him and he ducked behind me. I was a most ineffective shield and enjoying the feel of his warm, hard body against mine way more than I should. But tonight I didn't care. Tonight was for celebrating love, and family and friends and laughter. And right now, in this little group that we made as Greg and Anna joined us, we had every one of those things and I didn't think I'd ever been happier.

At the other end of the marquee, the local band providing the music shifted tempo and couples began to gather and fill the dance floor that Matt and Andy had helped put down the day before.

'Would you care to dance, my love?' Greg lifted Bronwyn's hand gallantly to his lips as he made his request.

'I would, thank you.' She tilted her head up to accept the kiss he now placed on her lips – her sons definitely got their height from the paternal line – before he tucked her arm around his and led her to the dance floor.

Anna let out a sigh. 'Do you think we'll be like that when we've been married as long as your parents?' she asked Andy as she watched her new in-laws walk away.

'Absolutely.' The one word was said without hesitation or

doubt. 'And right now, I think we should follow their example.' He held out his hand and she placed her own slim one in it, grinning happily as they threaded their way through friends and family – mostly on Andy's side – to join Bronwyn and Greg.

'Guess that just leaves you and me,' Matt said as he released me from the circle of his arms. The loss of his body close to mine left a coolness in its place and I tried not to mind.

'I guess so.' I smiled up at him as I turned, my dress making a satisfying swishing sound as I did so. 'Although I'm sure you probably still have a tonne of people here to catch up with.'

His blue eyes scanned the room for a few moments before the gaze landed squarely back on my face.

'Probably. But none of them are as pretty as you so I think I'm going to stay right here if that's all right.'

That was way more than all right as far as I was concerned and I felt myself flush at the compliment. Thankfully the lights were lower now and I hoped Matt wouldn't notice. One corner of his mouth lifted and I knew I hadn't got away with it.

'It's so warm in here, you wouldn't believe it was nearly October, would you?' I said, looking away from him and flapping my hand ineffectually.

'Lots of hot bodies in here.'

I turned back slowly to meet the mischievous grin and Matt waggled his eyebrows a couple of times.

'You should know,' I replied.

'Oh... is that a compliment?'

'Err...' Now that he mentioned it, it did sound exactly like a compliment.

He tilted his head a little, awaiting my next words with interest.

'Actually it was more an allusion to the fact that you're the one usually surrounded by all the hot bodies.'

'Fleur French, are you jealous?'

'No!' I laughed. OK, maybe I was a tiny bit on blue days but that wasn't the point. 'I know what a pain in the backside you really are, even if you look OK.'

'See, that's one of the things I love about you.'

'One of the things?'

His grin widened. 'Stop fishing.'

'Fine. What is it that you "lo-o-o-o-o-ove" about me?' I widened my eyes as I said the word, lengthening it as I did so. I really had had far too much champagne.

'That you keep me grounded. Even halfway up a mountain with you, my feet and ego are firmly planted.'

'I've known men half as good-looking as you whose egos are three times the size.'

'Have you now?'

'Yep.'

'Hmm.' He rubbed his jaw, clean-shaven tonight in honour of the wedding. And also for a quiet life, as Bronwyn had been on at both Andy and Matt ever since the wedding had been announced that they were both to have a decent encounter with a razor for the wedding day, with no sign of that stubble the two of them often sported day to day.

'Does it feel strange?'

'What?'

'This...' I ran my thumb along his jawline distractedly, feeling the smooth skin beneath. His head turned so that his mouth was against my palm, his eyes holding mine and his lips placing the softest of kisses on the palm of my hand. I stood there, hooked on his gaze, a thousand fireworks shooting and fizzing through my body as I sucked in a deeper breath. His hand closed around mine, turning it gently and this time kissing the back of it.

'Would you like to dance?'

I nodded, the smile spreading across my face as his bright eyes crinkled at the edges and his wide mouth, a mouth that had unexpectedly featured in dreams I hadn't even told Rumi about, smiled, revealing straight white teeth, contrasting with his summer-tanned skin.

'I was hoping you'd say that.' His hand moved again, this time enclosing mine as he led us both to the dance floor where the band had just begun another slow-paced song. Matt's arm slipped around my waist and with the other, he held my hand out, mirroring the stance of his parents. Anna, meanwhile, had both her arms looped around her new husband's neck and they were gazing at one another, oblivious to the people, and world, around them.

'What's wrong?' Concern swept away the smile as Matt looked at me, his arm still comfortably wrapped around my waist.

'I...' I glanced around and then went up on tiptoe, trying to reach his ear. He bent to help me. 'I don't know how to dance like this.' I returned my heels to the floor and looked up at him.

'There's nothing to it,' he said, his arm tightening around me momentarily in support. 'Just hold on and we'll be fine.'

The tension still filled my body.

'What's up?'

I shook my head and focused my gaze on our joined hands.

'Oink oink.'

The daft words were enough to distract me and I felt the glimmer of a smile play at the corners of my mouth.

'What?'

'You just told a porkie.'

'I did not.'

'Oink oink!' he said again, this time louder.

'Shooosh!' I said, feeling the giggles build.

'Are you going to tell me what's wrong?'

'It's nothing!' I said, tapping him lightly on the waist to emphasise my words.

I saw him begin to open his mouth and I knew what was coming.

'Don't!' I warned him.

'Then tell me.'

There was a pause and, eyes fixed on mine, he took a deep breath and opened his mouth.

'OK!'

He snapped his mouth closed.

'You are—'

'Undoubtedly I am whatever you are about to say, but I'd rather talk about you.'

'Would you now?'

He watched me for a moment as the vintage tune played, and the singer crooned about a moonlight serenade.

'Definitely.' The words were soft and low, and I felt... I wasn't sure what I felt, only that it was something I'd never felt before. Not really. And I had the strangest sensation it might be love.

'So, what's up?' he said as, with the gentlest of movements, he pulled me a tiny bit closer and I revelled in the spread of his warm, large hand on my back through the soft fabric of my dress.

'I suppose I just feel a bit silly.'

'For what?'

My shoulders shrugged. 'For not knowing how to dance like this.'

Matt shook his head gently. 'You don't ever need to feel silly about anything, Fleur. And as for dancing, I think you're a natural.'

'I know that was your foot I just trod on, so thank you for the compliment but this time it's you telling porkies.'

His laugh was low, deep and, oh, so sexy. 'Fair enough. But like anything, it just takes a bit of practice.'

'Are you offering?'

'Would you accept?'

For a moment it felt as if everything fell away, the people, the music, all sound except for my own breath. We'd both had too much champagne and the cynical part of me knew that it was unlikely any of this would mean anything tomorrow. If it was even remembered. But right now, I didn't care. I shoved all those cynical thoughts into a room in my mind and bolted the door on it, shoving a wardrobe in front for extra security. I wanted to enjoy this. I *wanted* this.

'Yes,' I replied. 'I think I would.'

'Good,' he said before tilting his head back up, pausing as his lips became level with my hairline and placing the lightest of butterfly kisses there before gathering me just that little bit closer as we danced on.

The band announced a break and in their place an MP3 player hooked up to the speakers began pumping out 'YMCA' and the dance floor filled quicker than you could say open bar. Anna grabbed my hand as I went to leave and I, in turn, caught hold of Matt.

'No way!' He laughed.

'Oh, no, if I have to do this, so do you!' I shouted above the music.

He let me pull him onto the dance floor. Both of us knew if he'd wanted to, he could have kept going and I'd have had no chance of stopping him. It was like harnessing a Yorkshire terrier to an ox cart. But he turned, dipping down beside me to make himself heard as hard muscled arms tightened momentarily around my waist.

'You owe me for this.'

'Oh, do I?' I shouted back as he stood.

'Oh yeah,' he called back and the promises wrapped up in those two words sent a rush of heat to my face – and a few other places. I danced opposite Anna, alongside the two brothers and we shouted the words of the song into the noise around us and absorbed the joy of it all.

* * *

Bronwyn had rostered everyone who was at the wedding off for the following day, and I, for one, was very glad. I woke up and cursed whoever had authorised the emergency roadworks in the village this morning. That was until I realised the searing noise I was cursing was coming from inside my own skull. I pulled the pillow around my ears as if that would help and turned over, groaning painfully as I did so. Which was when I came face to face with Matt Morgan.

'Oh, shit.'

27

'I have to say I've had more flattering greetings first thing in the morning.'

That I had absolutely no doubt of. He'd looked hot yesterday but now, sleep rumpled and morning gravel adding to the normal rough-edged voice, he was active volcano caldera hot.

'Sleep OK?' he asked when I remained mute.

'I think it was probably more akin to unconsciousness rather than sleep, if I'm honest.'

'I think you might be right.'

'Can I ask you something?'

'Yep.'

'And don't take this the wrong way.'

He did a lazy, sleepy half-smile that, had I had more energy and less construction noise in my brain, would have broken any and all reservations. 'This sounds like it's going to be good.'

'What the hell are you doing in my bed?'

'And good morning to you too.'

'Yeah, I know. Sorry. But...' Oh God. I peered under the

bedclothes, careful to keep my eyes focused forwards, and discovered I was at least clothed, albeit in one of my less salubrious T-shirts, which also appeared to be on backwards. Could have been worse.

'Are you... um...?'

'Boxers,' Matt replied, showing no intention of moving any time soon.

'Right. And where were you when I...?' I made a vague gesture over the area of my body under the bedclothes.

'Bathroom.' He nodded his head towards my cosy en suite.

'Ah. OK. And remind me again why you're here.'

'Because you asked me to stay.'

'I did?' Colour began creeping up my chest and filling my face at the thought of what else I might have asked him to do.

'Why?'

He shifted onto his back, arms folded behind his head, showing off impressive guns, which really wasn't helping matters. He rolled his head to the side so that he was facing me.

'Who am I to question your motives?'

'I don't have any motives!' I said in a pitch that was way too high for a Sunday morning, let alone a Sunday morning playing host to a raging hangover.

Matt winced.

'Sorry,' I said, returning my voice to its normal timbre.

''S OK.' His eyes were drifting closed again. I prodded him in the arm. 'Huh?'

'Don't go back to sleep.'

'Why not? It's Sunday. I'm tired. And I'm hungover.'

'And you're still in my bed!'

'Even better,' he said, sleepily through half-closed lids.

'Matt.'

'Hmm?'

His eyes were fully closed now and he looked so peaceful. Before I could speak again, his breathing slowed to the deep and regular pattern of sleep and I didn't have the heart to wake him.

Holding onto my head with one hand in an attempt to stop my brain shaking any looser than it already felt, I slid out of the bed and, stealing another look at Matt's sleeping form, padded over to the bathroom and closed the door. Slumping down on the loo seat, I rested my head on the cool porcelain of the vanity unit and pulled out one of the drawers beneath it. Two headache pills and several glasses of water later, I cleaned my teeth, had a shower and pulled the door open a crack. Matt was still out for the count. I crept out, opening the large armoire stealthily, praying it wouldn't creak. Snagging some undies, a cuddly jumper and some joggers, I did a cartoon Pink Panther stalk back to the bathroom and got changed.

When Matt woke again over an hour later, I was curled up in the armchair by the window reading. Apparently we hadn't got around to closing the curtains last night and he was clearly one of those annoying types who could sleep with them open.

'Hey, you,' the rough voice croaked out.

I looked up from my book. God, he looked good. Wa-a-a-ay too good. I set my expression to normal and gave him a brief smile.

'Hello.'

'What you reading?'

'A book called *Shadowlands*.'

'Sounds Hobbitish. I didn't think you were into all that.'

'I'm not. And it's not. It's non-fiction and about lost villages and ghost towns of Britain.'

'Now that sounds more like you.'

'Does it?' I asked, genuinely interested.

'Yep,' he said through a yawn as he pushed himself up in the bed exposing a rock-solid, muscle-sculpted chest. *Yeah, Matt. That's really helping matters. Thanks.*

'Oh,' I said, because frankly, with the surprise sight of Matt's half-naked body on display, that was all I could manage for the moment.

'How come you're looking as human as that and I feel like I just crawled out of the primordial swamp?'

If that was what men in there looked like, someone get me a cossie, because I was going in!

'Oh. Water. Lots of it, and painkillers.'

'I don't suppose you've got any more of those tablets, have you? It feels like I'm hosting the final of *Strictly* in my skull right now.'

A smile slid onto my face as I unfolded my tucked-up legs and stepped towards the bathroom. 'Argh!'

'Shit! Are you OK?'

I grabbed onto the bottom of the bed and hauled myself back up. 'Yep. Hadn't realised that leg was asleep.' I gave it a quick massage and felt the blood flowing through, bringing life back to my limb.

'God, you went down like a sack of spuds!' Matt's chuckle was deep, rough and annoyingly sexy.

'Flattering. Thank you. I didn't see you rushing to help me. Too busy bloody laughing.'

This made him laugh even more.

'And all in the pursuit of trying to help you. Hmmf,' I said, finally making my way to the bathroom now that both legs were back in working order. 'No good deed goes unpunished,' I called out as I popped out two painkillers and filled the glass I'd been using with fresh water before taking them both back to Matt.

'Thanks. You're a lifesaver.' He placed both pills in one hand and palmed them into his mouth, swallowing them with one large gulp.

'There's no point sucking up to me now.'

'Oh. Rumbled.'

'Completely.' I perched on the edge of the bed.

'Do you have plans for today?'

'Something quiet,' I said, holding my finger to my lips before pointing at my head.

'Sounds good. If you're free, I might know just the place.'

I flopped forward on the bed across Matt's legs, which were still buried under my duvet. 'Oh God.' My voice was muffled thanks to my face being smooshed in the bedding. 'Does it involve hiking? I can't...'

The way too pleasant sensation of Matt's large hand on my back stilled my thoughts, and my objections.

'No. It involves you and me going – in a car,' he emphasised, 'to get the second-best Sunday lunch in the county.'

'Why don't we get the best Sunday lunch?' I said, tucking my feet up and wiggling round to face him. His hand drifted from my back to my side and I happily let it.

'Because the best one is my mum's and she's off today.'

'Ah. Good point. So, where's this other one?'

'A cosy pub tucked away between the mountains that only locals know about.'

'And me, if I go with you.'

'You're a local.'

'Not really. I'm from London.'

'You're an honorary local.'

'Am I?' The smile spread on my face.

'Absolutely.'

'Ooh, thanks.'

His reply was a gentle squidge of his hand on my waist.

'So how come we're not going for breakfast?'

Matt stretched one arm out and snagged the clock from my bedside table. 'Because this.'

I was now propped up on one elbow, the weight of Matt's other hand still resting comfortably on my side, and my tired eyes focused on the clock, widening as the message meandered its way to my brain.

'That is *not* the time!' I said, grabbing the clock along with his hand.

''Fraid so,' Matt said through a yawn as he stretched again to return the clock to where it lived. 'Hence my suggestion of lunch rather than breakfast because I think we well and truly missed that window.'

A giggle escaped. 'Whoops.'

'Yep.'

'I have one more question.'

'You have no sympathy for a bloke with a raging hangover, do you? One question after another.'

'You have a lot of confidence for someone who's still lounging in someone else's bed.'

'What's the question?'

'Where were you supposed to spend last night?'

'Mum's spare room.'

'Are they going to notice you didn't stay there?'

'That's two questions.'

I pulled a face.

'No. They're not. I always leave it as tidy as I found it. Some old military habits are hard to shake.'

'Being tidy is one habit I'd be quite happy for a boyfriend to have.'

One dark brow rose, a sexy half-smile on the lips I'd spent

yesterday evening doing my best – which had turned out to be pretty poor – not to focus on.

'It's just an observation. That's all. But while we're on the subject... sort of.'

'I thought you said you only had one more question...'

'Yeah, well...' I waved my hand. 'Things change.'

Matt shoved himself further up in the bed so that the sheet now sat at the bottom of his flat abs. He was, undoubtedly, the hottest man I'd ever had in my bed. And I was no longer in it...

'OK. Let me have it.'

'Huh?' I said, my attention snapping back from somewhere it really shouldn't be. 'Oh.' I shuffled a bit more until I was sitting cross-legged on the other side of the bed. Matt was watching me with that slow, lazy smile, which really wasn't helping, considering the question I had currently bouncing around my brain.

'Wow. That bad, eh?'

'What?'

'The look on your face and that cute blush has given me a pretty good idea what this question might be.'

'Really?'

'Uh-huh.' He swung his legs out of the bed and hooked his overnight bag towards him. Reaching in, he grabbed a white T-shirt and pulled it over his head. It fitted in all the right places and I watched his back muscles ripple as he shrugged it down his body.

'So, are you going to tell me?' I asked as he shook out a just-battered-enough pair of pale Levis that, when he slipped them on, hugged his bum so well I was momentarily jealous of a piece of denim.

'And save you the blushes? Nope,' he said, turning as he did up the buttons. 'Why would I spoil that fun?'

'You're actually quite mean, aren't you?'

His eyes flashed with mischief as he fished out his tooth-brush and padded towards the en suite.

'You can have a shower here if you want.'

'Had one last night,' he said around a mouthful of tooth-paste. 'But thanks for the hint.'

'That wasn't what I meant!'

He peered around the door.

'It wasn't!' I insisted.

He disappeared again, brushing for another couple of minutes. Some splashing and a slightly shocked sound came as, I assumed, he washed his face in cold water, until he appeared in the room once more.

'I didn't mean you were smelly.'

'Sure, you didn't,' he said, calmly squirting a small amount of aftershave from a bottle I couldn't see the name of before dropping it back in his bag.

'I didn't!' I said, aiming to give him a gentle-ish thump to reinforce my words but his reactions were quicker. He caught my hand, clasping it firmly within his own. Before I could react, his other hand reached for my free one, gently pinning that to my side.

'Just in case I'm mistaken, why don't you tell me what it is you want to know?'

'Huh?' Right now the only thing registering in my brain was that I was remarkably close to a very hot man and neither of us, unlike last night, could blame it on alcohol. I raised my gaze and watched as his eyes met mine, then slowly lowered to my lips, lingering there for a long moment before they lifted again.

'Tell me,' he breathed.

'I... umm... I don't know.'

'Liar.'

Shit. I'd forgotten how good he was at sniffing out bullshit. Fine. Two could play at that.

'OK, then, Mr Smarty Pants.' I tilted my chin up defiantly. I still only reached his chest. Minor detail. 'You tell me.'

'You want me to tell you what your question was?'

'Well, you seem so sure I haven't forgotten it. Maybe you could remind me?'

'Maybe I could.'

Ha. He was totally bluffing. He had no idea. I knew it!

'Go on, then,' I said, looking as sassy as I was able to with my arms loosely pinned to my sides.

'You're wondering if we slept together.'

Matt's reply was a statement, not a question, as he was clearly aware he was hitting the nail squarely on the head with an enormous mallet.

'No, I wasn't.' I did my best to make my reply sound as cool and casual as possible – not easy when my face was burning so bright I was at risk of being mistaken by Search and Rescue as a warning flare.

'You feeling warm?'

'Nope. Cool as a cucumber, me.'

'By the fact you're asking, I'm assuming you don't remember a lot about last night.'

'Some. Just not... all of it.'

His broad chest expanded and then he breathed out, which really wasn't helping matters. 'I see.' Matt let go of my hands. 'Well, that is a shame.'

'It is?'

'Yep,' he said, reaching down for his bag. 'You ready to go?'

'What? No! Why is it a shame?' I scooted over and placed myself in front of the door. This was, obviously, like putting a dormouse in front of a hippo and expecting a favourable outcome but I had to make the effort.

Matt looked at me, looked at the door, and gave a small shake of his head. One point to the hippo. 'Do I look like a bloke who'd kiss and tell?'

'It's not kiss and tell when you're talking to the other person you may or may not have kissed!' I said, shifting to one side as his hand reached for the doorknob.

'That's true. Most of the time, the other person involved doesn't need telling but...' He let out a dramatic sigh and that was when I saw it. That hint of a smile.

'You lying—' I had no idea what word was coming next but, as it turned out, I didn't need to think of one because Matt conveniently cleared my head of all thoughts altogether. His mouth was soft but strong as his lips pressed against mine and my body responded, seemingly without need of instruction from my brain. My brain had in fact, decided it wasn't needed at all for the moment and was kicking back as the rest of my body was doing just fine without it. In one swift movement, Matt had scooped his hands under my backside and his body was now pressing mine against the door, my legs wrapped around his waist, as his lips moved from mine and I felt the loss of them before they reconnected with my skin just under my jawline. I tilted my head back a little to savour the feeling and he let out a small groan of pleasure as I did so, continuing the trail of kisses down to the hollow at my throat before sweeping slowly back up to meet my hungry mouth.

'So,' I said, slightly breathless as we both came up for air. 'Did we do this last night?'

'Oh God, yes. And so, so much more.'

'We did not.' I giggled as I wrapped my legs tighter. He slid his hands round to my thighs and met my eyes.

'No, we didn't. Unfortunately. You were completely plastered and I have strong rules about that.'

'Good to know you have ethics.'

'Yep. That and I don't like to waste my talents on someone
who's not even going to remember it.'

'You know you're setting yourself up for failure, don't you?'

He leant in and kissed just to the left of my mouth. 'I
promise I'm not,' he whispered before his lips met mine and I
lost all interest in food.

'We need to get you some lunch,' Matt said, pulling away
and helping me gently to the floor.

'Funnily enough, I'm not hungry.'

'You might not be right now but you will be.' He took one of
my hands in his and grabbed his bag with his other. 'You drank
a lot last night and I mean – *a lot*.' I gave him a gentle, but heart-
felt, thump and he gave a low chuckle. 'You need food.'

'Spoilsport.'

Matt closed his eyes and let out a breath before answering.
'Believe me, this is literally one of the hardest decisions I've
ever made.'

'Hardest, eh?' I giggled like a teenager.

The smile slid onto his lips as Matt quickly pulled me close
against him. 'So hard.'

With the evidence I had at that moment, there was no
option but to agree.

28

While Matt took a few minutes to make himself presentable by thinking about whatever it was that he needed to do the job, I dashed into the bathroom to whip off my jumper and joggers, and slip quickly into a ruffle-edged wrap dress I'd bought on my last shopping trip with Anna. The irony of me zipping out of view to change when I'd just been kissing Matt's face off and would happily have dragged him into bed that moment did not escape me but there we are. I was an enigma. Or in need of sustenance. One of the two.

'Nice!' Matt wiggled his eyebrows as I returned to the room and sat on the bed to pull my boots on, inadvertently giving him a flash of thigh. That was the only thing about wrap dresses. They were flattering on pretty much everyone but they were also the one item most likely to cause you to show your knickers to passing traffic on a breezy day. Luckily I'd bought new knickers when I'd been out with Anna too so at least there was that.

* * *

'Are you OK to drive?'

'Yep. All good. You OK to be a passenger?'

'Funny,' I said, belting myself in. 'I'd have thought you'd have checked that I wasn't going to throw up before you kissed me if you were that worried.'

He screwed up his face. 'Nice image. Thanks.'

I shrugged.

'But if you want to know, I hadn't actually planned any of that and frankly there wasn't a lot of thinking going on.'

He turned over the engine of the Subaru four-wheel drive, taking his own vehicle this time rather than the hotel's.

'I'm not quite sure how to take that.'

Matt turned, catching my chin in his hand and snatching another kiss. 'Believe me, it's a compliment. And also, all your fault.' He pointed the car up the drive and turned out onto the quiet road.

'My fault?'

'Yep.'

'How did I guess? OK.' I folded my arms. 'This should be good. Do tell how you pinning me against the door for a snog was in any way my fault.'

'Ooooh, you really liked that, didn't you?'

'Not the point,' I said, willing the satisfied smile threatening to spread all over my face to stay in my mind.

'Ha!' He laughed, a deep, warm, relaxed sound filling the car and wrapping itself around me. 'I knew it.'

'Stop avoiding the question.' Matt didn't answer. 'Oi.' I poked a finger in a rock-hard thigh.

'Huh. Oh, sorry. Just thinking about you against a door. Also, ow!'

'You're supposed to be concentrating on the road.'

'I am. I'm multitasking.'

'You can't. It's impossible. Except perhaps for mothers. Some of them seem to have superpowers. Otherwise studies have proved you can't. You actually just switch your brain to and from one task meaning you're not actually doing either task efficiently.'

'I hate to contradict these studies and I also agree about the mum thing. But there are times when being a soldier involves multitasking too.'

'Fair enough. There was actually something in the study that mentioned sometimes it's vital so...' I didn't want to think about Matt in danger zones. He didn't talk about it much but I knew from his mum he'd lost a couple of good friends in Afghanistan, one of whom was a local lad. Her eyes had filled when she'd spoken about him and I'd subtly changed the subject. 'But could you just do me a favour and think only about driving right now?'

Matt slid his hand over to my thigh and I laid my own hand over his. The movement had been natural, almost automatic, and he turned his hand to hold mine for a moment. 'It's a hard ask but OK.'

'How far is this magical place?' I said, nosing out of the window as we turned onto another, even smaller road.

'Almost there. Don't worry. It does exist, I promise.'

'Good. Because you can explain it to my stomach if it doesn't.'

'Not sure I'd want to. Sounds like you've got a grizzly bear tucked away in there.'

Matt slowed as we rounded a corner and there, on the left, stood a picture-perfect pub. Its Welsh-slate roof glinted in the sunshine and freshly painted white walls set off the host of bright, clashing flowers that had been planted in an array of containers from a pair of old wellies to a tin bath that I suspected had a history of its own to tell.

Matt pulled into one of the few remaining spaces and parked before leaning over and plonking a quick kiss square on my lips. With that he hopped out of the car and was round my side before I'd hauled anything more than a leg out. Taking his hand, I forced the rest of me out, helped by the delicious smell of roast dinner wafting on the crisp mountain air.

Matt locked the car, my hand still in his.

'You ready to go in?'

'Are we going to get a table?' I scanned the almost full car park.

'Yep,' Matt replied, catching hold of the twisted iron handle attached to the solid door and opening it. 'I messaged Owen earlier and he said he'd reserved one. After you.'

'It's obviously popular.' The place was full, from what I could see. 'Lucky he had one free.'

'A few years ago Andy and I were part of a mountain rescue team that found his boy and some friends after they got lost. The path had been washed away and it can be pretty hard to find the right way when that happens. Add in some bad weather that came in faster than predicted and it all got a bit hairy.'

'Were they all OK?'

'Yep. Good result. And worked out pretty well for everyone on the team as we all have an open invitation here. And the food is...' He did a chef's kiss and I giggled.

'Matt!' The man walked towards us, barrel chested, with a booming voice and, as I now found out, a good strong hand-shake. 'So good to see you. And is this Mrs Matt?'

'Oh... erm...'

Matt squeezed my hand with his free one.

Owen winked at me. 'We live in hope. Have a good time yesterday, did you both?'

'Yeah, thanks.'

'Well, you'll be wanting some food, then. Let me show you to your table.'

* * *

'You were right. That was second only to your mum's roast.'

'Good, eh?'

'Very. Thanks for bringing me.'

'Thanks for letting me. Room for pudding? They're just as good as the mains.'

I placed a hand on my tummy. 'Oh God, I couldn't. I'm going to go pop if I eat anything else.'

'Fancy a walk to help it go down?'

'I'm not sure about that. You might have to roll me out of here as it is.'

29

'This is stunning!' Below me an indigo-blue lake contrasted with the deep green of the grass and grey slate of the rocks around it.

'I'm glad you like it. It's one of my favourite places.'

'It's pretty hidden away,' I said, soaking up the crisp air that smelled so different from the air I'd got so used to over the years. It smelled fresh, and sharp and, well, clean. I sucked it down into my lungs.

'That's rather the point.'

I looked round to where Matt was now sitting on a large boulder, its once sharp edges smoothed away by centuries of rain and wind scouring its surface. He held out a hand and I found a foothold and clambered up to sit next to him, glad I'd worn flat boots. We sat together in an easy silence, staring out at the lake and the mountains that rose up behind it, Matt's hand resting at my waist.

'I spent a lot of time here when I got back from Afghanistan.' His face was still turned to the view and I remained silent, sensing there was more. 'Good hideout, plenty of tree cover. Not many people know about it.' He glanced across. 'It's not the easiest access route.'

'No.' I smiled. 'I can't remember the last time I had a piggy-back. And I'm pretty sure it wasn't over a mountain crevasse.'

His laugh was soft and he pulled me closer. 'It wasn't a crevasse.'

'It was massive! My legs wouldn't even stretch over it!'

'You just need longer legs.'

'Or smaller gaps in the mountainside.'

'But then everyone would know about it.'

'Fair enough. But don't fall out with me because I won't be able to get back!'

Matt brushed his lips against my ear. 'I have no intention of falling out with you.' His breath was warm and tickly.

'Glad to hear it,' I whispered back.

'Here.' He shuffled and I clambered over him to sit between his legs, now looking at the view from the same perspective. The downside was that I couldn't see his face but there was an upside in that I was leaning against his hard, muscled chest, his arms wrapped tight around me and, despite sitting on literally one of the hardest surfaces known to man, I don't think I'd ever been more comfortable.

His chin rested gently on the top of my head and we sat there, at ease with each other, listening to the birdsong and the soft rustle of leaves as a warm autumn breeze chased through the trees. I felt his breath, slow and steady.

'Did it make you feel better, coming here?' I asked eventu-ally, hoping I wouldn't break the spell but wanting to know more about this man I knew now for certain I was falling in love with.

'Mm-hmm.' He lifted his chin, kissed the top of my head and adjusted his arms as he moved. 'It did. Different people find different ways to process stuff. For me, the best thing was getting out into the landscape, away from the popular spots, and just walking. Looking at these views, taking in that big sky. Sometimes it's hard to believe that, at the same point in time, you have beauty and stillness in one place and absolute chaos and trauma somewhere else.'

I remained silent. There was nothing to say. I couldn't imagine what Matt had been through, what he'd seen, and there was no point pretending I could. Moving my arms, I tightened our embrace a fraction more. Matt kissed the top of my head again in response. We sat there a while longer, watching the scudding clouds cast shadows on the surface of the lake, deepening the blue of its waters, making them almost black before the sun chased them away, both of us absorbing the peace. I was hesitant to move, feeling the calm in this man who meant more and more to me each day.

'Matt,' I said eventually.

'Hmm,' he replied.

'I can't feel my bum.'

* * *

'This is nice.' Matt took my coat from me and hung it on the hook in the hallway as I peeked into the lounge.

'Want to see the rest?'

'Obviously.' Like most people, I was curious to nose around other people's homes and see what their style was, and, most importantly, what books they had on their shelves.

'And this is the main bedroom,' he said as we finished the tour.

'It's lovely, Matt.'

I meant it. The house had a good feel to it although Matt's

style was what one might kindly call utilitarian. One side of his mouth tilted up.

'You can be honest.'

'What? I am.'

The blue gaze hooked onto mine.

'OK. It's very... functional.'

'Mum says it looks like a barracks room expanded into a house.'

'She did? Oh. Well, I'm not sure about that. It's just... well, it's certainly not cluttered.'

The smile evened up.

'OK, fine. Personally I think it could do with a bit of colour and some soft textures, but each to their own. You know I love your mum to bits, but this is your house and if this is your style, that's perfectly OK.'

'I wouldn't say it's my style.' He gave a shrug as he led the way down the stairs and into the kitchen. 'Coffee?'

'Yes. Thanks. What do you mean, it's not your style?'

'It's not a "style" at all,' he said, making the gesture with his fingers after flicking on the kettle and, taking my hand, he pulled me towards him. 'It's just what I need.'

'If you're happy with how it looks and feels that's all that matters. Other people's opinions are just that. Their opinions. It's your house.'

'It's boring. And not very homely.'

'So.' I shrugged my shoulders. 'Make it homely.'

He stared down at me for a moment and the next moment I was in his arms and being plonked, albeit carefully, onto the sofa. Matt stood back, admiring his handiwork.

'It's looking better already.'

I made myself more comfy, tucking my socked feet up underneath me. 'Flattering, but that's not what I had in mind.'

'I know you didn't. But it's still an improvement.'

'Yeah. Well. The last time I lived with a bloke, it didn't work out so well.'

'Yes, it did. It worked out perfectly.'

'Matt. I got dumped, fired and evicted all in one go, in front of a packed restaurant.'

'Which left you free to move here and to go out with me.'

I looked up through my lashes at him. 'Are we going out, then?'

He knelt one knee on the sofa and leant forward, a straining biceps now either side of my head.

'You're going to make me ask, aren't you?'

'Absolutely.'

'Fine.' Matt leaned closer and brushed my cheek with overnight stubble growth as he kissed the sensitive part of my neck, just below my ear. 'Fleur French—'

'Actually, it's Richard. Technically speaking.'

He blew out a sigh but I felt his mouth curve into a smile against my skin. 'Fleur surname-to-be-determined, would you please go out with me?' His mouth moved down my neck as one hand teased the strap of the dress I'd worn under an open shirt, his lips following the same track, butterfly kisses flitting along my collarbone and shoulder, the straps of both my dress and bra being gently encouraged to slip. He was still bracing himself with one arm, his other hand momentarily gripping the side of my waist before it slid inside my dress and moved slowly upwards, his thumb brushing skin until it grazed the underside of my breast through the fine satin of my bra, setting free a bolt of heat throughout my body that escaped with a moan from my lips. Matt's mouth moved quickly to cover mine as he repeated the touch, this time brushing the tiniest bit higher. I moaned into his mouth and wrapped my legs around him, pulling him closer.

'Is that a yes?' he asked, pulling back, eyes now blazing with heat, that sexy half-smile on his mouth.

'It is.' I hooked my arms around his neck and gazed up. 'But I can always change my mind...'

Before I could say another word, Matt had flipped us both so that I was now sitting astride him, leaving both his hands free.

'Oh, I see. You want me to do all the work?' I teased, sliding my hands under his T-shirt and pushing it up to expose granite-hard abs and a line of dark hair trailing its way to the button fly of his jeans.

'Absolutely not. I just have plans to make sure you don't want to change your mind.'

'Oh, yes?' I did my best to maintain a dignified tone, but his fingers had moved fast, sliding up my back and unhooking my bra with a speed I wasn't going to question, merely appreciate as his hands cupped my breasts and began to tease them.

'Mm-hmm,' he said, skilled fingers still moving, 'and those are exactly the words I want you to be saying all afternoon.'

'All afternoon?' I forced out, my voice sounding hoarse and low, and unlike my own.

'At least,' Matt whispered as his hands moved towards the other strap of my dress...

* * *

'Wow. This is so yum! I didn't know you could cook.'

'You've met my mum, right?'

'And?'

He shrugged as he dexterously twisted spaghetti onto his

fork. 'She taught us both to cook when we were kids. Said she wasn't going to have sons who were a burden to their partners.'

'She did a good job.'

'I guess so. I've haven't poisoned anyone yet.'

I put the fork down and grabbed at my throat, my eyes bugging out as I did so.

'Funny girl.'

I grinned and picked my cutlery back up.

'Well, I'm very grateful to your mum.'

'I'll pass that on.'

I focused on my food.

'OK. So, what happened there?'

'Huh?'

'One minute you were fine and now you've gone all introspective.'

'I have not.' I had. Completely. But that wasn't the point.

'Sweetheart, I have certain skills and one of them is knowing when people are lying to me.'

That wasn't the only skill he had, that was for sure. No! Focus, Fleur.

'It's not lying. That makes it sound awful.'

'That's not how I meant it, Fleur.' He pushed his empty bowl away as I finished my last mouthful.

'I'm OK,' I replied with a laugh that I put all my effort into.

Matt pushed his chair back, reached over to the seat of mine and pulled it closer to his. Taking my hand, he pulled me gently onto his lap.

'You know you can tell me anything, right?'

'Mm-hmm,' I said, nodding, my fingers busying themselves with the toggle of the hoody I'd borrowed from him and was currently swimming in. His hand stilled mine and I looked up.

'I just...' I gave a small shrug. 'I don't know if your parents will be very impressed about... this.'

'This?'

'You, me... doing this.' I slid off his lap and padded over to the window, looking down the long garden and out onto the adjoining fields. A couple of sheep were up against the fence, chomping on the grass that grew there.

'OK. And what exactly are we doing?'

'Erm... having sex? I'm pretty sure you were there!' I turned back to face him.

'Yep. I was definitely there.' His back was straight and his gaze laser-focused. 'But,' he said, standing and taking the couple of strides necessary to close the distance, 'I was under the impression that this was way more than just sex. It is for me anyway.'

'That's not what I meant.'

'OK.' His voice was even, and when I looked up at his face, I couldn't tell anything from that either. 'What did you mean?'

'I... just. I don't want to upset your parents. They've been so good to me.'

A smile broke through the mask that had slid into place. 'You think this would upset them?'

I wrapped my arms around myself. 'I don't know. I think, maybe, I should have, you know, perhaps, thought about things more. The consequences of things. Before...' I flapped my hand between us.

'Before...?' He tilted his head.

'Before I seduced you.'

The laughter was sudden and warm and booming as Matt's hands settled at my waist and lifted me onto the nearby work-top. His eyes were still smiling as he dropped his hands down to rest on the top of my bum and positioned himself in front of me.

'What's so funny?'

'You. You're funny. And bright and beautiful. And sexy and cute.'

'Thank you. But you don't think I'm capable of seducing anyone, apparently.'

'Nope. That's not what I said at all. I think you're more than capable. I think you're super hot but you still didn't seduce me.'

'I didn't?'

'No. This…' He slid me closer and I automatically moved my legs so that he could stand between them, lessening the distance between us as much as I could. 'This, to me is so much more than just sex. I hope to you too but that can only be your decision. And for the record, my parents are nuts about you and have been trying to get us together pretty much since you arrived.'

'They have?'

'Yep.'

I looked down at where my hands rested on my lap, one fingernail agitating the thumb. I recognised it as a stress response and made a conscious effort to spread my hands on my thighs. 'Is that why I'm here now?'

Matt curled his finger and gently tilted my chin up towards his face.

'Oi.' The word was soft. 'You've known me for a while. Surely you know by now that I no longer take orders from anyone.'

My cheeks tinted pink. 'Not exactly true.'

There was that laugh again. 'Fair enough. I no longer take orders unless I am completely besotted with the woman directing me. Better?' His eyes flashed at the recent memory but my brain had got hooked up.

'Besotted?' I asked quietly.

'Totally,' he replied, resting his forehead against mine. 'Absolutely. Utterly. Incomprehensibly besotted.'

'I don't think anyone's ever been besotted with me before.' The smile was widening.

'Hard to believe, but also good. Saves me having any competition to dispose of.'

'Dispose of!' I squeaked.

He stood back, holding his palms up. 'I'm joking! Totally joking!'

'Yeah, well, you shouldn't say stuff like that when you're capable of doing it!'

He returned his hands to my back. 'Fleur, if I was going to do it, I'd have done it with that Jasper arsehole and, frankly, done the world a favour. Anyway, where was I?'

'Being besotted with me and assuring me your parents wouldn't mind.'

'Oh, yes. OK, so just to be clear – when I met you for the first time...'

'Yes?'

'Massive crush. Right there and then.'

'Really?'

'Yep. No word of a lie. I walked up and saw you and thought all my Christmases had come at once. And then I realised you weren't alone so I kind of had to stuff that all to the back of my brain and be completely professional.'

'You did a great job. I had no idea.'

'Training for keeping control of your emotions can come in handy in all sorts of situations.'

'I guess so.'

'And then you split up. Part of me was pleased.'

'Matt!'

'I know! I'm a horrible person. I felt bad for not feeling bad, honest. But he treated you like shit and, whatever the situation, you were better off without him.'

'And also homeless. Wait... was it your idea to get your parents to hire me?'

'Nope.' He held up his hands and I felt the loss of the warmth of them around my backside. 'Absolutely not. I actually warned Mum against it.'

'Wow. Thanks.'

The broad shoulders gave a shrug. 'I'm not a romantic. I didn't think, oh, wow, this is meant to be. I still thought you were lovely, but I also thought you'd probably end up going back to him. Frankly, when I took you back to London the next day, I didn't really think I'd be bringing you home again.'

'You thought I'd stay with Jasper.'

'Unfortunately, yes. Blokes like him tend to get what they want.'

'Maybe he did. I'm not convinced he wanted me back anyway.'

'Sweetheart, he absolutely did. Why do you think that woman was there? Why do you think he was so mad at me turning up? He was jealous as hell.'

'I just assumed he'd already moved on. And grumpy. You and I weren't together then anyway.'

'No. Much to my disgust. I thought I'd better give it a while before I showed any hint of what I felt. I didn't want to be a rebound.'

'You're most definitely not a rebound.'

'Glad to hear it,' he said, lacing my fingers through his own.

'And you think your parents will be OK?'

'Yesterday, just before the wedding, my mum came up to me and told me that if I didn't ask you to dance soon, someone else would and that would be that.'

'I see.'

'I couldn't risk that. So I asked you.'

'Lucky for you you're hot, so I said yes.'

His lips brushed mine. 'And the rest, as they say,' he whispered, 'is history.'

I hooked my feet around him and pulled him as close as I could, my hands going to the back of his neck, my fingers tracing the muscles there as we kissed. Matt's hands roamed up and down my legs before finally sliding up and under the oversized hoody. I let out a moan, my hands moving to grip his shoulders as he continued his exploration beneath the fabric.

'Any more orders?' he whispered.

30

'Oh my God!' Anna squealed as soon as I answered the video call.

'You're supposed to be on honeymoon,' I replied, laughing.

'I know, I know. And it's gorgeous. But this is amazing!'

'Is it?'

'Of course! Oh my God. He's had *such* a crush on you, hasn't he, love?' Andy's face appeared beside his wife's.

'Yep,' he agreed, sucking on a straw that led into a highly decorated cocktail.

'What's in that?' I asked, laughing. Andy was strictly a pint man.

'No bloody idea but it's delicious and alcoholic and that's enough for me.'

'So?' Anna asked. 'Have you...?' She raised her eyebrows.

I felt my cheeks redden.

'That's a yes, then.' Andy chuckled. 'Maybe he'll stop being such a grumpy bugger now.'

'He's not grumpy!' I said, automatically defending Matt.

'Not with you, he's not. He wants you to like him.'

'Oh, just ignore him,' Anna said, gently pushing Andy away. 'So? Are you happy?'

'Yeah,' I replied. 'Yes. I really am.'

And I was. I'd found my family and spoke to them every day. And now there was Matt.

When we weren't working, Matt and I had spent as much time together as we could, and when I stayed at his place, it felt natural and relaxed. I didn't feel like a visitor there. I felt as though I belonged. He'd even asked me to go shopping with him for some soft furnishings. I'd found a good, kind man I truly loved, and who loved me back for who I really was.

* * *

'Wow.'

Anna and I exchanged glances.

'Surely it can't be legal to have legs that long,' I said. 'Do you think part of her gym routine is on the rack?'

There was no doubt that Melanie, the TV starlet signed up to be filmed leisurely hiking the famous Welsh 3000s, guided by Matt, had a gym routine. There wasn't a bit of her that wasn't toned or perky. To top it all, she even looked good in a bobble hat.

'So, Matt darling, could we just have you over here?' The producer gave a vigorous headshake to the make-up chap who was desperately, albeit in vain, attempting to apply some powder to Matt's face. A face that right now looked thunderous. He held up a finger to them and instead strode over to where Andy, Anna and I were watching proceedings.

'I will never forgive you for this.' He ground out the words quietly as he stood face to face with his brother.

'Stop making such a big deal about it. It's going to be great publicity for the business.'

'We don't need any publicity.'

'Don't be daft, man. Every business needs publicity, especially if it's good. And that woman has billions of followers on social media.'

'Billions?'

'Well… I don't know. It's a lot. I know that.'

'Is that so? All the outdoorsy type, are they?' I was surprised Matt was getting any words out at all, considering how tight his jaw was. 'Hardly appealing to our ideal demographic.'

'Look, stop moaning and just get your arse over there. The sooner you do it, the sooner it's done and you can thank me later.'

'There's a reason I said I didn't want to do this and I still stand by it. Thank you? You're lucky I don't break your other leg.' He spun on the heel of his hiking boot and stomped towards the impromptu television set.

'It's her I feel sorry for, stuck with him up a bloody mountain,' Andy grouched.

Anna and I exchanged a look. The woman looked anything but unhappy about the possibility as she draped herself over Matt and the photographer snapped away for publicity shots.

'OK. Great! You look so good together,' he enthused. 'Right, shall we go and get some outside shots now?'

Matt threw me a glance but his face was impassive.

'I'll be there in a minute,' he told the photographer, who looked, momentarily, about to argue with him but decided against it. Wise move. Matt strode back to where his mum had now joined us.

'I'll see you in a bit, OK?' he said, apparently addressing all of us, but his eyes shifted to me. 'I don't want them to know about you and drag you into this circus too.' Matt flashed his brother another dirty look but Andy shrugged it off.

'You'll thank me in time,' he reiterated.

'Don't count on it.' With that Matt turned and walked back to where Melanie had chosen to wait for him. Flashing him a laser-white smile, she tucked her arm around his and together they left for the next photo shoot.

'Who is she, again?' Bronwyn asked.

'She's off one of those reality shows. Seems to be everywhere at the moment. It's great publicity.' Andy was sticking to his theory.

'Well, I'm glad you're not going, if I'm honest.' Anna's words were out before she thought them through. 'I mean...' She turned to me, her face full of heat. 'I didn't mean that anything's going to happen.'

'It's fine. As Andy says, it could be great publicity for you all. I'm sure the fact that they're both good-looking won't harm ratings for the TV, either.'

'Yep. Obviously they'd have been higher if I was doing it,' Andy said. Bronwyn laughed and I leant round Anna and flicked him on the ear.

'Wow, she's already posting things on her socials and tagging us in it. This is great,' Andy said, rubbing his ear.

We all leaned in to peer at the Instagram account Andy had pulled up on his phone. There was Melanie, looking trim and fit and beautiful with a smile a foot wide and Matt, looking far less cheerful but still incredibly hot. The photographer was right – they did look good together. But I trusted Matt. I trusted his decision not to disclose our relationship in case the production crew began bothering me. Although I did wonder if he had been open about it, perhaps Melanie would be less interested in climbing him rather than the mountains.

'Don't worry about it,' Anna said. 'She's not his type in the slightest.'

'What? Young, slim, fit and beautiful?' I gave a laugh but I wasn't convinced my heart was in it. Although I trusted Matt implicitly, there was no denying his companion was interested. 'It's all for the show,' Anna made another attempt. 'I saw her last boyfriend and he was kind of skinny. I don't think he's her type either.'

Oh, good. So she was single too. This was getting better all the time. 'Well, I'd better get on and start setting up for lunch.'

* * *

'The views up here are just spectacular.' Melanie posed to the lens as it panned around the landscape before finally settling on Matt, who, apparently unaware of the camera, slid his rucksack off his back, laid it against a rock and took a long pull on his water bottle. 'See what I mean?' Melanie said in a lowered voice, looking right down the camera lens before giving it a wink.

'Why are you even watching?' Anna's voice made me jump.

'Shit!' I picked up the phone off the floor. 'Stop ninja-creeping up on me.'

'Sorry. I did say hi but you were engrossed.'

'I'm not engrossed. I'm...'

The truth was, I didn't know what I was. The filming had been going on over a week now and I'd barely seen Matt other than on the screen. The 'team' had decided that it would be great for him and Melanie to spend time together outside the trekking. Initially they'd suggested he and Melanie share a hotel suite, but Matt had vetoed that immediately and no amount of cajoling or pouting by Melanie would change his mind. So that was something. But by the time he'd finished having dinner with her every night, with that being filmed to chop into the footage of the actual hikes, he was exhausted. I got the feeling it wasn't the hiking wearing him out. I knew he'd done the 3000s before in less than a day. I sensed the bigger problem was being constantly surrounded by the TV crew without getting any time to himself in the evening to decompress.

I'd gone over a couple of nights at his request, as my shifts worked out in time for me to see him, but conversation had been limited and, although there had been nothing obviously wrong, he'd seemed tense. He'd told me before that he still needed time to himself at times, to think things through, or conversely to not think at all.

'Would it be best if I left?' I'd asked.

'What?' Matt had been right beside me but miles away. 'No. No, sorry, sweetheart. It's just been kind of full on. I'm bloody mad at Andy for lumbering me with this.'

'I don't think he broke his leg on purpose, and you're nearly done now anyway. Didn't you say tomorrow was the last peak?'

'Yeah. I know. It's just shitty timing of him. That's all. This isn't my thing at all.'

'But you're a big proponent of exercise for mental health. That could be a good message from this.'

'You're right,' he'd said, throwing his arm around me. 'Sorry, I don't mean to be a grumpy bugger. How was your day?'

'It was OK. Same as usual really.' I'd snuggled in against the hard body and felt the security I loved as he'd wrapped his arms around me. 'Is she that bad, then?'

'Who? Melanie?'

'Yes.'

'No, not at all. She's nice, actually. I suppose it just goes to show you can't tell what people on telly are really like.'

'No... I suppose not.' We'd sat there for a little longer and Matt's breathing had settled in a steady rhythm. I'd known without looking that he was asleep. Carefully unwinding myself from his arms, I'd kissed his lips lightly and let myself out of his house.

* * *

'Hey.' I turned at the deep voice. 'What happened to you last night?' He kept his voice low and his body language neutral. Melanie was the other side of the restaurant, sipping on a camomile tea. They were tackling Crib Goch today and she was nervous. I'd made her the tea and told her it might help calm her nerves. She'd smiled but I saw through it. She was scared and I didn't blame her.

'He knows what he's doing,' I'd told her. 'You really couldn't be in better hands.' I'd regretted my particular choice of words the moment I'd spoken them but the sentiment was right.

'Yeah. I know. Thanks. I, like, totally trust him but I've seen the pictures of the ridge thing and just think shit!'

'It is kind of intense.'

'Still, I guess it's a good excuse to get closer to Matt if need be!' She'd laughed and I'd dredged up a smile. 'Not that anyone would need an excuse. I'm kind of surprised he's single, actually.'

'Oh... he is?'

'Yeah. That's what he told us.'

'You're right, that is surprising.'

I continued on with my task now. Matt touched my arm. 'Hey.'

'Hello.'

'What's up with you?'

'Nothing.'

'How come you left last night?'

'You fell asleep and I can get a better sleep in my own bed than on your sofa.'

'Are you going to actually look at me today?'

I turned around.

'Why didn't you wake me up? We could have gone to bed together.'

'I had an early shift and you were obviously tired.'

'I'm never too tired for you, you know that.'

'Melanie's over there. She's nervous about today so I made her a camomile tea and told her you'd look after her.'

'Is this bothering you?'

'Nope.'

'You're acting like it's bothering you. What are you worried about?'

'I'm not worried about anything,' I said, moving him out of the way to begin laying the table behind him.

'You're acting weird.'

'I'm not the one *acting* at all.'

'What's that supposed to mean?'

I didn't answer. After a couple of seconds, I saw Matt glance around then snag my hand and lead me into the snug. Closing the door, he turned back to me.

'OK, what's going on?'

'Nothing, but I need to finish setting the tables.' Matt mirrored my step as I moved to exit.

'Is this about the TV thing?'

'Nope.'

'I told you I didn't want to do it.' he continued, dismissing my answer.

'It was all arranged. You couldn't back out.'

'OK. So what's the problem because, honestly, Fleur, I'm not really in the mood for theatrics.'

'Says the man spending all his time with a woman off the TV.'

'This is about Melanie? For fuck's sake, Fleur. I thought you were OK with this.'

'Well, I had to be really, didn't I?' I threw up my hands. 'You didn't even speak to me about it.'

'Yes, I did!'

'No, Matt. What you did is told me you were doing it. And while I would never stand in the way of anything you wanted to do, if we're supposed to be together, then, from what I understand of *healthy* relationships, people talk about stuff. Discuss things. They don't just state that they're doing them.'

'I didn't have a choice. Andy bloody lumbered me with it. You know that!'

'I do, but that doesn't mean we couldn't still have a conversation about it! How do you think I feel with you going out with a woman like that every day? Spending every free moment with her?'

'There's nothing going on, Fleur. I was with you last night.'

'Yeah, and you fell asleep!'

He bent his head, thumb and forefinger pinching his nose. 'I don't have time for this, Fleur. Not today.'

'That's fine. You'll have more time now you're single anyway.'

His face screwed up. 'What?'

'Yeah, I was chatting to Melanie this morning and she was singing your praises, and told me it was hard to believe you were single. I had to agree, it was. But actually, now I'm finding it far more easy to believe.'

He shook his head. 'Jesus, Fleur. I just told them that so they wouldn't sniff around and bother you!'

'Oh, right, you did it for me.'

'Yes!'

'Nothing to do with wanting to let Melanie know there were no obstacles?'

'No!' He ground out the words. 'This is ridiculous. This is about you and your insecurities.'

'Oh, is that so?'

'Yes. You have a fear of abandonment and right now you're projecting that onto this situation.'

'I am not, and don't try and pretend you understand something you know nothing about!'

'Fleur—'

'No!' I said, pulling away from him. 'Don't you dare act like you know me. You grew up surrounded by a loving, supportive family. It didn't matter what you did, you knew you could always come back to them. That they'd be there. That you'd have someone who loved you no matter what. Do you even know how valuable that is?' Whether he did or not, I didn't wait to find out and he made no attempt to interrupt me. 'I doubt you do. You just take it for granted. Like you take me for granted.'

This time he made a stand. 'No, I don't!'

'Really? I think you do. And I think you took it for granted that I wouldn't mind that you'd gone around telling everyone in this bloody TV crew, including Melanie, that you're *single*!'

I saw realisation dawn on his face.

'Well, guess what,' I said, poking him in the chest hard, which probably hurt my finger more than him but still. 'I do mind. I've spent my life trying to be what everyone else wanted me to be. Hoping that by doing so I'd find someone to love me. But all it did was bring me unhappiness. And I'm not doing that any more. I'm not going to pretend I'm OK with you denying you're in a relationship and so now you don't have to.'

'Fleur... I—'

'Oh!' Melanie stood at the door, looking super cute in pastel-coloured, high-end branded walking gear. 'Am I interrupting?'

'Not at all!' I slapped on a smile. 'We were just having a discussion about dinner tonight. I thought you and Matt should eat here, you know? Maybe sing the praises of the hotel a bit? He disagreed.'

'He did?' Her wide-set blue eyes flicked between us.

'I know, right? Don't you think it's a great idea? Play on the whole family link of the businesses.'

'Oh God, yeah. You're so right. Matty... Are you being a grump?' she asked in a babyish voice as she pouted at him and I nearly threw up on the spot.

'Have a good day. Don't worry about the hike. It'll be great.' I smiled widely and walked back out into the restaurant and straight through, up to my room. There were still tables to set but right now I needed to make a call.

31

'Fleur, darling, how are you?'

'I'm OK.'

'What's wrong?' For the relatively short time she'd had the role of being my mother in anything other than title, Elodie had learned remarkably quickly.

'I was just wondering if I could come and visit you both.'

'Of course, of course. You know you never need to ask. Is something wrong?' she persisted.

'I... I think I just split up with Matt.'

'Oh, my darling. Do you want your father to come and get you? He's saying he can leave right now.'

'No, no, it's fine,' I said, not knowing whether the tears tracking down my cheeks were from pain at losing Matt or joy at having found my parents and knowing that they, at least, wanted me. 'I'll drive to you.'

'Are you sure? We don't want you driving if you're upset, my darling.'

'I'll be OK. I promise.'

'Well, you know there's a room here that is always ready for you for as long as you want.'

'Thanks.' I swallowed. 'Thanks, Mum.

Through her own tears I heard, 'You're welcome.' It was the first time I'd ever called her that. It hadn't felt right immediately. I'd had stuff to work out in my head before I could. Blame I needed to assuage. But, like Matt, I'd found solace and peace in the countryside. My mother had been so young and she'd tried so hard, but sometimes it didn't matter how hard you tried, things didn't work out. I understood that now. Far too well.

I'd been wary of getting into something with Matt because of his connections to the place that was my home and my job. But his family had been so happy and so enthusiastic, I hadn't put up much of a fight. Now that had come back to bite me. But I was an adult. We both were. Once the emotions settled I was sure we would be able to function and go about our daily lives without it causing a problem.

'Fleur?' Anna tapped on the door and then poked her head round. 'Are you OK?'

'Yep, I'm fine.'

Anna stepped into the room and closed it behind her. 'Clearly you're not.' She glanced at the suitcase. 'You're leaving?'

'Only for a short time. I think we both just need a break. Matt's caught up in this programme and I'm missing my parents. We're both tired and it's just come to a bit of head with everything today. We'll be fine.'

'I know,' Anna replied, certainty in her tone. 'You're meant for each other.'

I wasn't sure I believed in the whole soulmates thing but Anna did and, right now, I didn't have the energy to argue with her.

'You are,' she said again when I made no reply.

I tossed over a brief smile in the hope that that would placate her and continued with my packing.

'You know he didn't want to do this, right?'

'Yes. I know.'

'He's still really cross with Andy.'

'I know,' I repeated. 'Look,' I said, straightening and turning to Anna. 'None of this is your or Andy's fault. No, it's not ideal that Matt's had to take part instead of Andy and I'm not thrilled about him saying he was single, but I know he values privacy so I can see the reason for that too.' I moved closer to Anna and reached out for a hug.

'I hate that you've argued,' she said. 'Andy feels awful.'

I moved her back so that I could look her in the eye. 'He doesn't need to. OK? We're both adults and I'm sure we are going to have the odd blip. Everyone does. But that's between him and me and is no one else's fault.'

'But you're still leaving?'

'Temporarily. I need a bit of space. Just for a few days.'

Anna nodded, her empathetic soul still causing her to look troubled as she headed out of the room.

Closing the door behind me, I made my way along the corridor and down the stairs to find Bronwyn. I felt bad leaving her in the lurch but right now I just needed to get away for a few days and had to hope she'd understand.

'Oh, Fleur love, there you are. I was just coming to find you. Are you all right?'

'You've seen Matt, then?'

She nodded.

'I'm sorry.'

Bronwyn shook her head. She was, unquestionably, fond of

me, but Matt was her son and I'd hurt him. Although, if I took a break from adulting for a moment, he hurt me first.

'I thought you two were so good together.'

'I did too.'

'Are you sure it's not just a misunderstanding?' she asked as we stepped into the restaurant.

'I hope so. I think a bit of space will—'

We both halted as we entered the dining room. Framed by the sunlight streaming in through the window was a picture that burned itself into my brain. Melanie's arms were around Matt's neck, and his hands rested on her hips as the two of them shared a kiss that was definitely more than just walking partners.

'Oh!' Melanie giggled as she pulled back, her fingers still teasing the soft fuzz that was Matt's buzz-cut hair squared off exactly at his neck. 'I didn't realise we had company.'

Matt's head turned sharply, his eyes meeting mine.

'Take as long as you need, Fleur.' Bronwyn's voice was quiet. I leant over, kissed her cheek and picked up my case from the hall. Two minutes later I was in my car.

'Fleur.' Matt stepped out in front of my car. 'We need to talk.'

I kept my eyes focused forward, looking past him, my doors locked.

'Fleur!'

'Oh, Matt, there you are. We need to get going.' The producer looked at Matt, then my car, then back to Matt.

'Matt?' Melanie strode out, adjusting her pink and silver bobble hat.

Matt waited but I refused to meet his eyes. After a few more moments he stepped to the side and I accelerated up the driveway. *Do not look in the mirror. Do not look in the mirror…*

* * *

Dear Bronwyn,

I'm so sorry to leave you in the lurch like this but I'm afraid I am unable to return to my position at the hotel. I had no intention of leaving permanently when I spoke to you but, as things have turned out, I think it is for the best.

I'd like to take this opportunity to thank you and your family for the incredible kindness you have shown me and wish I wasn't repaying you for all that in this manner.

I can send a courier to collect the rest of my things if you would be kind enough to box them up for me. If this isn't possible, I will come and get them myself if you let me know the best time for me to do so. As I'm sure you can understand, I do not wish to see Matt at present so would like to time the visit accordingly.

Dear Fleur,

Please find enclosed the rest of your things. I'm so sorry things ended like this. It certainly wasn't what any of us had hoped for.

I'm glad you have your family around you now but please remember, we all still love you and always will. I hope in time we will get to see you again.

Lots of love,
Bronwyn

The programme was a hit – as was Matt apparently – but I chose not to watch it. Getting over Matt Morgan was the hardest thing I'd ever had to do in my life but I was getting there. Kind of.

'Oh my God, I love it!' The client stroked the velvety flock of the wallpaper on the feature wall behind her bed. Peacocks strutted across it, trailing vermilion and blue tails of tactile fabric, the rest of their plumage picked out in a reflective gold, all of it adding to the lush feel of the bedroom she'd hired Elodie's Interiors to design. And between us, Mum and I had nailed it.

When I left Wales that day, I had no plan further than the next few hours. To drive to my parents', spend some time with them and then, after a cry, some hugs and several buckets of tea, tackle sorting the rest of my life out. Once again, I had managed to get myself into the position of falling for a man and, when it all went wrong, I was without a job and a place to live. I'd thought I'd learned my lesson after Jasper. I'd fully intended to. But that plan hadn't figured Matt Morgan into the equation. We'd been friends. That was all it was ever supposed to be. Instead it had turned out to be full-blown, messy, wonderful, break-your-heart-into-a-million-pieces love.

'I have to give most of the credit to my daughter.' Mum beamed as she slid her hand around my waist and gave it a squeeze. 'My original idea was to go in a different direction, but Fleur sourced that wonderful wallpaper and we went from there.'

'Oh, I'm so glad you did,' the client enthused. 'I mean, I know whatever you would have chosen would still have been amazing, Elodie. It always is, but I am absolutely in love with this room.' She sat on the chaise longue I'd had re-covered in an emerald-green velvet to match the green of the peacocks.

'It's beautiful. Thank you both so much. I know I'm going to love being in here now. It just feels so utterly luxe.'

Mum and I said our goodbyes and walked back through the leafy streets of South Kensington to the Tube station. From there we'd make our way to St Pancras and catch the next train back from London to Cambridge. Spring was announcing its presence in the bright green of the new leaves unfurling on the trees and delicate shades of white and pink blossoms dancing upon the cherry trees. Tourists were becoming more plentiful both here in London and in the city of Cambridge. The place I now called home.

Most people my age would probably be horrified at the thought of living with their parents. Then again many of them would likely be in a relationship, possibly with kids of their own. But I didn't care. I loved it. I knew Mum and Dad did too. There was an unspoken sense of all of us making up for lost time, lost experiences.

'I am so proud of you!' Mum took my hands between hers as we sat at the café in the station, passing time before our train left.

'Thanks, Mum. I can't believe how happy she was with it all. I was so nervous.' I'd been working with Mum ever since I returned 'home'. She hadn't forced me. They'd, very kindly, told me I didn't have to work at all if I didn't want to. Dad had asked if there was anything I wanted to study, seeing as I'd missed out on university earlier in life. But the truth was, I didn't feel as though I'd missed out. There was no subject that gripped me enough to call me to its study for three or four years and I'd had absolutely no idea what I wanted to do with my life. I'd drifted into hospitality and that was where I'd stayed – until Jasper. But the less said about that particular episode, the better.

Working with Mum had been great and I finally felt like I'd found my niche. I got excited about colours, and seasons, and styles. Mum and Dad took me to a tonne of historical houses around the country, allowing me to absorb different styles as well as learn about and enjoy the sense of history that lay behind them. We went to Paris for the weekend on the Eurostar and took a trip to Spain, visiting Gauguin's creations in Barcelona and the colours and culture of Madrid and Seville.

I'd spent a lot of time reading, and walking. Cambridge had a distinct lack of mountains but I'd never been a massive fan of hills anyway. Most of the time Matt had had to half drag me up them. To be fair to him, the views had been worth it, but exploring my new home had been exciting too and the difference between the city and the mountains had been beneficial. It was too different to risk comparison. There was lots to learn, explore, and Dad had taken me on a tour of Christ's College, which was amazing. The reactions and greetings he'd garnered as we'd walked around had shown he was respected and well liked, which didn't surprise me but only made me prouder and, as Mum took a business call, I people watched and recalled the conversation Dad and I had the first time he'd shown me around.

'Dad?'

'Yes?' He'd looked up , over the top of his reading glasses at me as we'd sat in his office looking online at a menu for later.

'Are you disappointed I didn't get a degree?'

He'd snapped the laptop shut. 'No.' He'd reached out and taken my hand, wrapping it tightly within his own. 'No, no, no! You mustn't think that. Have I given you that impression?'

'No, not at all. I just...' I'd looked around at this world-renowned institution of learning. 'This is your life and I don't really...'

I'd stopped, as he had already been shaking his head. 'This is not my life, Fleur. Yes, for a long time it was. It felt like it was all I had. I'd lost your mother and I knew I would never, ever love anyone as much as that again, so I didn't put much effort into it. I made education my life because it was the only thing I loved. But then I found Elodie again and then I found out about you. My own darling girl.' He'd lifted my hands to his mouth and kissed them.

'Sorry, I didn't mean to embarrass you,' I'd said, keeping my voice low in deference to the surroundings. His door had been open – he'd said he preferred it that way so that should any student want to speak to him, it would, hopefully, feel less intimidating.

'You could never embarrass me. I am so proud of you, Fleur. So, so proud.'

'Of me?' I had been truly surprised. 'For what?'

'For being who you are. For taking the difficult start you had and not letting it sour you. For being the wonderful woman you are, that you've become all by yourself.'

'I guess I had good genes.'

'Well, yes, there is that.' His laugh had been gentle, aligning with his nature, but it had had a giggly, infectious quality and there we'd sat, in a cornerstone of learning, giggling like a couple of kids.

* * *

'Thanks, Mum,' I said as we walked back to my car, having disembarked at Cambridge. Dad had insisted on buying me a new one after it had been decided I would stay. There had been much protesting on my side but Dad had won out.

Mum smiled as she got in, swinging her legs in elegantly

after her. 'What were you thanking me for?' she asked as I belted up.

'For letting me become part of this. Working with you, I mean.'

'Fleur... I can't...' She smiled across at me then dived into her tan leather handbag for a tissue. She began again. 'There is nothing to thank me for. I am just so happy you enjoy the work. You're naturally talented.'

'Do you think so?'

'Did you not hear the client today?' she replied, laughing as I pulled out of the station car park.

'Well. Yeah, but—'

'There is no but, Fleur. You created a room that the client loved and you did that alone.'

'I had you to ask. That's kind of a big help.'

'I never told you yes or no. Just to go with your instinct.'

'Yeah... for future reference that was really annoying.'

'Aha,' she said, and gave a small Gallic shrug. 'But it worked, *non*?'

'I guess so. *Oui*.'

That was another thing that was new in my life. I was now almost bilingual thanks to Mum's patient tuition. Dad also spoke French so we often practised at home. The rusty French I remembered from school was polished up and improved upon and I'd just read one of my favourite romcom novels in French and only had to look up a few words. Apparently on our next trip to Paris, I was going to be doing all the talking. We would see about that, but the thought that I probably could brought me a feeling of pride I'd been lacking my entire life.

'Are you OK, Fleur?' Mum's soft voice floated into my thoughts.

'Huh? Oh. Yeah, yeah. Fine.'

I was fine. I was absolutely fine. Except... I wasn't. Putting the car into park, I exited and beeped it locked.

'Are you sure you feel quite well? You look a little pale.' Mum's youthful face studied me as she laid the back of her hand against my forehead.

I was staring at the car on the drive.

'It's been a long day. Let's get you inside and... oh, hello, darling!' Mum's face lit up as Dad appeared at the door, but quickly became serious as his greeting smile, unlike usual, was brief and troubled. 'Ralph, what's wrong?'

Dad looked to me. 'Fleur. I think you'd better come in.'

32

Andy and Anna stood as I entered the room. Anna's eyes were rimmed with red and Andy's expression was fixed and stoic but I'd had a lifetime of reading faces and what I read was pain.

'Oh... Fleur.' Anna moved towards me, tears flowing.

I stepped back from her. 'No...' I shook my head. 'No!' I shouted, my voice cracking on the word as my heart, the heart I'd thought broken before now, was crushed into powder in my chest. Turning, I pushed past my parents and out through the hallway, into the kitchen and out of the back door into the large garden. The last rays of evening spring sunlight wound themselves around the mature trees, filtering through the branches as I made my way to the biggest oak and sat heavily on the wooden swing strung to its strongest limb. Dad had made it himself when I'd moved in. For someone who had never done any DIY in his life, it had not been without incident, but once Mum had assured him it was just a small cut and his finger was still in place, he'd collected himself and returned to the job in hand.

I clung to the ropes that secured it, gripping them until my knuckles were white. I knew there was something wrong. That feeling I'd had when I saw the car, the pain behind Andy's eyes and Anna's flowing tears... Matt was gone and I wasn't sure I could bear it.

'Fleur?' Anna's gentle voice carried on the evening breeze. 'Fleur, where are you?'

My throat was swollen with unshed tears so I pushed myself off the swing, allowing her to see me, careful to retain my grip on the ropes. Right now they were the only thing keeping me upright.

'Fleur.' Anna ran towards me and flung her arms around me. I couldn't respond. I wanted to but there was nothing in me. Nothing but pain.

'We need you to find him. If anyone can, it's you.'

A shard of light sliced into the darkness of my heart.

'He's...' I croaked out.

'Missing.'

'Not...'

'No.' Her voice was strong now. Determined.

'You don't know that for sure though, do you?'

'He's not.'

We stared at each other for a long moment. 'Why don't you come back inside and we can talk?'

I hesitated, images, words, feelings all tumbling through me before I took Anna's hand and she led me back inside.

'I've tried everywhere I can think of but no luck.' Andy's attitude towards me was cool. 'Anna thought you might be able to help.'

'How long has he been missing?'

'Six days.'

'I'm sure he's fine. He's had survival training.' I wasn't sure if I was trying to convince them or me.

Andy shook his head, standing as he spoke. 'Come on, Anna. I told you she wouldn't be interested in helping.'

'Andy—'

'Now just hang on a minute, young man.'

'Dad, it's OK.'

'No, it's bloody not,' he said, his eyes locked with Andy's. 'I completely understand that you are upset and extremely worried about your brother but it's not my daughter's fault—'

'Yes, it is! He was happy. Finally!' Andy turned to me. 'I don't know what you did, but it was like you chased away the ghosts that still surrounded him. Once he let himself go and fall in love with you, he was like a different person. There was a light back in his eyes that I haven't seen since before he was deployed. And then you left! You left him and they all came back. Those and worse.'

'I can't be responsible for another person's happiness, Andy! That's not fair. And do you think leaving was easy? How do you think I felt seeing that woman drape herself all over him, and him apparently not objecting?' I took a step towards the man that had been my friend. 'How do you think I felt never seeing him, instead seeing cosy dinners for two plastered all over her Instagram account, and when I did see him all he did was fall asleep? And sorry, but I'm pretty sure you were there when we walked in to see him snogging her! So, as much as you want to blame me for whatever's going on with Matt, it's not my fault. I loved him with everything I had. More than I thought I was ever capable of. I felt like I was one side of the coin and he was the other. So don't.' I poked him in the chest. 'You.' Poke. 'Dare.' Poke. 'Accuse me of not caring about him.' Poke.

Andy glared down at me and I glared back.

'Ow,' he said eventually. The dam I'd been building was breached and a single tear trickled from my left eye and raced down my cheek. Andy's own eyes filled. 'Please, Fleur. I don't know what else to do.' All our anger gone now, his arms wrapped around me and I returned the hug, both of us clinging to hope for the man we loved so deeply.

'Matt was as shocked as we were, apparently, by that kiss,' Anna said, speaking quickly. 'Melanie was playing up that side of it to add spice to the programme. Or at least that's what she told us she'd been encouraged to do. And she admitted she fancied Matt, so it wasn't exactly a hard ask. So far as she knew he was single, so she hadn't thought it was a problem.'

'He told them he was single?' Mum asked.

Andy took up the story. 'Matt was worried about people digging into his private life and wanted to protect Fleur.'

'Having dated a journalist once, I think he had the right intentions. They'd have mined your background for fodder, I'm afraid, Fleur,' Anna added.

'My background?'

'Yes. I know it looked bad but I do believe Matt was doing what he felt was right for you. To protect you.'

'I don't need protecting.'

'That's as may be. But Matt has worshipped the ground you walk on from the first day he met you. It's his nature to protect those he cares about. And he would have done anything to protect you.'

'Then why hasn't he contacted me to try to explain?'

'Would you have believed him?' Anna asked, not unkindly. She was probably right.

'They wanted to do a second series, the response on social media was so good, but Matt said no straight away. When they tried to push him – always a big mistake – he told them that taking part at all had been a mistake and because of it he'd lost the best thing that had ever happened to him.'

'Oh...'

'He's barely spoken to me since.' Andy's normally smiling features were swathed in sadness.

'Really?' Since I knew how close the two brothers were, this took me by surprise.

Andy's shoulders slumped, his brow furrowed. Anna held his hand but the misery was still etched in his features. 'If I hadn't got us involved in that programme in the first place, he wouldn't have had to cover for me and, in his eyes at least, you'd still be together.'

'So, what happened?'

'He just didn't show up for work one morning and his phone was off. I managed to get one of the guys to cover and went round to his house. He was so angry with me, he'd taken my key back, but Mum still had one. Most of his stuff was still there. But his hiking boots were gone and some of his hiking gear. But not much else.'

'So he's just gone on a long hike. To clear his head. He told me he did that a lot when he came back from deployment.'

'He's never gone without telling anyone before. Even back then. He wouldn't have put our parents through the worry.'

'Maybe he's gone to a hotel for a bit. Just needs a break.'

'His car is still parked outside his house and he hasn't used his bank cards.'

'How do you know that?'

'Officially I don't. Unofficially a girl Matt and I went to school with works at the local bank and she checked. You can't tell anyone because she'll get fired. Look, hopefully he's fine and he'll wonder what all the fuss was about when he turns up, but right now I've searched everywhere I can think of and there's no sign of him. Mum isn't sleeping and hasn't left her room for the last two days and Dad's trying to be stoic but...'

Andy paused, dipping his head for a second, his swallow audible in the silent room. 'Fleur. My family is falling apart and you're the only one that can help.'

'No.'

All of us turned to my dad.

'I'm not letting you put my daughter in danger. She's gone through quite enough thanks to this man!'

'Dad. It's OK.'

'No. No, it's not OK. We've just found you. I'm not prepared to lose you on some wild goose chase.'

'Oi!' Andy's hackles were back up and I put a hand on his arm to stop him taking the step closer to my dad that he had in mind.

'You're not going to lose me, Dad. I promise.' I wrapped my arms around his neck and looked up. 'But the problem is – I still love that bloody wild goose.'

* * *

I pushed on, my throat and chest burning with effort and exhaustion, but I was nearly there – I hoped. I'd refused the offer of anyone else coming with me. If Matt wasn't where I was going, then I had no clue where he would be either. But if he was, I didn't want his secret place revealed.

'Shit.' I looked down over the split in the rock that Matt had piggybacked me over before. My legs hadn't grown in the past several months and a normal step wasn't going to do it. I tilted my head back, scanning the sky before looking ahead of me, focusing on the way forward. 'You'd better bloody be worth all this, Matt Morgan.' And then I ran.

'Ooof!' Pushing myself up, I brushed some dried mud off my trousers and smeared some of the damp mud further about.

Grabbing the rucksack I'd flung over first, I slid it back onto my shoulders and pushed on.

I was close now. This was the spot, I was sure of it. But there was no sign of Matt. Was that the remains of a fire? So he had been here, but he wasn't now. I dropped my pack to the ground and sank onto my knees. A sob, strangled and raw, escaped. I'd been so sure. I'd had to be sure. It was what had kept me from falling into the abyss. I might not have been with Matt any more and I'd done my best to come to terms with that, but I still loved him. And now... now it was likely he was gone. The demons had returned too strong to beat back and part of that was, albeit unintentionally, my fault. Another sob broke as I flopped back onto my heels.

33

'Fleur?'

My head snapped up and met Matt's shocked gaze. 'Fleur!' he repeated, joy mixed with confusion in his expression as he hurried to me and hefted me up to my feet. 'Are you OK? What are you doing here?'

I'd thought I was exhausted but where there's a will there's a way and the thump landed square on his chest, actually producing an oof. 'Where the bloody hell have you been?'

'How did you get up here?' He looked around me. 'Who's with you?'

'I climbed, and no one. People have been looking for you for days! Do you know how worried everyone is about you? What the bloody hell are you playing at?' I was screaming at him now through a flood of tears. He'd caught my hands and was holding onto them after I'd landed a few hefty punches.

'I'm sorry. I didn't think...'

'No. You didn't think about anyone but yourself! Your mum is beside herself. Did you think about that? She's already been through you being deployed. Dreading that call, and then she gets you back, safe, only for you to pull this stupid stunt! I thought you were bloody dead, you idiot!' Unable to thump him, I gave him a good kick on the shin instead.

'Ow! Jesus,' he said, through a laugh that was swallowed by tears. 'I'm definitely sure I liked you better when you wouldn't say boo to a goose. How did you get across the gulley?'

'I ran for it and hoped for the best.'

Matt stared down at me for a full minute before wrapping his arms around me and holding me so tight I began to have some concern for my ribs. But a cracked rib was nothing when it came to what might have been. I'd found him. And he still loved me.

'Why didn't you bring Andy?' he asked when he finally loosened his grip and, with a gentleness that belied his size, moved the hair that had fallen across my face with all my exertions.

'Because he obviously doesn't know about this place.'

Matt shook his head. 'I don't understand.'

'It's your secret and you shared it with me. It's not my secret to tell. But I need to let them know you're OK now. It's not fair on them.'

'No... I know. I guess I have a lot of apologies to make.'

'Yep. And you owe me a few nights in a really swanky hotel for a start to make up for all this.'

'You... does that mean we're...?' He swallowed.

'Yes. As you eruditely put it. We are. If that's what you want.'

He crushed his lips to mine, pressing me against him as though he couldn't get close enough. I knew how he felt and returned the kiss with as much passion, and desperation, and hope as he did.

'You're piggybacking me on the way back down, though. You know that, right?'

'We could always stay up here a night.'

'OK, don't take this the wrong way.'

'Uh oh.'

'I love you and everything.'

'Good. Same here.'

'So this is said with all the love in the world.'

That deep, sexy laugh I'd missed so much tumbled out. 'Fleur. Spit it out.'

'You seriously need a bath.'

* * *

Having apologised to everyone, and taken the much-requested bath, Matt sat with me on his sofa and we talked about everything. The shadows of times past he thought he'd conquered, the situation with the filming, my new career and the places I'd travelled to. We shared everything we'd missed since I'd left and more.

'I thought if I sat up there long enough, away from everything, everyone, I'd figure it out.'

'You can't rely on me for your happiness, Matt.'

'No, I know. That's not fair on you. I see that now. Can I tell you something without you thumping me again? You know you left bruises, right?'

'Oh, pffft, I did not.'

He hiked up the leg of his jogging bottom to show me the large bruise flowering on his shin.

'Oh. Sorry. But on the other hand, you kind of deserved it. What do you want to tell me?'

'Don't be mad.'

'You're making it worse.'

'OK. I was going to head back shortly after you arrived

anyway. I'd figured out what I needed to. It had taken longer than I'd expected and I hadn't planned on being away that long. But I'd figured out that, one, I need to talk to a professional about some stuff. And two, that I needed to see you. To at least try and explain things and ask, beg if necessary, for a second chance.'

'You were about to head down?'

He winced.

'I risked life and limb for nothing?'

He tugged me onto his lap. 'Not at all.'

'I could kick you. Again.'

'I know. Which is why I'm holding onto you.' The sexy smile loomed dangerously close to my lips. A very unfair tactic on his part. 'But you're right. You can't rely on one person for your happiness. You have to find that within you. And I have. But when I'm with you, everything is just so much brighter and better. You make everything brighter and better for me. And I love you. I'd fallen in love with you within about ten minutes of meeting you, which was a bit awkward. But then you stayed and I had to give you time to adjust and find who you really were. And when you did, I loved you even more. I hadn't thought it was possible but it happened. And now? Just when I thought I couldn't love you any more, you do something that changes my mind and it's worth the bruises.'

'Well. I should bloody well think so too,' I croaked out through a tear-roughened throat.

'Fleur?'

'Yes?'

'I'd love to meet your parents.'

'Good. Because my dad wants a word with you.'

'That's good because I have something to ask him too.'

EPILOGUE

Matt did meet my parents. Having given him a good telling-off first, by the end of the afternoon, they both loved him. He and Dad even went off to play a round of golf the next morning.

'Thank you.' I'd kissed Matt as he took my dad's clubs out to the car for him.

'No problem.'

'So, when are you going to tell him you hate golf?'

'Not for a few years yet.'

We were still working out the logistics of things. I loved the career I was finally building and Matt needed the open air and space for his mental health as well as because he loved his job, but we'd work it out. We'd have to, I thought as I held my hand out in front of me and watched the facets of the pear-shaped diamond catch the light. My fiancé watched me for a moment then leant over to kiss me as our joint families chattered and laughed around Bronwyn's big farmhouse table. Rumi and her family had finally been able to come over and she and Anna were chatting about the trip to India they were planning for a joint textile project while Andy advised Ayaz on the best way to get to Fairy Glen the following day.

My face hurt from smiling. This was where I was supposed to be. With the man I was supposed to be with. This was who I was.

ACKNOWLEDGMENTS

Another book baby out in the world. The excitement, and nerves, never seem to change. I hope you enjoy your trip to Snowdonia with Fleur and Matt and I'd like to take this opportunity to thank a few people who've helped this one find its way into the world.

First of all, the incredible team at Boldwood Books, including my sooper-dooper editor, Sarah Ritherdon, who is always supportive and understanding and reassures me when a wobble threatens to raise its head. I am so grateful to be in cahoots with this amazing group of people. Thank you.

Thanks to my fellow writers who are always ready with a listening ear. Rachel, Nat, Rachel, Sarah and Rachel, plus anyone else I've forgotten. You're all stars.

Thanks to Jo who has been a supporter from the beginning. I hope you enjoy this one too, my lovely. Thanks for all your encouragement and wise words.

A huge thanks goes to D who introduced me to Snowdonia when I was in dire need of the healing power of nature. It was exactly what I required at that moment so thank you so much for letting me invite myself along and also for not leaving me on a mountain. I'd also like to thank you for all the help with the geography of the area and the names. Should I receive any complaints and/or corrections, I will, of course, be blaming you entirely. Big hug!

And last but never least, thank you to James for everything. You are the reason any of these books exist.

MORE FROM MAXINE MORREY

We hope you enjoyed reading *You've Got This.* If you did, please leave a review.

If you'd like to gift a copy, this book is also available as an ebook, large print, hardback, digital audio download and audiobook CD.

Sign up to Maxine Morrey's mailing list for news, competitions and updates on future books.

http://bit.ly/MaxineMorreyNewsletter

Explore more uplifting reads from Maxine Morrey.

ABOUT THE AUTHOR

Maxine has wanted to be a writer for as long as she can remember and wrote her first (very short) book for school when she was ten.

As time went by, she continued to write, but 'normal' work often got in the way. She has written articles on a variety of subjects, as well as a local history book on Brighton. However, novels are her first love.

In August 2015, she won Harper Collins/Carina UK's 'Write Christmas' competition with her first romantic comedy, 'Winter's Fairytale'.

Maxine lives on the south coast of England, and when not wrangling with words loves to read, sew and listen to podcasts and audio books. Being a fan of tea and cake, she can (should!) also be found out on a walk (although preferably one without too many hills).

Instagram: @scribbler_maxi (This is where she is to be found most)
Facebook: www.Facebook.com/MaxineMorreyAuthor
Pinterest: ScribblerMaxi
Website: www.scribblermaxi.co.uk
Email: scribblermaxi@outlook.com

Boldwood

Boldwood Books is an award-winning fiction publishing company seeking out the best stories from around the world.

Find out more at www.boldwoodbooks.com

Join our reader community for brilliant books, competitions and offers!

Follow us
@BoldwoodBooks
@BookandTonic

Sign up to our weekly deals newsletter

https://bit.ly/BoldwoodBNewsletter

Printed in Great Britain
by Amazon

27159384R00188